AM I

THE

ONLY

ONE

new york times
bestselling author

e.k. blair

Am I the Only One
Copyright © 2020 E.K. Blair

ISBN: 978-0-578-72131-6

Cover Designer: Emily Wittig Designs
Interior Design: Champagne Book Design
Editor: AW Editing

To my husband

You laid the path so I could chase my dream.

AM I

THE

ONLY

ONE

PROLOGUE

Washington DC, a city filled with prestige and corruption, American dreams and political fallacy. Money was the blanket hidden agendas lay beneath. It seemed if you wrapped yourself in designer labels and surrounded yourself with the proper society, people were willing to turn a blind eye to live in their false reality of perfection. Who wanted to disrupt a seemingly charmed life and risk social disgrace?

No one wanted a scandal; that's why people lied. God forbid we weren't all perfect. Emma wasn't attempting perfection though. Instead, she was a mule for someone else's modus operandi.

But Emma knew this. She was a smart girl, always excelling in her studies while in high school, earning a substantial academic scholarship to the distinguished Georgetown University. It was almost three years ago when Emma packed her bags, said a tearful goodbye to her family, and left home in Tennessee to chase her dreams in the nation's capital.

Rain fell in a soothing patter on top of Emma's umbrella as her high heels tapped against the wet pavement of the empty sidewalk of the city. It was late, and she picked up the pace against the chill of the night. Snow patches still lined the curb, and when she rounded the corner and spotted the upscale hotel she'd been instructed to go to, her steps slowed.

The lights from inside cast a soft glow through the fog-covered windows. She couldn't see through the glass, but Emma knew he was in there. From everything she'd been told, he would be eager for someone just like her. He, who'd been graced with power and admiration, elected by the people to uphold the law and fight for justice, garnered a certain . . .

1

je ne sais quoi. Maybe it was confidence, maybe arrogance, maybe entitle-ment. Or maybe it was a mixture of everything, creating an intoxicating elixir to get punch-drunk on life's delightful sins.

Opening the door, Emma stepped out of the rain and into the warmth of wealth.

"Evening, Miss."

She looked up as a man in a suit stepped behind her to assist in the removal of her coat.

"Thank you," she murmured as she slipped out of the wet garment and handed over her umbrella.

When he strode off to check her items, she turned to scan the room. Since it was nearly empty at the late hour, it took only a moment to spot him across the grand space. He was the only one sitting at the bar, suit coat draped over the back of his chair, tie loosened, sleeves rolled up. Making her way through the room, she watched as he slipped off his glasses and rubbed his forehead.

"May I?" she questioned softly, looking to take the seat next to him.

"Um, of course . . . yes."

She smiled at his flustered demeanor. Stress and a lack of sleep carved the lines around his eyes, which beamed all-American blue. His briefcase was open opposite him to show stacks of files and papers.

"Working off the clock?"

He looked over to her, smelling of spiced cologne and scotch. "In my line of work, there are no clocks."

"What can I get for you?" the bartender asked, pulling Emma's attention as he set a cocktail napkin in front of her.

"Grey Goose martini, up, stirred, with a twist."

When she looked back to the man whom she already knew so much about, he was wearing a slight smirk.

"So, no clocks," she started, picking up the exchange. "How do you know when to stop?"

The clink of the martini glass being set down sounded at the same moment his eyes landed on her cleavage.

"I'm not a man who likes to stop."

ONE

Carly

Two months earlier . . .

Looking over the suit-jacketed shoulder of my husband is a view I've come to know well. No longer in front, no longer beside, but always one step behind. I stare out into the sea of eyes, which are filled with hope as they watch the man I fell head-over-heels in love with nearly thirteen years back. This wasn't my world before him, before we crashed into each other after a conference he was the guest speaker for at the community college where I used to work.

It was after our cars collided in the cramped parking lot that I got my first look at him. His tailored suit screamed *I'm out of your league,* but the charm in his smile soothed my insecurity. A whirlwind romance it was. He whisked me away into a world I knew nothing about as I clung to his reassurance that I belonged wherever he was.

My heart beat in an unexplained rhythm for William Montgomery III, the Ivy League alum who adopted the nickname of Tripp during his college years.

He adored me.

I adored him.

It was nothing short of a fairy tale, and seven months later, Tripp could no longer hold on to his heart. My world went spinning off its axis the day we were enjoying a peaceful afternoon at Dumbarton Oaks Park. He couldn't keep his hands and lips off me. When the clouds severed and the rain poured down, the slow, sensual mood

3

eclipsed into my squealing and laughing as we ran, bolting across the gardens hand in hand. Soaking wet with the sky filled with our abounding mirth, he grabbed me, awed delirium in his eyes.

"What are you doing?" I had asked breathlessly, but Tripp had been too busy watching the heavens rain down on my face as I had smiled up at him.

"Marry me," his heart spoke.

Two simple words.

That was all he needed.

I knew he was it for me. His were the only hands I wanted on me, so without hesitation, my own heart replied, "Yes!"

We never made it out of the rain that day; instead, we ran through the flowers and escaped into the Orangery greenhouse where Tripp pushed me against the vine-covered wall. He couldn't rein in his desire, and neither could I. Unfastening his pants in a rush, Tripp hoisted me off the ground, pushed the skirt of my dress up, and yanked my panties to the side. The two of us had made love in a frenzy of raw ecstasy.

That was then, and this is now.

Spontaneity has been exchanged for schedules. Lost are the days of decisions made purely from our carnal desires when we loved beyond love's capacity to love—boundlessly and freely.

"It's time to take the next step," Tripp announces to the crowd, snapping me out of my remembrance. "It's time to put a true anti-corruption expert in the governor's mansion."

The crowd's applause spreads like wildfire, growing louder at each of Tripp's strategically placed pauses.

"I am running for governor, and I intend to win. You have my word that, as governor, I will work for the citizens of Maryland with a level of intensity, tenacity, transparency, and rigor that this state has never seen before."

Roars erupt when Tripp takes a step back to soak in the peoples' encouragement. It's a moment he's been striving toward for a long time. After ten years of working for the state as one of its leading prosecutors, he won the vote of the people to become the state's attorney general, but his term is coming to an end, and he has his eyes set on becoming governor.

He turns to me, takes my hand in his, and raises them up as a symbol of our united promise to the people. I knew my husband and I would be presented as a package deal. He will be running for governor, and I will, in turn, have to gain the confidence of the people that I can hold my own as First Lady of the state of Maryland.

So, I smile to the crowd and take the kiss my husband proffers, a kiss that was discussed and choreographed the night before. It wasn't a spontaneous gesture of love and devotion, but rather a plotted act of American family values to give the perception that he's a loyal and faithful husband—a man people can trust.

I wanted to express my concern that the kiss would look too staged, but I've learned through the years that any opinion of mine that contradicts Tripp's parents' was null and void. So, I keep my behavior proper just as my mother-in-law had pressed, and when Tripp pulls back, I gaze up and give him an adoring smile.

And with that, I nail the performance.

After the rally, we go back to the house for a little breather before we head to DC where Tripp's parents are hosting a large celebratory party. While Tripp is on a call with his campaign manager, I slip out of my conservative attire and put on the deep-red dress that I bought for this very occasion. It isn't my typical color, but this isn't a typical day.

I'm able to take one glance in the full-length mirror before Tripp calls out from downstairs, "We need to go. Are you ready?"

"Coming."

After grabbing my clutch, I head downstairs with a little more bounce in my step than usual, excited to show off my new outfit to my husband. I spot Tripp from across the room, wearing the new tie I picked up for him. He's on his phone and barely glances my way when he grabs the car keys and mouths for me to come on.

Disappointment returns. It's a feeling I've become familiar with, especially lately. Trailing behind him, I slip on my wool coat before we head out. The drive is a little over an hour, but Tripp spends the whole time on the phone.

I get it. He just made his big announcement and people are excited, but with how busy everything has been leading up to this point, and knowing that, moving forward, it's only going to become even more hectic, I was hoping to snag a little of his attention on our drive.

Just because I'm irked beneath the surface, I go against my instinct to say something because I know it would wind up coming out accusing or snarky, so I opt to keep a tight lip. This is his moment, after all, not mine.

We hit some slight traffic in the city, so when we arrive, we are a bit late. Even though I'm exhausted and the last thing I want to do is to mingle with the influential people of Maryland and DC, I'm ready to dazzle.

Walking hand in hand as we enter the house that's even grander than ours, we're immediately greeted by Tripp's father.

"There you are, son," William says with a clap to Tripp's shoulder. "And Caroline," he continues, taking both my hands in his as I grit my teeth in distaste for the name he insists on calling me, as if saying *Carly* would stain his tongue in low-society tar. "Lovely as always."

As he kisses my cheek, I hold my breath against his robust cologne before pulling back with a mock charmed smile. "Thank you, William."

"Oh, you two finally made it!" Eloise, Tripp's mother, croons with outstretched arms as she approaches.

After a kiss to her son's cheek, she turns her attention to me. I'm not surprised when she gives me a once-over before hugging me and remarking in distaste, "Red is quite a bold statement."

All I can do is force a smile. No sense in poking the beast.

Of course, she would only view me in red as whorish or cheap when my true intention is to give a fashionable, patriotic nod to the Republican Party, which the Montgomery's are known to be a part of.

William leads Tripp away to introduce him to a few old colleagues from his days when he held political office, leaving me to mingle alone.

It doesn't take long until I'm joined by few wives of my husband's colleagues. These aren't friends by choice, but necessity. When I married Tripp, the women welcomed me into their sorority because that was what was required of them. It was what their husbands expected.

The evening draws on, and I find myself scanning the room for Tripp, not having seen him in nearly an hour. My smile holds with the women, but on the inside, my frustration with my husband grows.

"Please excuse me," I politely interject. "It was lovely seeing you all tonight. Thank you for coming, but I should greet some of the other guests."

Wanting a moment to myself, I set down my champagne flute and slowly make my way to the other side of the house. I close the bathroom door softly behind me and take my time freshening up. I spend an extra few minutes behind the heavy mahogany door, checking my makeup and hair, but I know I need to return to the party.

As I open the door to the restroom, I expect to hear the soft tunes from the baby grand piano in the living room, but instead, I hear a woman's laughter from down the hall. It's odd that anyone aside from family would be in this section of the house, so I head toward the muffled voices. Approaching the cracked door to one of the spare bedrooms, my breath catches in my throat when I peek in to find Tripp with one of his staff.

Olivia.

His campaign scheduler.

My skin pricks in chills as I find my husband cupping her cheek in his hand. The heaviness of my gut at the sight turns me lightheaded, but I can't look away. It isn't that I'm shocked to see Tripp with another woman; I've been suspicious of it for a long time.

Too many unexplained late nights.

Too many cancelled dates.

Too many days without a kiss, a touch, a look.

I've yet to see it with my own two eyes, though, and it isn't something he openly flaunts like other politicians. Quite frankly, I'm peeved that he would choose an event like this to be so blatantly disrespectful and risk being caught. Rage and jealously boil from beneath the surface, furious at the man Tripp has turned into. A man just like his father. I bite my lip to keep from snapping like a lunatic as I watch the twenty-something-year-old with red hair and red lips run her hand down the length of my husband's tie.

"Come, dear," Eloise murmurs from behind, startling me. She places her hands on my shoulders and guides me away from the door, saying, "Boys will be boys."

Stunned that Eloise can be so cavalier about what her son is doing steals the words from my tongue. I can hardly speak. Everyone knows the rumors of her husband's affairs through the years, but is she really condoning the same behavior from her son? She leads me back to the party, and it's then that I truly realize I hold no value in this family.

"Tonight is a very important night," Eloise condescends as if I don't know. "The men have it easy, but it's us who have to win over the wives of all those powerful men. And you know how women can be."

It's sickening how dismissive Eloise is being, but at the same time, I'm mortified. Too mortified to say anything to her. To stand up for myself. The desire to prove that Tripp and I have an unbreakable love has always been stronger than anything else inside me. I've always wanted to prove that we are nothing like his parents. But the cracks are exposed, and I'm too embarrassed to acknowledge it. So, I simply smile and follow my mother-in-law across the grand room where caterers in black ties serve the finest of hors d'oeuvres and champagne on polished silver platters, all the while, swallowing down the sheer outrage. It runs deep through my core, causing my palms to tingle with hostility.

"Ladies, I'm honored to introduce my son's wife, Caroline." Eloise beams in fakery to a group of women.

Another stab of irritation at the name *Caroline* cuts me even though I should be used to it by now.

The women greet me as etiquette would instruct: warm smiles, gracious handshakes, light hugs, and what would appear to most to be genuine compliments that aren't only for me, but my husband as well. To smile hurts, but I endure the pain through every emotion that's roiling within me and carry on as if thoughts of what Tripp is doing with that girl on the other side of the house aren't playing in 3-D inside my head.

"Whatever you saw, dear, let it go. You have a job to do," my mother-in-law whispers into my ear, jabbing the knife deeper into my heart.

I stand strong, refusing to let Eloise see me falter. She treats me as if I know nothing about what it means to be a politician's wife, when, in fact, I know all too well what it takes to swim with the sharks. These women love to present as refined, but behind the doors of their privileged societies and clubs, it's the gossip and scandal they love to sink their fangs into.

Luckily for me, I've been able to distance myself for the most part. Ladies' luncheons are easy to get out of when you have a job, which I do. Years back, William and Eloise pushed me to quit, insisting that the public wanted to see a wife that was devoted to her husband's career. At the time, I was able to argue that, as Republicans, we could appeal to the Democratic population if I kept my job at the university. William agreed with the logic, but it still wasn't good enough for Eloise, who saw my job at the university as trivial. And to be honest, it is trivial. It isn't a high-paying job, and it certainly isn't the career I hoped to have, but at least it was mine.

This was never my dream. My dream was to open up my own private practice, to build my career from the ground up. I took the initial steps by securing a lease on an office space years back, but the endeavor had proven to be more time-consuming than I anticipated while also supporting my husband's goals.

Tripp's career has and will always come before anything else.

As it stands, I only have two clients, and I pay more for the rent than what they pay for sessions.

A big part of me has wanted to go back to school to get my doctorate, but the moment Tripp left his job as a state prosecutor and started his path in politics, it was no longer about us or me—it became all about him.

In turn, my life has become a joke, leaving all my goals in the dust to make sure Tripp could achieve all his.

"You're up early," Tripp remarks as he walks into the kitchen while I'm screwing the lid onto my coffee mug.

"The weather is supposed to turn bad later today, and I have a lot of work I need to get done so I can leave before the snow hits."

"This winter has been brutal."

"Which is why I need to get going." I grab a few student files and tuck them into my bag.

"Not so fast," he says, pulling me in by the waist. "You looked amazing last night."

Memories of that redhead swarm, and I have to temper my fury so I don't snap at him. I want to ask why he couldn't have expressed this compliment to me last night and why he felt it necessary to sneak alone time with that girl instead of me.

"So, you liked the red?" I pretend to flirt. It's pathetic, really. My having to tuck my tail between my legs for the tiny bit of hope that my husband will give me the attention I'm so desperate for.

"Loved it."

Tripp grips my hips tighter and kisses me. I want to get lost in the kiss the way I used to, but I can't. All I can feel is tension, all I can see is him with *her*. Wanting so badly to erase the images that are taunting me, I push myself into him in an attempt to spur even a shred of passion.

"Whoa, don't get too worked up," he lightly jokes as he pulls back. "What'd you put in your coffee?"

Sometimes he makes me feel so stupid.

My response is curt, "Nothing. Just forget it."

"What's wrong now?"

I gather my belongings and dodge the fight that's brewing by avoiding the true issue at hand. "Lack of sleep. I'm just exhausted and running late."

"Okay. Be careful driving."

Slinging my bag over my shoulder, I barely peck Tripp on the cheek. "Will I see you when I get off work?"

"I have a four o'clock meeting with Bradford."

"In the city?"

"Yes. Dad wanted to come, so I agreed to meet them there."

"Well, try not to stay too late. The snow is forecasted to start around four."

With a fleeting kiss, I'm out the door and on my way to Georgetown. I'm able to suppress my irritation, but it always has a way of quietly brewing inside me. The once vibrant girl who lived on life's euphoria is now a thirty-nine-year-old who can only find diminishing glimpses of the rapture that once was.

"Good morning, Mrs. Montgomery. I watched your husband's speech on TV yesterday. For an old guy, he's kinda hot," Jenny says when I walk into the waiting room of my office.

Jenny is a freshman who answers the phones and schedules appointments through the university's work-study program.

"Old? Really, Jenny?" I tease the perky nineteen-year-old.

"You know what I mean."

I laugh as I pick up a stack of mail that's on the filing cabinet. "Well, enjoy your youth before *things* start to droop."

"O-M-G! That's so gross."

"Tell me about it."

This time, we both laugh as I make my way into my office to check emails before my first appointment arrives.

TWO

Emma

"That's it," I exhaust as I toss the letter onto my bed. "That was the last one."

"Are you sure?"

"Yes, Luca. I'm sure. I've applied for every loan, scholarship, and grant that I'm eligible for." The burning heat of tears threatens. "I don't know what else I can do. This isn't fair."

"Can you talk to the university again and explain the situation? Your parents died; it isn't as if your grades fell because you were out partying."

All it takes is the mere mention of my parents to rattle my heart.

"I've been on academic probation, Luca. They gave me a semester to pull my grades back up, and I blew it. They aren't going to give me another chance. The scholarship is gone."

"Will your boss let you switch to full time?"

A defeated laugh breaks through. "Tuition is around forty grand a semester. Even at full time, it won't come close to what I need. Unless I start hooking in the evenings, no one is going to pay me that amount of money."

Luca's oblivion to the cost of Georgetown annoys me. His parents are rich, alive, and pay for everything. I, on the other hand, have worked my ass off to earn my way into this private university on a full academic scholarship. But when my parents died in a car crash just shy of a year ago, my grades slipped. Despite his ignorance, I love Luca. He's been my closest friend since I moved to DC.

We met freshman year, both of us majoring in culture and politics. Luca is assuredly attractive with his dirty blond hair, tall stature, and bone structure fit for the runway. He's also a tomcat, which killed the hope I once had that he could be someone who could commit. The fact that we've never crossed that line made it possible for us to connect and build a solid friendship. Luca has always trusted me enough to be unguarded and transparent. I used to give him the same in return, but after my parents died, all that changed.

He takes my hand in his. "What can I do?"

"I don't know."

"You can stay with me if you need a place to live."

As much as I hate feeling like anyone's charity case, I understand that living with Luca is going to be my only option if I want to stay in DC after I get kicked out of my dorm.

"Thanks. I might just take you up on that."

"If you need anything, you know I'm here for you. You're my only true friend."

"Whatever," I tease, nudging his shoulder. "You're a socialite; you have hundreds of friends."

"Those aren't friends. They're just people."

Through my sadness, a smile grows for the guy who's holding my hand. It's a strange mixture of emotions that dangle heavily in my chest as I speak around the knot lodged in my throat. "You're all I have, you know?"

Luca moves in closer and holds me in his arms. He has become so important to me this past year, more than simply a friend. He's my everything.

"I'm sorry," I say as I pull back. "But I have to get going."

"Where to?"

"I have my counseling appointment."

Luca watches me as I pull on my snow boots and apply concealer under my tired eyes.

"Did you see her husband on TV yesterday?" Luca asks.

"I missed the speech but caught a few clips on the evening news." I swipe on a little lip gloss.

"I bet you he ties his wife up during sex and spanks her."

My jaw drops. "What?"

"Oh, come on, Em. A guy of power like that, you know he has to be controlling in the sack."

Shaking my head, I laugh.

"Have you ever checked out her wrists?"

"No! God, that's so weird."

He stands to meet me face to face, and I can tell he's happy to make me smile. Luca then rests a still kiss to my forehead the way he always does, and somehow, it soothes.

"Thank you," I whisper.

"For what?"

"For *you*."

"She'll be with you in just a moment," the girl from behind the desk says after I check in for my appointment with Mrs. Montgomery.

Taking a seat in one of the chairs in the waiting area, I scroll through my emails to busy myself. I started coming to therapy after my parents died because there was no doubt I needed help. In the blink of an eye, I lost my family—my world. Never have I felt so alone. Lost, really. We used to meet at her other office, but since I'm always on campus, she thought it would be more convenient for me to start having our sessions in her advisory office. So, I come here every week and talk through my issues with Mrs. Montgomery in an attempt to piece my life back together. Instead, it continues to crumble even further apart.

She has done what she could to help, going as far as to petition the university on my behalf for an additional semester of leniency due to my personal hardships.

The request was denied.

It's frustrating because, while this prestigious education is being handed to most students on a silver platter, I have to fight for it.

"Emma, good to see you."

Mrs. Montgomery is standing in the doorway to her office, and I slip my phone into my bag before following her inside. She takes the seat behind her desk, and I take my usual spot on the leather couch by the window that overlooks the parking lot.

"So, how are you doing today?"

"Been better." I exhale deeply, feeling entirely defeated. "I wasn't able to get the grants or supplemental scholarships I needed to cover my tuition."

"I'm so sorry," she says, and I can tell in her tone that she truly means it.

"I guess that's how it goes for people like me."

"People like you?"

"Poor people."

"You're far from poor, Emma."

"I'm even further from rich," I retort. "Let's face it, maybe this was just a pipe dream—working in politics."

"It doesn't have to be a pipe dream. You could always transfer."

"I already looked into that. The thing is, most of the courses I've taken are so specific that there aren't equivalents at most universities, which means that practically all my credits are non-transferable. It would mean starting over from the beginning."

"Have you considered student loans?"

"I won't be able get any student loans because my credit is screwed, and I don't have anyone to co-sign for me. Plus, my part-time job only pays enough to keep my gas tank full and food in the fridge." I grow more frustrated as I speak. "I am *three semesters* away from graduating, and I'd have to start all over. Plus, the resources that Georgetown has would guarantee me landing a good internship. This is all I've ever wanted since I was old enough to vote, a career in politics." Slumping my shoulders, I sigh in resignation, adding, "It sucks to be so close but to know that it isn't going to happen for me. I'm surrounded by students wasting this opportunity, who don't really care that they're here, when I'd do just about anything to stay."

She shifts in her seat, asking, "If your mother were alive, what do you think she would tell you?"

15

This is the very thing that upsets me most. "I wouldn't be in this situation if she were alive."

"Possibly, but people can lose scholarships for all sorts of reasons. So, just humor me." She crosses her legs and sits back in her chair. "What would she say to you?"

I don't want to admit that I can almost hear my mother telling me not to give up. But my mom is no longer here, and the world is no longer the same in her absence, so what's the point of considering a dead person's thoughts?

I swallow the emotion lodged in my throat and state, "It doesn't matter what she would say, or what anyone would say, for that matter. It isn't their life; it's mine."

"True, but I wonder if you don't want to consider her opinion, not because it doesn't seem relevant to you but because of the feelings it might bring up."

She hits the nail on the head.

"Is that the case?" she questions when I don't react to her statement.

"Not everyone wears their emotions on their sleeves."

"You're right, but you shouldn't be scared of them either."

"I'm not scared," I defend, even though we both know I am.

"Then what is it?"

My sadness isn't something I want to show to others, yet she continually presses me to be more vulnerable. The thing is, I used to be able to drop my guard and expose more, but after losing my parents, I can't.

I'm scared of opening myself up to only be hurt in the end. If there's one thing life has taught me this past year, it's that nothing lasts forever. One way or another, all relationships eventually come to an end, and I know all too well the pain that comes along with that.

"Like I said, it isn't their life; it's mine," I state with a bloom of defensiveness.

She nods. "So, what are you going to do with your life?"

Looking away into blank space, I try and fail to hone in on an answer. "I don't know. All I do know is that I want a better life; that's why I came here. I want to be a media strategist for politicians; a respectable job that I would enjoy waking up every day to do. I don't want all my time and hard work here at this school to be taken away from me when I'm so close to graduating."

My words come out in desperation, and I can clearly see Mrs. Montgomery's sympathy, which bothers me because I don't want people feeling sorry for me.

When the hour is up, she assures that our standing appointment will remain.

THREE

Carly

It's evident how upset and disappointed Emma is about losing her scholarship. If there were anything I could do for her, I would do it. But it wouldn't be ethical. I just hate seeing her dreams being crushed right in front of her eyes.

I have two more appointments on the schedule today, and as the hours pass, the sky darkens with thick, low-hanging snow clouds.

"Jenny," I call through my opened office door.

"Yeah?"

"Why don't you go on before the snow gets worse?"

"Are you sure?"

"Yes. I have a few more things to take care of, but then I'll be leaving myself."

Jenny gathers her belongings and pokes her head inside my office before heading out, asking, "What about tomorrow?"

"If the campus doesn't close, I'll email you and let you know if I'll be coming in."

"Okay. Be careful driving home," she says as she wraps her scarf around her neck.

"You too, Jenny."

When the door closes, I pull out my cell and call Tripp.

"William Montgomery," he answers formally, which irritates me to no end.

"Yes, I know. Didn't my name pop up on your phone?"

"Hi, sweetheart. Sorry, I didn't even notice."

His lack of attention, being purposeful or not, scratches through the soft scab the day was able to form over our earlier rift.

"I'm heading home in a few minutes. Are you still having that meeting later?"

"Yes."

"Can't you reschedule? The weather is turning bad."

"No reason to reschedule. If the roads get too bad, I'll get a room for the night," he tells me distractedly before talking to someone else.

"Well, what time do you think you'll be home?"

He continues talking to whomever is in the room with him before responding, "Honey, I'm swamped right now. Can we talk later?"

"Sure."

I toss my phone into my handbag, frustrated that, once again, his work is more important than I am.

The drive takes longer than usual with the heavy snow, and when I finally make it home, I'm exhausted. I change out of my work clothes, heat up some leftovers for dinner, and get lost in mindless television. The house is empty and quiet as I make my way upstairs to lie down. It's now close to ten thirty, and I've yet to hear from Tripp. I should be worried, but I'm too busy being annoyed, wondering what's so hard about sending a text to let me know he's running late. This type of annoyance isn't anything new. Tripp has made a habit out of staying out late these past few months, claiming that the upcoming campaign is taking up more of his time than he expected. I used to buy into his lies, but I know all too well that it isn't his job that's keeping him out so late.

There was a time I was his priority. Tripp used to make me feel as if nothing mattered more to him than I did. He placed the pedestal in front of my feet, took my hand, and helped me step up. Foolishly, I thought I'd remain there forever, that Tripp would walk through fire to keep me as his priority no matter what anyone else thought.

Closing my eyes, I drift back to when nothing mattered more to Tripp than my happiness.

"Why didn't you tell me this was what you wanted?" Tears stream down my cheeks when Tripp walks into the bedroom. I take a seat on the bed, entirely distraught as I hold the large manila envelope my soon-to-be mother-in-law gave me when we were out to lunch earlier.

"Baby, what's the matter?"

Tripp rushes over to the bed, but the moment he reaches for me, I slap the envelope against his chest, shoving him away. He stumbles back, shock clear in his eyes as he catches the envelope before it can fall.

"What happened? Why are you crying?"

"You honestly thought this wouldn't upset me? If this was what you wanted, why couldn't you have talked to me about it in private instead of having your mother do it for you?" The words rip out of me harshly.

"Do what?"

"Do you have any idea how humiliated I was to have my future mother-in-law tell me that my fiancé wanted me to sign a prenup?"

At my words, his hands move fast, ripping open the envelope. His eyes skitter across the first page as his neck reddens in anger.

"I never ... baby, I promise, I didn't know anything about this," he insists as he sets the papers down.

Looking over my splotchy face, he sits on the edge of the bed in our brand-new home and pulls me in next to him. He holds my face and wipes my tears, assuring, "I have never, not once, considered a prenup. The thought never even crossed my mind because that isn't what you are to me. Nothing about you and me is a business deal. I'm in this for life because you are all I will ever want in this world."

He speaks firmly, needy for me to believe him, and I do. I can see the truth in his worried eyes.

His hands cup my cheeks, and I grip his wrists to hold him to me, needing to rest in his comfort. The comfort of his words, but mostly, the comfort of his touch. When he pulls me closer and presses his lips to my forehead, my body sinks into the heat of him.

Minutes pass in silence as I allowed him to soothe me before my voice cracks, asking, "Do your parents not like me?"

"Baby, no. Don't think that."

"Then why?" Pulling back, I look him in the eyes, desperate for understanding.

"I'm sure her heart was in the right place. She was probably thinking she was protecting me."

"Protecting you from what? From me?"

"I'm not defending her. What she did was out of line, but she and my father . . . they aren't like us. They don't have what we have. But I don't want you to think that my parents don't love you. They do."

I know Tripp isn't being honest. One time, while at their house for dinner, I overheard his parents telling Tripp they were worried about me not fitting into their family. Tripp defended me. He doesn't care that I didn't grow up with the upper echelon, didn't care that I graduated from a state university instead of an Ivy League, didn't care that I worked a job that would never pay our bills. He once told me I was the most authentic person he had ever met, that my love was the purest he'd ever known.

He opened up to me, admitting he had dated his fair share of women before me, but that they were just consumed with the idea of becoming Mrs. William Montgomery III. He saw the spark of living the "good life" in their eyes. Their love was one of agenda.

I've never asked for anything from him. I was happy and content living in my one-bedroom flat in the city. I don't care about his name. To me, he's simply Tripp Montgomery—a guy who's head-over-heels in love with a girl—me.

Later in the evening, I overhear Tripp on the phone in his study. I listen to him as he raises his voice in disapproval to his mother, chastising her for going behind his back and upsetting me. My heart swells in knowing that, no matter what, Tripp has my back and supports me.

While Tripp is still on the phone with his mother, I pull out the contract that outlines the provisions should we ever divorce. I skim the pages and, even though Tripp is against having a prenup, even though I am against it, I sign anyway. The last thing I want is for anyone to think I am after the Montgomery money or that I have any ill intentions. But there's something else to me signing, something that makes me feel a step ahead of Eloise, that, aside from the fact that she's been caught and berated by her son, I know I'm not signing the contract out of persuasion or intimidation. I'm signing of my own free will.

The dip of the mattress stirs me back to the present. I can smell the faint scent of Tripp's cologne as he lies on the opposite side of the bed.

Tired of feeling lonely and neglected, I give in to my irritation and mutter beneath my breath, "You could've called."

"Stop."

"Why?"

"Because it's late, and I'm tired." His tone is that of annoyance, which instantly pisses me off because I'm the only one with a reason to be annoyed.

My frustrations seep out as I roll over and mumble under my breath, "You always have an excuse."

"What?"

"Nothing. Go to bed if you're tired."

"Carly, it's two o'clock. I've been working all day," he shoots back.

"Well, maybe you should stop working so late. Then you wouldn't be too tired to spend time with *your wife*."

Tripp turns the lamp on and tempers flare.

"You really want to go there, Carly?"

"It's been four weeks."

"What's been four weeks?"

Tossing the covers off me, I sit up and glare at him before snapping, "Since we've had sex, Tripp!"

"This again? In case you haven't noticed, I've been working my ass off. And let me tell you something else, your constant insinuations that I'm not being honest or faithful is a fucking turnoff."

I lose my composure as anger bursts from within. "You seem to have enough time for Olivia."

"Nothing worse than an insecure wife who has too much time on her hands."

"I saw you!" I accuse, sitting up and looking down on him. "What were you doing with her alone and on the opposite side of the house with her last night?"

This has him pushing up to sit next to me. "If I didn't want you, I wouldn't come home to you every night."

"If you wanted me, you'd have sex with me, touch me, kiss me, *something*! And I'm not talking about a staged, closed-mouth kiss to impress your constituents or get votes."

We continue slinging our words back and forth, pressing each other's buttons and hitting below the belt. But just because I've never outright caught him in the act, it doesn't mean I don't know that he's cheating.

I've found questionable texts on his phone, the lingering scent of women's perfume on his shirts, and after he changed his password to his email accounts, I knew he was hiding something.

"I just feel so far away from you," I confess, finally lowering my voice and giving up on the fight.

"I'm right here. Life is busy and stressful, but I'm here, and I need you. I need your support."

"You say you need me, but I need you too."

"It won't always be like this."

I don't believe him, though. I sense myself approaching my end with him and our marriage that has turned into a joke. It takes everything in me to keep the peace and not lash out at him on a daily basis.

"How much longer will it be then?" I mumble as I lie back down. "Because I'm sick of waiting."

Tripp doesn't respond, and no other words are spoken as we lie on opposite sides of our bed.

FOUR

Emma

"**W**hy are you studying so hard for finals?"

Looking up from my textbooks, I glare at Luca and respond, "Because maybe, just maybe, if I make high enough marks on these last exams, the university will take pity on me and reinstate my scholarship."

"Is that even a possibility?"

"I have no clue, but I'm desperate for anything at this point."

It's been a couple weeks since receiving the last of my rejection letters and, even though I've been doing everything I can to pull my grades up, I'm still falling beneath the GPA requirements for my scholarship.

Luca walks across my dorm room and sits next to me on my bed. "My mother was asking about you."

"When?"

"She called me last night."

"You didn't tell her anything, did you?"

"No, but I wish you would let me," he says.

Luca's mother has always liked me since I am the one and only consistent girl in her son's life, and one who's far from the unwitty tarts Luca often finds himself falling into bed with. His mother respects my tenacity and hard work, often teasing Luca that he could learn a thing or two from me. I have a feeling that she likes me enough to offer to lend me the money I need to finish my degree, but the last thing I want is a handout, so I made Luca promise to keep his mouth shut.

"She was wondering if you were going to make it to the New Year's Eve party."

"Crap. I totally forgot to RSVP."

"So, you're coming?"

"Of course I'm coming," I say. "That's one party I refuse to miss. Plus, it's become our one date of the year."

New Year's Eve would forever be our night together. After the first one we spent together, Luca told me that he refused to share that holiday with anyone other than the person who meant the most to him, and it's likewise for me as well.

"What are you going to say when my mom asks about school, because you know she will."

"Hopefully, I can get a plan in motion in the next couple weeks so that when she does ask, I won't seem so adrift. But first, I have to ace this last final," I tell him. "And you need to get off your cell phone and start studying too or else your mom won't even care about my issues because she'll be too busy jumping down your throat if you screw up your GPA."

Pausing whatever he's doing on his phone, Luca peers over at me, teasing, "I do a lot of screwing, we both know that, but never with my grades . . . only chicks."

"You're disgusting." I scoff, scrunching my nose and closing my books.

"Where're you going?"

"I need a break. I'm going to run out and grab a coffee. You want anything?"

"Nah." He flops back onto my bed, distracted once again by his phone.

"What's got all your attention on that thing?"

"Some girl I met at The Tombs last Saturday."

"Of course," I reply with a roll of my eyes. "I'll be back in a few."

Pulling on my snow boots, I laugh to myself when I hear Luca's delayed, "See ya," before I leave.

The bitter cold bites my cheeks when I walk outside, and I

tighten my scarf around my neck as I head to a local coffee joint on foot. A light snow falls, planting icicle kisses on my face as I walk. I've always enjoyed the cold winters. It's as if I'm living among the dead for a moment, all the while knowing rebirth is just a season away. If only human life could be the same. If only we could wipe the slate clean after each year to have our own rebirth, a chance to start over and erase the faults from the months past. I wish my own year would die just as the blooms that lie in their grave beneath the snow I now walk upon.

When I step into the bustling coffee shop, warmth thaws my cheeks, stinging the cold away. The line isn't that long, and I take my spot, waiting for my turn to order an extra hot hazelnut latte. After I place my order and the barista announces my drink is ready, I look over and spot my therapist sitting by the oversized brick fireplace.

"Mrs. Montgomery, hi," I say as I approach.

"Hello, Emma," she responds, looking slightly surprised to see me. "Join me?"

I slide onto the couch next to her and nod to the shopping bags by her feet. "Christmas shopping?"

Looking down at the bags, Mrs. Montgomery smiles, answering, "I wish. I haven't bought a single thing yet. My old snow boots bit the dust this morning." She angles her foot out to show me her new designer chocolate-brown boots. "So, I splurged on these."

I smile. "Nice." Then I take a sip of my latte.

The past few sessions, Mrs. Montgomery has been focusing on having me talk through the emotions of my parents' death. The appointments have been intense, so it's a huge relief when she indulges me in light conversation, asking simply, "So, what have you been up to today?"

With a heavy sigh, I relax into the plush leather couch. "Studying. I had a final yesterday, and my last one is tomorrow morning."

"How do you feel about yesterday's exam?"

"Good. I mean, as good as I can considering the semester I've had."

"With all you've been through, you've held up remarkably well, Emma. I only wish the university could extend you a little more of a grace period. I'm impressed by your determination. Most would've just given up on finals if they were in your position."

I take a moment to digest the complimentary words but find difficulty in accepting them. "I'm probably—subconsciously, at least—taking this opportunity to ignore the reality that none of this really matters anymore."

"It does matter. Maybe the grades don't, but it says a lot about your character. You aren't a woman who gives up. I admire that about you."

The heat of my cup warms my hands as I mindlessly pick at the cardboard sleeve. "You won't be admiring much when I'm degreeless and working some dead-end job that will never be enough to pay off all the debt I have, which I'm only digging myself deeper and deeper into because I can't even make the minimum payments."

The expression on Mrs. Montgomery's face transforms to that of . . . *pity?* There's nothing worse than being felt sorry for, but I see it in her eyes, and I don't like it.

"It was good running into you outside of your office," I say as I stand in an attempt to remove myself from her dolent gaze. "But I really need to get going."

She then grabs her shopping bags. "I should probably get back to work as well. Did you park out back?"

"I walked."

"You walked?" she gapes in surprise. "It's freezing outside."

"I like the cold. Plus, I needed time to clear my head."

"Let me at least drive you back. I insist."

Reluctantly, I agree, and we make our way out to the back lot, but before we get two steps out the door, Mrs. Montgomery stops dead in her tracks, causing me to bump into her. There's a strange expression on her face, so I follow her line of vision, which points to her husband holding a woman in his arms. Mrs.

Montgomery looks on with horror as her husband embraces the girl, who looks to be around my age with vibrant long red hair.

The embrace doesn't last long before he pulls back and brushes his lips across the girl's cheek in a sweeping kiss before he opens the passenger door to the SUV and helps her inside.

To say this situation is uncomfortable would be a drastic under-statement. Mrs. Montgomery is speechless as she stands next to me, both of us witness to her husband's betrayal. And now it's me who has pity in my eyes as I look at her.

"Men are assholes," I whisper, more to myself than to her, but Mrs. Montgomery hears and responds, "It's probably nothing."

The saddened disgust splayed across her face tells me she doesn't believe her own words. That she knows damn well that it isn't *probably nothing*.

"Are you okay?"

"Let's get you back to your place," she deflects as she watches the SUV disappear when it turns the corner.

The drive back to my dorm is filled with uncomfortable silence. She's trying her best to appear unaffected and poised, but her façade is terrible. I can see right through it and straight to her mortification.

"Maybe she was just a friend who was in trouble," I mutter, break-ing the silence in an attempt to go along with the theory that it wasn't what it looked like. "It did look like the girl had been crying."

Mrs. Montgomery's response is that of a simple nod.

"I'm sorry. I don't mean to be intrusive."

"Emma, it's fine. You need to focus on your last exam and let me focus on whatever happened back there, which like I said, was proba-bly nothing. My husband is a busy man who deals with many people, so . . ."

"Of course," I agree, not wanting to upset her any more than she already is. "I didn't mean to overstep."

"It's fine. Now, which building is yours?" she asks when she pulls into the campus housing where I live.

I direct her to my building, but before I get out of the car, I turn to her. She still wears the mask of indifference, yet her eyes expose the nasty beast of horror at what the both of us just witnessed.

"I guess I'll see you later this week at our normal time?"

"Yes," she responds with a forced smile. "Good luck on your exam tomorrow."

FIVE

Carly

When Emma shuts the door and walks into her building, I drop the façade of calm I'd been clinging to. My hands grip tightly around the steering wheel as my arms begin to shake. I allow the heat of my wrath to emanate from the core of my soul, the one piece that is most tender, the piece I felt safe enough to hand over to Tripp only to have him incinerate it.

I've tried so hard, exhausting myself to keep my world from falling apart. Holding tightly to my temper, I rarely ever let my frustrations boil over. I'm always the one to swallow the bitter pill of hostility to avoid a quarrel, but I'm at the end of my rope. How much longer do I have to stand by while my husband gets to live out his fantasies with women I can't dare to compete with? I don't compare to the twenty-something floozy he's fucking around with when I'm fast approaching my forties. No amount of nips, tucks, or Botox can reverse the years that have etched their existence on my body.

Tears run rivers down my cheeks as I drive back to Maryland. Tears that hold everything I've been hiding. Each one is a salty cocktail of anguish, hatred, loss, jealousy, desperation, and animosity. His audacity to bastardize our marriage rips fissures inside me. Wounds I doubt he could heal because, in this moment, my whole world, the world I built around my love for Tripp, completely disintegrates.

So I cry.

That's all I can do because no amount of screaming can erase the asshole my husband has turned in to.

With every blink, I see him with *her*. Static clips of him undressing *her*, kissing *her*, touching *her*, pushing into *her* play in color the whole drive home. I move in a haze through the home we've made together, up the grand staircase where he made love to me the first time he brought me to this house, and through the French doors of our bedroom. There isn't a single room that is untouched by the burning love we once shared.

Now, I stand and stare at our bed in dead silence. A room that used to be filled with laughter and passion is now filled with cunning jabs and insults, lies and deceit. In a crashing instant, the overwhelming feeling of loss sends me to my knees, and I wail my pain out, loud and ugly. My cries echo through the house as I sob and sob until I eventually wear out and force myself to my feet. Needing to distract myself, I move to the kitchen, grab a glass of wine, and bury myself in work until the sun sets and the night closes in.

Hours have passed with no word from Tripp—not that I want to hear from him. When I decide to turn in for the night, I lie in bed and curl into myself. There's no concept of time as I brood in the darkness. My mind is a labyrinth of agonizing torment. I laze in it because, what other choice do I have? I give in, allowing it to fester and create the fuel I need to find strength, hardening my softest parts and sharpening my once-smooth edges.

The stairs creak under Tripp's feet, and my stomach churns in disgust at the thought of what he's been doing that has kept him out till nearly one in the morning. I pretend to sleep as he makes his way into the closet and strips out of his clothes. When he finally comes to bed, I fear this marriage is over. That very thought makes it impossible for me to think about anything other than the memories of how our marriage began.

"What are you doing in here? You're not supposed to see me! It's bad luck."

"Fuck luck," Tripp says when he closes the door behind him, turning the lock so no one can barge in.

I stand in nothing but my undergarments, uncomfortable with my flaws even though Tripp worships my body as if it were a shrine built solely for his worship.

He walks across the room, which is one of many in his parents' home. The home in which he grew up. The home in which I will marry my love today.

Knowing that his language only turns crude when lust ignites in him, I grow tense when his hand touches the bare skin of my hip.

"Stop. Your parents are downstairs. What if—"

"What?" he interrupts. "What if someone catches me making love to the woman I'm about to marry?"

"Well . . . yes."

His smirk is devilish. "That's what locks are for."

"Tripp."

"Mmmm, say my name again."

The way he's teasing me is sweet. I give into the comfort of knowing he craves me and wrap my arms around him, whispering, "Tripp."

"Don't make me wait until tonight, baby."

And I don't. We're like two sex-crazed teenagers with each other, living in bliss, eager to love beyond our ability. Professing our devotion and making promises of eternity before friends and family isn't enough, so we love even harder.

After, when we're both spent, I rest my hand upon his chest so I can feel the life pumping inside him.

"It's yours, you know," he confesses.

"What is?"

"My heart. It's always belonged to you."

I relish in the tenderness my soon-to-be husband openly displays to me. It's a stark contrast to the cutthroat prosecutor he is in the courtroom. His track record for wins is more than respectable—it's impressive, and his trajectory is set. It's the future his parents had groomed him for, and Tripp only has one more case left before he will officially announce his candidacy for Maryland's Attorney General.

I know his goals well and will support him and encourage him. Together, we are powerful as we move forward to achieve our dreams.

When Tripp falls asleep, I stare up at the ceiling, knowing I need to take control of my situation. I won't confront Tripp about what Emma and I saw at the coffee shop. What would be the point? He would simply deny whatever accusation I made. All I can do is pick one of two options: stay or leave.

Taking my time, I think through both possibilities and consider them carefully. If I stay, either I will have to confront him and hope that, through therapy, we can rebuild our marriage or I will stay quiet and remain as I have been—the good wife. I mean, it isn't uncommon for wives of politicians to do, and maybe I could if he would keep it under wraps the way he used to. But now he's flaunting his indiscretions, and I have more self-worth than to let my husband treat me like this. It's a life I refuse to live no matter how prestigious this life might be.

So, that leaves only one choice—leave.

But it won't be that simple. I've created a world that revolves around my husband, and I've lost myself along the way. If I leave him, I'll have nothing to call my own. All because I signed that stupid prenup out of spite for Eloise. Not that I want to get my hands on the Montgomery money, but I do want what is rightfully mine from everything the two of us have built together over the years.

My thoughts and emotions run rampant, and I grow even more frustrated. Rolling onto my side, I listen to Tripp's breathing as it evens out.

I'm already doubting myself.

Maybe I'm reading too much into things and all my suspicions are in my head. My mind fumbles between so many conflicting thoughts that it has me questioning the things I already know to be true. Before I know it, I'm slipping out of bed and quietly making my way into our closet. I close the double doors quietly behind me, and then flick the lights on. It takes a second for my eyes to adjust, but once they do, I look around the large room and spot his suit and tie that are crumpled on the floor, the clothes he wore today.

I pick up his button-down dress shirt, look it over, and then bring it to my nose. My heart roars when I inhale the unmistakable sweetness of perfume. My hands clench the shirt with hostility, causing my knuckles to burn and strain before I sling the shirt across the small space. Fire ignites rage; my palms tingle as I hold in my hysterical screams.

I hate him.

In this moment, there's no denying how much I hate him.

The deceit brings me beyond tears and drops me right into white-hot fire, scalding me from the inside out. How dare that bastard lie, cheat, and destroy the life he promised me? The life I've clung to and relied on to keep me safe. The life that's nothing but a cover for his own selfish gain while he has his cock buried in everyone but me.

Taking in deep, steady breaths, I affirm my conclusion: I will leave him.

SIX

Emma

"You can't spend Christmas alone, Em."

"I'll be fine. Plus, I need to unpack and settle in."

"You have three boxes," Luca says, clearly annoyed by my stubbornness. "You'll be unpacked in thirty minutes, so stop being a brat and come home with me. My mother keeps asking to see you."

I look around my new room, the room I had no other choice but to take. As soon as I knew I was being kicked out of the dorm, I went to my boss to see about switching over to a full-time position but was told that none were available at the moment. Broke and desperate, I took Luca up on his offer to move in with him.

"Luca, please," I murmur as I sit on the edge of my new bed, shoulders slumped.

He walks across the room and sits next to me. I can barely burden the weight that's pressing down on me, and he sees it.

"Come here." He breathes the words as he pulls me into his arms. "I just don't want you to be alone."

"I'm fine. Really."

My words are worthless; I'm far from fine. My last hope was hanging on my finals, and although I scored impressively on them, the university was unforgiving and pulled my scholarship anyway.

On top of the stress of having to quit school, losing my place to live, and finding a job that will support me, this will be the first Christmas without my parents.

"You're a shitty liar, you know?"

Pulling back, I tell him, "I'm not lying. I'm actually going back home to Tennessee to spend Christmas with my brother and his family."

"Well, if you change your mind, I don't leave until tomorrow afternoon."

"Thanks, but I really think that it'll be good for me to go home for a little while." It isn't the truth, but I tell him the lie anyway.

Luca gives me an agreeing nod, and I watch as he walks out of the room. When he closes the door behind him, I fall back onto the bed and think about my brother, who is the same one I just lied to Luca about. The one with the family that doesn't exist—never has. Matthew is the true reason I fight so hard for a better life, the reason why I refuse to throw in the towel.

Luca was right when he said it wouldn't take me long to unpack, and less than an hour later, I'm lying on top of my bed while night casts its haunting glow through the windows. The wind howls with unforgiving force through the bare trees, and I shiver with a chill that prickles along my skin. My chest feels hollow; it's felt this way for days as I fight to bury despair and feign indifference to my situation. Even more, I'm fighting the hardest to run from the absence of my mom and dad.

It's been nearly a year since I lost them. I've been doing everything I can not to think about it, but it's impossible when all my body has to feed on is the sadness that dwells inside me. It's a painful ache that constricts around my lungs as I push back the tears. I wish to be stronger than my weakness. I wish to be free from the sadness.

Something pulls me out of bed. Maybe it's the longing for solace . . . maybe it's restlessness, I don't know, but I walk to my door anyway. The hardwood floors are cold under my feet as I allow sorrow to carry me to comfort. The clock reads after midnight, and when I peek into Luca's room, he sits awake on the edge of his bed, staring out at the snowfall.

He turns to me when he hears me enter. "Are you okay?"

I don't want to show my fragility, but I can no longer hang on to my deteriorating strength. In my defeat, I let go of the fight for a brief moment and admit, "You're right. I'm alone."

Luca's eyes soften as I stand here, heartsick.

"And I'm sad," I speak on a broken voice. "I'm so sad, Luca."

"Come here."

He holds the covers back for me, and I climb in next to him.

He's warm.

He's comfort.

Luca's strength bands around me when my body trembles. Silently, I pray for him to take my pain away—to heal me entirely. But my heart continues to break within his arms.

Pressing against him, I search for comfort within his hold. It's the craving to simply belong when I'm so lost. My legs tangle with his, and when his hand moves to cradle the back of my head, my body slacks and relaxes fully.

"I've got you," he whispers, tucking my head under his chin. "You aren't alone."

With those words, I hang on even tighter because I'm scared he might be wrong.

"Will you talk to me?"

I shake my head like a coward, but he only holds me closer.

"We always used to talk," he says.

And he's right. But, ever since my parents' death I've been shutting him out more and more. I even refused to allow him to come to the funeral when he wanted nothing more than to be there for me. I'm too scared of ever feeling the pain of abandonment again. But it isn't just Luca, I've shut everyone out. If I can build a wall around myself, then I can protect myself from ever getting hurt.

So, that's what I do.

After ten long hours in the car, I arrive at my brother's exhausted and park in front of the facility that's been his home since shortly after our parents died. It wasn't my choice for him to be here, but I had no other option. It broke my heart when the transition had to be made from my parents' house to a state-run facility for the mentally disabled. Matthew is low-functioning autistic and isn't able to live or make sound decisions on his own. After the accident, the state stepped in and took the house and cars to pay off my parents' debt, making it so that we were barely even able to pay for the burial plot and funeral.

That wasn't the hardest part, though.

After their deaths, I did everything I could to win guardianship of my brother. I put myself in debt with all the court and attorney fees I racked up because there was no way in hell I was giving that right to the state of Tennessee. He's my brother, and I have a responsibility to take care of him any way I can.

Since I can't afford to put him in a private facility, he stays here, where the state picks up the majority of the cost, leaving me with the rest. The amount of credit card debt I've racked up this past year has been monumental. He's the reason I've been fighting so hard to stay at Georgetown. All that is over now, but no matter how bleak my future looks, I'll do whatever I can to get him out of this derelict place and into a private facility.

I called last week to let them know that I would be taking Matthew for Christmas, so when I walk in to sign him out, the director is waiting for me to discuss Matthew. It comes as no surprise that the setbacks outweigh the progress. Matthew doesn't handle change or stressful situations very well. They trigger his anxiety and temperament.

"Emma!" Matthew exclaims when he enters the director's office with his duffle bag slung over his shoulder. "Why weren't you here at five o'clock when you said you would be?"

I wrap my arms around my big brother and squeeze him. "I'm sorry. I got a late start this morning, but I'm here now."

"But you said you'd be here at five."

"I know." I drop my arms from around him and step back, seeing the annoyance in his eyes.

"It's after six. It isn't five like you said."

Resting my hand on his shoulder, I nod as I release a breathy chuckle. "I know. I'm late."

"Yeah, because it isn't five."

"Matthew, sometimes people run late," Mrs. Nguyen says as she stands from behind her desk. "I know you were expecting her at five, but we have to remember to be flexible, okay?"

Matthew nods. "Yeah, okay," he says before adding, "But she said five."

I shake my head and smile, taking his bag for him and pushing on his shoulder to lead him out.

"Why didn't you call?"

"Because the roads are bad and I just wanted to get here as soon as I could."

"You should've called," he continues, unable to let it go.

It doesn't bother me at all. According to Matthew, you better follow through with whatever you tell him because he will make sure you know if you mess up.

"Come on. Get into the car so we can check into the hotel."

Excitement lights his face, and as we head to the hotel, he rambles on and on about going swimming.

"It's an outdoor pool, buddy. It's way too cold to go swimming."

"But I want to go swimming. It isn't *that* cold."

"Dude!" I exclaim. "Do you not see the snow falling from the sky?"

"It still doesn't feel *that* cold."

Matthew may be four years older than I am, but I've always felt like the big sister. Like it's my job to protect him because he only functions at a child's level, which is why he will never be able to be self-sufficient. It's another layer of pressure weighing on me. I'm all he has.

After we check in and Matthew has claimed his bed, we head out to grab a bite to eat. While we wait for our food, he tells me in extreme detail about the last movie he got to watch during the facility's monthly outing to the theater. I forgo mentioning that I've been wanting to see the film as he reveals the whole plot, including the ending.

I smile as I listen, but when the waitress delivers the mac and cheese and Matthew's expression drops, so does my smile.

"Is there anything else I can get for you two?" the woman asks, to which I quickly shake my head as he stares in disgust at his dinner.

"It's white," he complains. "It's supposed to be orange."

"I know, but remember, we have to be flexible. Try it. You might actually like it," I attempt to encourage, but I know better. My brother isn't one to be swayed at all.

"No." He pushes the bowl away. "And the pasta is shells. I only like elbows."

"It's all the same."

"It isn't." His voice notches up an octave. "It's nasty."

"You haven't even tasted it, so how do you know it's gross?"

"It looks gross."

I pick up his spoon to hand it to him, but he pushes it away. Out of the corner of my eye, I can see several people staring at us, most likely wondering why a grown man is throwing such a childish fit. Their stares annoy me, as they always have, and I have to temper my urge to scream, *"He's autistic, so stop judging."*

I then dip the spoon into the bowl and scoop up one shell, encouraging, "Just take one bite."

"No!" He shoves my hand away, sending the lone piece of pasta to splat onto the table.

"Well, this is dinner. If you don't eat now, you'll be hungry later."

"I want normal mac and cheese."

It's useless to push him, so I drop it and eat my dinner while Matthew throws his fit, banging his palm against the table while everyone around us whispers in scrutiny.

Heat flares up my neck in embarrassment, but I shove it down and smile at my brother. "Why don't we go to the store after this and buy a Christmas tree?"

His eyes brighten in excitement and the fist-banging comes to a stop.

With that, I pay the check, and I can't get out of this restaurant and away from all the invasive stares fast enough.

"Why can't we get a real tree," he asks when we arrive at the store to buy Christmas decorations. "We always get real trees."

"The hotel won't let us have a real tree. It's a fire hazard, so we either get a fake tree or have no tree at all."

"Fake trees suck."

"Hey!" I scold as he walks ahead of me, but I understand. Everything about this Christmas feels wrong.

Every year, Mom and Dad would drive us out to the tree farm to pick our Christmas tree. Even after I went off to college, I could still depend on all the same family traditions when I came home for the holidays. My mother loved Christmas. She always went above and beyond. The house was always so warm and alive with music playing, the fire crackling in the hearth, and there was always something yummy baking in the oven.

I quickly brush away a rogue tear at the memories, and my heart sinks even lower.

"Look at this one!" Matthew shouts as he points up to a ginormous fourteen-foot tree.

"That's way too big. We need something more like . . ." I stroll down the aisle, and then point to a small five-foot, pre-lit tree. "This one."

He claps and smiles, pulling out the item slip for us to take to the registers.

"We need ornaments too."

"I want red ones," he says.

After grabbing some ornaments, a couple of stockings, and a few decorations, I put everything on my credit card, which I have no money to pay off, and we load up and head back to the hotel.

I do my best to recreate Mom's festive spirit. We find a Christmas movie on the television and work together to set up the tree and decorate the room with cheap tinsel garlands. Once the stockings are on the posts of our headboards on our beds, I take a quick shower and slip into my jammies. Matthew is hyper-focused on his tablet, watching YouTube when I slip under the covers.

"Hey, Em," he says from his bed. "Did you know that sixty percent of tray tables have traces of MRSA."

"That's disgusting," I mutter as I plug my phone into its charger.

"Also, airplane blankets are only washed every five to thirty days."

I look over to find him reading something on his tablet. Matthew has been obsessed with *everything* airplane related for a few years. Ask him any random question, and chances are, he already knows the answer. Before airplanes, he was fixated on hot air balloons. I don't know what it is about air transportation that captivates him so much, but it's more than just an interest; it's more of an obsession. Last month, when I visited for Thanksgiving, I took him to the airport. We weren't allowed past security, but Matthew still had fun watching everyone at the ticket counters and baggage claim. He even got to meet a pilot, which thrilled him like none other.

"It's getting late," I say while stifling a yawn. "You need to get your pajamas on, okay?"

"I'll do it later. I'm not tired yet."

"Can you just go ahead and do it now?"

"But I'm not ready to go to bed."

"I know, but you'll forget. I don't want you to fall asleep in your clothes."

Frustration tangles his words when he argues, "I won't forget. I'm not dumb."

"I never said you were dumb, but you *will* forget, buddy. You always do."

"Ugh," he grumbles, tossing the covers off his legs. "Fine."

When he's back in bed, I turn off my lamp and roll over as he continues watching airplane videos.

"Em?"

"Yeah?"

"What about presents?"

His childlike dreams for Christmas morning tear at the wound on my heart, and my throat grows thick. How do I reason with him without disappointing him? How do I explain the amount of debt I've racked up just to ensure he has a decent place to call home? That I'm shacking up with a friend because I lost my dorm and my scholarship? That I'm drowning in his living expenses and housing? That I'm barely hanging on?

"We'll figure it out in the morning." I brush off his question before closing my eyes and drifting away into a fit of sleep.

The following morning, I wake before Matthew does and make the decision to take him to Five Below, which is basically like an upscale dollar store.

When we arrive, I explain again, "Remember, you have to stick to the forty-dollar spending limit."

He smiles, taking this pathetic excuse for gift shopping as a challenge. "Got it."

We each grab a cart and split in opposite directions. I grab him some candy, a T-shirt, a couple of games, a new case for his tablet, and some new headphones. I toss a few more things into the cart, and when I hit my spending limit, I head to the registers, check out, and wait for Matthew to finish his shopping.

"Don't look!" he exclaims when he makes his way to the front of the store.

Covering my eyes with one hand, I say, "I'm not," as I hold out the credit card with my other hand to give to him.

Once back at the hotel, Matthew wraps the gifts in the room while I wrap in the bathroom so our presents will be a surprise for each other. Once they're under the tree, I notice a small box with a tag that says: To Mom and Dad. Pressure mounts from under my ribs as my eyes heat with unshed tears.

"Are you trying to guess what I bought you?"

Blinking back the pain, I swallow hard. "Do you remember that time you snuck into the living room in the middle of the night and pulled back the tape on the presents to see what all you got?"

He chuckles. "How could I forget? You narked on me! I would've gotten away with it if it weren't for you."

"Whatever. You got caught because you did a crappy job taping them back up."

"What about when you snuck into the advent calendars and ate all the chocolate, including mine?"

I bust out laughing. "What can I say, I have no self-control when it comes to chocolate." As our smiles fade, I look at my brother as he stares into the tree. "I saw you bought them a gift." He looks at me, and I clarify, "A gift for Mom and Dad."

His shoulders slacken, and after a stretch of silence, he asks, "Do you think we'll ever see them again?"

Death isn't a concept he's ever been able to fully grasp.

"That isn't how it works, buddy. It isn't like the video games you play. In this world, you only get one life, and when it's over . . . it's over."

His chin trembles as my words sink in. I've told him this before, many times, but he still doesn't fully understand.

"You still have me," I tell him, straining to get the words out without crying.

"You're never here."

"I know, but everything I'm trying to accomplish in DC is for us. And, one day, we will be back together."

"I hate where I live. It's always so loud, the food is crap, and everyone who works there sucks."

"It's only temporary." I try to assure him. "I promise you, I'm going to get you out of there and into a private facility, I just need to graduate and make a little money."

"How much longer?"

"Soon." The lie gnaws at the scar tissue of my broken heart, which is barely surviving. I don't know what else to tell him. I'm so lost and so defeated. I can't stomach the thought of having to tell Matthew that I've failed him miserably and that the shit hole he's living in might become his permanent home.

The sound of an airplane flying overhead catches his attention, pulling him off the bed and over to the window as he stares up in wonderment. I wish I could give him a better life, one more like the one our parents had given him. Everything used to be fine . . . he was so happy and well taken care of, and now . . . now everything is a colossal mess.

"Did you know that the back of the plane is the safest place to be if it crashes?"

I force a tight smile when he glances back at me. Little does he know that the metaphorical plane we are on is in a nosedive and we both have first-class seats.

SEVEN

Emma

"Emma," Luca's mother, Gloria, greets as she leads me through their doorway. "I am so glad you made it. Luca said you spent Christmas back in Tennessee with your brother's family. I hope you had a nice visit."

"I did, thank you." I slip off my scarf and wool coat.

"Let me take that for you," says one of the many catering staff that's working the party, and I hand over my stuff with a soft, "Thank you."

Gloria takes a look at my gold beaded cocktail dress, complimenting, "Beautiful," before asking, "School must be keeping you busy; it's been a few months since I've seen you. How did this last semester go?"

"Good," I lie. "It's becoming more time-consuming the closer to graduation I get."

"Only three more semesters," she remarks excitedly, and I mirror her smile with my own.

"I know. I can hardly believe it."

"Believe what?" Luca questions as he and his father approach, looking dapper in their tailored suits.

"Graduation," Gloria remarks as Martin, Luca's father, greets me with a kiss to my cheek.

"Have you started prospecting internships?" Martin asks.

Luca's eyes catch mine before I turn to his father, answering, "I've only just started researching ones I might want to apply to."

Shifting in my high heels, I wring my hands nervously as I dump my deceit all over their questions.

Thank God for Luca, who grabs my hand and excuses us.

"You're a life saver," I tell him as we make our way to the back of the house and into the grand living room, which overlooks the dock that leads out to the bay. "I feel like such a fraud, lying to your parents."

"Then why lie?"

I peer at him out of the corner of my eye. "You know why, Luca."

"Your pride is a bitch, ya know?"

A server passes, and I pluck a glass of champagne off the polished tray he's carrying, murmuring, "Yeah, I know," before taking a much too big of a gulp.

"Bottoms up. Are we getting wasted?"

I shake my head and let a smirk play across my lips. "I wish."

"Did you have a good Christmas?"

"I did. It was great seeing everyone. You?"

"Yeah, it was fine," he says, slightly distracted as he peers over my shoulder.

I turn to see who he's looking at, and I have to do a double take when my attention snags on familiar red hair. "Who's that?"

"Olivia. Her parents are old friends of the family," he tells me, and when the two of them catch eyes, he gives her a nod, saying to me, "I haven't seen her since she graduated a couple years back."

"Why not?"

Olivia starts walking in our direction.

"She wanted more," he says under his breath as she nears us.

"Luca," she drawls, holding out her arms and then giving him a hug. "Oh, my gosh, it's been forever!"

I catch a hint of her subtle perfume, but it isn't until she turns to me that it finally clicks. It's the girl Mrs. Montgomery's husband was with the day at the coffee shop.

"Olivia, this is my friend, Emma," he introduces.

"It's good to meet you."

"Likewise," I say as I secretly judge her.

"Are you at Georgetown too?"

"She is," Luca answers for me. "She's actually my roommate."

Olivia glances between the two of us, curiosity gleaming in her expression, to which Luca clarifies, "Just roommates."

"Whatever you say."

I wonder if Luca knows that Olivia is just as slutty as he is and is having an affair with a married man.

"So, do you live in the city?" I ask.

She takes a sip of her red wine. "Bethesda, actually. But I'm in the city a lot for work."

"What do you do?"

"I'm a political schedule coordinator. I'm currently on the campaign staff for William Montgomery."

She's on a lot more than just his campaign.

"Luca," his father calls, waving him over to where he stands with a group of men. "I want to introduce you to someone."

Luca excuses himself, leaving Olivia and me alone.

"That sounds like a great job. Do you like it?"

"It's extremely stressful, but yes, I love it. And Tripp is great to work for."

"Tripp?"

"Oh, sorry. Yeah, it's what everyone calls William." She takes another sip of her wine. "What about you? Do your interests lie in politics?"

We find ourselves strolling lazily toward the windows that boast a spectacular view as we chat.

"Yes. I'm actually studying to be a media strategist."

"Impressive," she notes. "How much longer do you have?"

"Three more semesters."

"It'll be here in no time."

I smile and nod, knowing all too well that those dreams are dead and gone. Unless a miracle happens, I'll never see myself in my dream job or any job that will pull me out of the gutter I'm sinking deeper into. "I actually know William's wife."

"That's right; she works at the university."

"So, you know her too?"

Shrugging, she responds, "Not really. With the election coming up, work keeps me very busy, plus I travel a lot. So, there isn't much time left for a social life, if you know what I mean."

Her job for the campaign is a side-by-side one, so wherever William is, she'd be right next to him, making sure he's exactly where his itinerary says he should be.

"If you want," she adds, "I can talk to Frank. He's the media specialist on Tripp's campaign. Maybe you could shadow him one day. Get some inside knowledge on the job."

I nod, intrigued to get a closer look, not only for the job I doubt I'll ever have but also because I'm nosy and want to know more about what's going on between Olivia and Mrs. Montgomery's husband.

"That actually sounds amazing."

"Great," she says, pulling out her cell phone. "What's your number?"

I give her my contact information, and a few seconds later, my phone vibrates inside my clutch.

"I just texted you, so you have my number as well. I'll talk to Frank and get back to you." She slips her phone into her purse. "And if I can manage to sneak away from work, maybe we could grab lunch sometime."

"Yeah, that sounds great."

She smiles, and I wonder how many people she's fooled into believing she's just as charming as she appears.

"Well, if you'll excuse me, I should probably go mingle," she says before strolling across the room to a small cluster of people standing by the baby grand piano.

My eyes linger as I sip my champagne. Her wavy red hair cascades down her back as she laughs at something someone says.

I startle when Luca sneaks up behind me and grabs my hand.

"Shit, girl. Why're you so tense?"

"I'm not."

He quirks a brow at me and tugs my hand, silently urging me to follow him. "Whatever."

"Where are we going?"

"Upstairs."

I'm completely okay with ducking away from the party, and I don't look back as we head up to his room.

"Holy shit!" he exclaims, shutting and locking his door before raking his hand through his perfectly imperfect hair.

"What?"

"My dad just introduced me to George Wilcox, the director of Command Consulting group, and he just offered me a paid internship for this summer."

"Are you serious? Doing what?"

"Working in security and global affairs."

I plaster on a smile that just might be as fake as Olivia's. Ironic how his exciting news cuts so deeply that the blade slices straight through to my truth. I love Luca, but jealousy runs viciously through my body.

"That's so great." I try to grin and do my best to force the words out, but they crack under the weight of my sadness.

"Emma," Luca says heavily, his smile falling into pity when he sees past my weak façade.

Slowly, he begins walking toward me

"No, it's fine. I'm happy for you."

Sitting next to me, he takes my hand. "That was really shitty of me. I'm sorry."

"What for? Being excited about a great opportunity? Luca, you have nothing to apologize for. I should be the one apologizing for being so self-centered."

His hand squeezes around mine, and I take the comfort, allowing my head to fall onto his shoulder. We sit in silence for a moment before he breaks it. "Why won't you let anyone help you?"

Because my situation is a thousand times worse than anyone even knows.

"By *anyone* you mean your parents?"

"Yeah."

With a hopeless sigh, I slacken into him more.

"Or what about your brother? Have you even told him about your situation?"

"It's complicated."

"You know, you don't have to pretend to be this pillar of strength. It's okay to ask for help."

Lifting my head, I look him in the eyes. "Who says I'm pretending? Is it so hard to believe that I *am* a pillar of strength?"

"We share a wall."

"What's that supposed to mean?"

"I hear you late at night."

My eyes hold steady when he reveals this. It's my defense, to prove that even though he hears me crying when I should be sleeping, I'm still stronger than my moments of weakness.

"I'm not judging you," he defends. "But I can't shake the feeling that there's something you aren't telling me."

He's right. As much as I love Luca, there are truths I've kept from him. My problems are my own, and the deeper I get, the more embarrassed I am to admit that I've fallen so far, so I cover that shame with lies.

"You know me better than anyone," I tell him because, even through the lies, it's the truth.

"Do I?"

"Of course you do," I exhaust. "You know you do, but I'm not taking anyone's handouts. I'm not a dog begging for scraps."

"That's harsh."

"It's the truth, Luca. You know just as well as I do that image is everything in this city."

"Those images are pure bullshit and everyone knows it."

"Yet, they still matter," I tell him. "It's easy for you to say it's bullshit because you don't have to worry like I do."

"Says who?"

I cock my head. "Are you serious? Look at you. Look at your family. They have clout. I mean, come on. Just look at the guests downstairs. My God, you were just offered a *paid* internship. I don't have those opportunities coming my way. I'm at a major disadvantage here. I've lost my parents, I've lost my scholarship, I've pretty much lost everything. You are the only reason I'm somewhat staying afloat."

He squeezes my hand again, giving me an optimistic, "We're going to figure this out."

Shaking my head, I bite my words, saying, "There's nothing to figure out, Luca. My dreams at Georgetown are done, and I don't have money to go to another university." Frustration rankles beneath the surface, and I stand, taking a few steps before turning back to Luca. "Look at me. Could you imagine what the people downstairs would say if they knew I had to go to a second-hand consignment store just to buy this dress? It's humiliating."

"You still stopped people dead in their tracks when they saw you."

"Like I said, image is everything, even if it's covered in lies."

He releases a sigh, knowing damn well that everything I'm saying is the truth. Standing, he slips off his suit jacket and loosens his tie as he walks over to his dresser. He pulls out a vape pen and then opens the double French doors that lead out to a small balcony that overlooks the side yard.

He takes a long pull off the pen and, after a few seconds, exhales into the outside air. When he extends the pen in my direction, I go to him and take it. This isn't anything new. Luca gets high often, but he never gets totally blasted. Again, image is everything.

I hold the fumes in my lungs long enough that my head is already swirling by the time I release it.

"So, this is your solution? Getting high?" I hand him back the pen.

"Got any better ideas?" He smirks before taking another hit.

We lower ourselves to the floor and lean our backs against the wall.

"I didn't mean to ruin tonight," I tell him, kicking off my heels.

"You didn't."

We continue to sit, silence expanding between us for god knows how long as I linger in my blissful high. My lids fall shut, but vertigo kicks in, forcing me to open them back up with a slight giggle.

"What's so funny?"

I look at my best friend with a lazy smile I don't have the strength to straighten.

"You're fuckin' stoned."

Nodding, I agree, "Yeah. That hit me hard this time."

We then hear the muffled voices from downstairs of everyone counting down in unison.

My brows cinch in confusion. "Have we really been up here that long?"

Luca nods, and when the guests erupt in celebratory cheers, Luca wishes me a happy new year. And like he's done on this night for the past couple of years, he holds my cheeks in his hands and kisses my forehead, saying, "I love you."

"I love you too."

But unlike the past, this new year no longer holds the hope of a better one ahead. Even in my current state, my high can't withstand the heavy weight of my despair. So I lean into my friend in an attempt to regain the comfort that no longer exists for me. Instead, I'm greeted with the dread that shadows my future.

EIGHT

Carly

My thumb nervously drags back and forth along the gold-plated rim of my coffee cup. Ribbons of steam float up, eventually extinguishing into the chill of the air that surrounds me as I stare into the eyes of my one and only dear friend.

I'm sick to my stomach—sadness and anger gnaw at my gut, and I'm wasting away.

Margot's silvery-blue eyes that reflect her steely personality don't give much away. Hard as stone—that's Margot. She's the one person who comes from Tripp's world that I've become true friends with. The one person I feel as if I can trust, which is why we are here today, lunching at The Oval Room.

"Aren't you going to say anything?" I question on a vacillating whisper.

After setting her teacup onto the saucer with a delicate *clink*, she folds her hands on top of the white-linen-covered table. "He's a bastard." Her tone is soft but stern.

"So, what do I do?"

"Well," she starts, adjusting herself in her chair, "you can do what everyone else does—what the public is used to seeing—and what's best for his career."

"You mean, play the good wife? Keep my mouth shut, smile at the masses . . . be made a fool of when speculation begins to stir? Become another politician's wife, turning a blind eye to her cheating husband?"

She leans in. "It's our world, Carly. It's what we agreed to when we said 'I do.'"

"No," I bite, sharply. "That isn't what I agreed to. That isn't who I am."

"But it's who you are now." She pushes her tea aside. "Look, the last thing you want to do is ostracize yourself by not handling this properly. You'll lose everything, including your reputation and most certainly your job. Tripp is adored—he's the one who holds the promise of a better tomorrow, and you hold nothing but his hand. Without hard evidence to back your accusations, you're disposable—not him."

"Why? Because he's a Montgomery?"

"Exactly. That family is a legacy."

I look around the room as people hold their quiet conversations and eat their award-winning lobster and duck confit. Most of these men are probably funding my husband's campaign. Tailored suits, strong egos, powerful influence, and members of the good ol' boys club. This is what I'm up against.

"It's all bullshit," I seethe under my breath.

"Not to them. We're merely ornate figures in their world. But that is what gives us power."

"Power?" I contest with a defeated shake of my head. "What power do I possibly hold over him?"

"A lot more than what you think." She takes a quick glance around the room before meeting my eyes again and lowering her voice, "You have the power to destroy him."

"If I destroy him, I destroy myself too. His family will make sure I pay for whatever damage I do to Tripp's reputation and career."

"Perhaps, but you're smarter than that."

"I don't understand."

"People underestimate you because they don't know you—the real you. The girl who grew up poor and did everything she could to build a better life for herself. They all see you as Tripp's arm trophy—quiet, supportive, and demure. And you have those qualities, but if

55

they were to dig down to your roots, they'd find someone much different. Am I right?"

I soak in what she's saying and nod, wanting to believe she's right. I've lived in this glass world for a very long time, long enough for memories of the past to fade. I grew up far from privileged. Heck, there were times I lied about how the vending machine ate my money just so I could get a dollar to use to put food in my belly. My lies were small in comparison to the other kids I went to school with, but it was only because I was too terrified of getting caught to try anything else.

"Tripp knows who I was before him. He knows I'm not a doormat."

She cocks her head, and with condescension dripping from her tongue, she remarks, "And, yet, here he is, treating you as such, wiping the shit from the bottom of his polished loafers on you every time he leaves *her* to come home to you."

Her words are sharp, cutting straight to the truth I haven't been brave enough to see on my own.

"He's a politician, Carly. He only cares about himself."

"And what about your husband?"

A glint of a smile creeps onto her lips. "You don't think I play that man like a fiddle? I may portray the good wife on the outside, but behind closed doors, I'm a snake, and he knows it." She takes a sip of her tea before adding, "Ours is not a marriage of love; it's one of opportunity. We're more powerful together than what we are apart, and we both signed up for that."

"So, you just use each other for your own personal agendas?" I question, not entirely shocked. Margot is feisty and opinionated, always holding strong against the men in our world. I just didn't know that her marriage was one of convenience.

Her wink confirms.

"Why have you never told me this before?"

"Why should I? I mean, it isn't like I'm unhappy. I love my life. But every marriage is different, and this is the one I *choose* to be in."

"I don't know if I could be in a marriage like that."

"You already are," she states. "He doesn't love you. I hate to be so blunt about it because I know that deep down you still adore him. You want to paint him in colors that don't exist. But that man doesn't love you if he's fucking other women, and that right there should be enough to harden your heart to him."

I swallow hard as she touches the gaping wound that I so desperately want to heal. I don't want to love him, but I do, and it's killing me. *He* is killing my heart.

With devastation seeping out of me, I admit, "I don't want this. This isn't the life I dreamed of when I married him. I don't want to be this woman who sits at home and waits for her husband while he's with other women, but if I leave, then what? Where do I go? What do I do? I have nothing. Everything is in his name. Do I really start over from scratch?"

"Don't even consider that as an option. You should look into hiring a private investigator," she suggests, but what she doesn't know is that, over a year ago, I trudged down that avenue just to have it blow up in my face. "Don't let that man get off with just a slap on his wrist. He took the life he promised you and flushed it down the toilet."

"But he's in the middle of his campaign," I stress under my breath. "He's running for governor, for Christ's sake. I don't want to be front-page gossip. Maybe I should wait."

"For what?"

I hesitate as I consider how much worse it will be if I do wait. If he's governor, it will only make the gossip worse.

"Look, whatever you do, just be smart. Make sure this only affects him and not you. Your husband deserves to pay not only for what he is doing but also for what all these men are doing," she says, eyeing the room, insinuating that they are all up to the same game, which they most likely are.

The thought scathes beneath the surface, making my skin crawl. I hate that Tripp has done this to us, ripped us apart at the seams. That he has thrown away our marriage for some twenty-something-year-old. Margot is right, though. Why should I have to suffer for his wrongdoings? I never asked for this, so why should I be the one left with nothing? There is no way his parents are going to stand by while I divorce their son. I know them well enough to know they will do anything to destroy me in the process. Destroy my finances, destroy my career, and destroy my name.

Reaching across the table, Margot lays her comforting hands over my restless ones. "You know that I support you no matter what, right? I'm a vault. I'll never say a word."

"You don't even need to say that. I know you wouldn't betray me."

"Just remember . . . whatever you do, keep your hands clean."

Her words circulate in my head, again and again and again. They stay with me when I get home and into the night. The sun set long ago, and my husband hasn't returned any of my texts and, when I call, his phone goes straight to voice mail.

The house is dark and silent, but our last few fights echo in my head, stirring my anger into resentment. I'm so anxious that I've nearly picked off all the polish from my nails; there's a tiny pile of flakes by my feet.

He promised me we'd never become his parents, but here we are, a reflection of what I never thought we'd be.

I hate that I signed that stupid prenup. God, what was I thinking?

I wasn't, and that's on me.

However, it's his parents who pose the biggest roadblock of all. They would never stand by and allow me to simply walk away from their son not even if they wish I had never come into his life. In their eyes, it would be a double insult for me to do so. They would rather keep me around than to have me divorce their son in the public eye and tarnish their name any more than I already have. They would turn on me and make sure that they spun the story to make me look like some cold-hearted gold digger who took advantage of their son.

So how do I ensure my future if I leave? How do I keep my integrity and my reputation intact?

If Margot were willing to get involved, she would've offered her help, but there is no way I would even ask that of her. She comes from a legacy family just as Tripp does, and I know she'd walk through fire to avoid a scandal.

What I need is someone who can help me prove he's a liar and a cheater so that the prenup becomes null and void.

Margot mentioned hiring a private investigator, and it is a good idea. A good idea I've already had and one that has already blown up in my face.

I've been anxious all day as I wait for Gerald to call me. Having to hire a private investigator has been a nerve-racking ordeal. I never thought I'd find myself needing to do so, and now that I have, I feel dirty. Everything about this feels dirty, but I have to know for sure—I need proof that I can see instead of just my gut instinct. I need it in order to break the fidelity clause in the prenup I signed.

Today is day one, and I'm a basket case, busying myself around my office at the university, wondering if Gerald has been able to dig up any evidence. He told me that it could take time and to be patient with the process, but that's easier said than done.

I'm on my knees and riffling through one of my filing cabinets when I hear a familiar voice in the waiting room. Leaning back to peer out of my office door that's open, I see my mother-in-law talking to the student receptionist.

My chest constricts.

What is she doing here? She's never, not once, come to my office.

I push myself to stand just as my office phone rings.

"Yes?" I answer.

"There's a woman named Eloise here to see you."

"Send her in."

I hang up, and not a second later, she walks in, dripping in a de-signer-labeled dress and blazer. She closes the door behind her, and when she turns to me, she's stone-faced.

"Eloise, what are you doing here?" I question, keeping my tone as polite as possible.

She doesn't return the pleasantries as she stalks across the room to where I stand nervously. I swallow hard as she opens her pocketbook and takes out a check.

My check.

The one I wrote to Gerald.

She holds it out for me, but all I can do is stare at the check I gave him a couple of days ago.

"Well," she says, "aren't you going to take it?"

My perturbed eyes lift to meet her cunning ones.

"Go on," she urges, nudging the check toward me. "It is yours, isn't it?"

Fear makes me want to lie, but my signature is inked on the bottom line. Slowly, I take the check, and when I do, I see fangs as she steps even closer.

Her demeanor turns menacing, and with a low, stern tone, she says, "If you ever think about crossing this family again, I will single handedly dismantle your life, piece by piece, until you're left with nothing."

Venomous fright slithers its way around my body, chilling my skin into a cold sweat.

"Don't ever doubt my ferocity to keep the Montgomery name an honorable one. Not only are we powerful but we're also well-connected," she tells me, adding, "Gerald is an old family friend, and his loyalties are solid." Her voice drops another notch. "Tread with caution, my dear, because I will ruin you if you even think about crossing my son again."

The moment she turns, I find my voice. "I didn't—"

"I'm confident you won't mention this little visit to anyone," she says before opening the door and walking out.

That moment with Eloise was all it took for me to surrender and keep my mouth shut. I feel so foolish for putting my trust into the man who carries the name I now resent. My heart, my life, my money—everything. Tripp has always taken care of me, paid all the bills, made all the investments. Here I thought we were building a life for us, but it's only been for him. I deserve what is rightfully mine, and people deserve to know the truth about the man who will most likely be elected as their governor.

Headlights pierce through the windows of the formal sitting room, blinding me for a moment. When the dark spots fade, I look out to the driveway but don't recognize the white car that's idling in front of the house. I walk across the room, lean against the wall, and discretely peek out the window. My gut somersaults in putrid hate for my husband, who is sitting in the passenger seat next to *her*—the red-headed bitch.

God, he isn't even trying to hide this from me. He might as well just slap me across the face with his adultery.

My palms singe in disgust when he leans over and gives her a hug. From this angle, I can't tell if they're kissing. It's taking every morsel of self-control not to run out there like a crazed housewife and cause a scene. But damn it, the urge to claw into the two of them is running rampant through my veins.

I duck back out of view when he gets out of the car. I want to move, but I can't. Paralyzed in my rage, my chest trembles as I try to take in a solid breath. The door opens and he calls my name as he walks into the foyer, but I don't answer.

I can't.

Shit, I can hardly even breathe as emotions combust inside my chest, aching against the bones in my body as I do everything I can not to fall to my knees. When he turns and spots me with my back braced against the wall, he opens his mouth to speak, but I'm quick to cut him off.

"Why are you doing this?"

His shoulders drop. "Seriously. We're doing this again?"

Looking into his eyes, seeing him for what he is, all the pain and sadness that's been drowning my heart morphs into something I've never felt before, something that scares me. At the same time, it fuels me with the strength I need to step away from this wall. With steady legs and a heart that's pumping venom, I find the courage to be exactly who Margot was telling me to be.

Because I'm better than this.

Soft and demure, no more. I want nothing more than to punish him, to pulverize the pathetic, picture-perfect world he's living in. This man I once loved is now the man I want to see rot in front of my eyes. But I want the satisfaction of knowing that his demise was all my doing.

For now, I'll keep that to myself and swallow every hateful word I want to throw at him.

"I'm sorry," I say gently as I walk over to him. "I overreacted."

He shifts in his stance, surprised that I'm not fighting with him.

"I've just been sitting here, worrying about you. When I couldn't get ahold of you, I thought the worst. That maybe you'd gotten into a car wreck or something."

"I'm fine. I'm sorry, my phone died, and I left my charger in my car that wouldn't start, so I got a ride home from one of the staff."

When I'm close enough, I see the apprehension in his eyes as he looks at me, but I soothe him with lies, saying, "I'm sorry I snapped at you."

"Are you sure you're okay?"

A smile lifts my lips for reasons he's ignorant to.

"Never better."

And this is the moment I say goodbye to my good side. Being kind and loyal has only gotten me hurt.

With a sweeping kiss to his cheek, I seal the decision to make the man I once thought as my savior into my enemy.

NINE

Early

The ticking of the antique grandfather clock is the metronome I've been pacing to for the past hour. I've practically chewed every one of my nails down to the quick. Maniacal . . . that's the best way to describe my current state of mind that has me questioning my sanity.

Am I really considering doing this?

I didn't sleep at all last night. Lying next to Tripp, I stared at the ceiling as my mind ran rampant, trying to figure out my solution to this situation he's created for me.

Trying to figure my way out.

Trying to figure what my first step will be.

He slept soundly, barely even shifting his body. I'm furious that he remains solid and content while I'm losing my mind in a panic. My palms ached to slap him—they tingled for it, which only acerbates me to the point of wanting to jump off a cliff, headfirst.

I don't have a lot of people in my life I can turn to, and I wouldn't dare ask Margot to get behind the eight ball for my sake. Hell, her husband works as a United States senator. But there is one person I know who just might be desperate enough. I wavered for hours last night when I considered how she could help. I'm still wavering because, even if I just broach the idea with her, she could easily go to the media for a payout, so I have to be very careful about how I present this to her.

I've weighed as many options as I could come up with, carefully taking into consideration how to keep my hands clean and not leave any trail that could lead back to me. This isn't some small-time con to get a few bucks for food. This is severely risky, and the consequences are unimaginable. If I can pull this off, I won't be forced out of my career and shunned from society. I mean, let's face it, if word ever got out about my involvement in this, I would lose everything including my integrity. Who the hell would even trust me as their therapist? I have absolutely no fallback but I also have absolutely no other option.

Walking into the formal dining room, I grab a bottle of scotch from the liquor hutch and pour two fingers worth. I'll take courage from wherever I can, even if it's from a bottle. With a release of a deep breath, I take a gulp, cringing as the burn makes its way down into the pit of my empty stomach.

Now or never.

I call my office at the university, and after the second ring, Jenny answers.

"Academic advisory office. How can I help you?"

"Jenny, it's Carly. I need you to pull Emma Ashford's file and call her to schedule a time for her to meet me at my other office."

"Your private practice?"

"Yes. I am free all day today, but if she's busy, schedule at her earliest convenience."

"All right, let me see what I can do."

"Just call me back after you get ahold of her, okay?"

"No problem."

The phone nearly slips from my hand when I end the call. I can't believe how badly I'm shaking. It's a vibrant terror I've never felt before, and I'm freaking out.

"What the hell am I doing?" I murmur while considering another shot of scotch. Instead, I step over to the French doors that lead out to the grand backyard. I stare out over the bay to where our boat—*his* boat—is tied to the dock. It's the middle of winter, and he'd forgotten to have the crew put it in dry rack storage. A tiny piece of me hopes the haul cracks and the damn thing sinks.

The boat was a gift he'd skillfully bought as a surprise for me, yet it's in his name and was bought with his money, which makes it protected per the terms of the prenup.

Jumping when my cell vibrates in my hand, I see it's my office and quickly answer. "Hi, Jenny."

"Hi. I got ahold of her. She's free today, so I scheduled her for two o'clock this afternoon at your other office."

"Thank you. I have to swing by the university later, so I'll see you then." I hang up and drop the phone onto an end table.

"Shit." I try to breathe as I begin to pace back and forth again.

Oh my god.

Am I really doing this?

This is crazy. This is insanely crazy, but Margot is right. I have to stand up for myself. No longer will I be Tripp's doormat. I won't let him take everything from me in our divorce. I refuse to walk away with nothing when I've devoted the past thirteen years of my life to this man, sacrificed my career for him, and allowed my goals to take a backseat to his.

Looking at the time, I rush upstairs to pull myself together as best I can, despite not getting a minute's worth of sleep. No amount of concealer is going to hide the dark circles under my eyes, but I do my best. I opt for casual clothes in hopes that she will see me in a less authoritative position and more on her level. Just one woman asking for another woman's help.

I know it's bullshit that I'm about to ask this girl to toss every moral she has out the window, but I'm going to do it anyway.

My hands brace themselves on the sink the moment the reality of what I'll be asking her to do creeps in. With my head hung, I take in a deep breath in a meek attempt to calm myself, but too soon my cell rings again.

I cringe when I see that it's Eloise.

"Eloise, hi. How are you?" I greet, all the while gritting my teeth.

"Caroline, I'm glad I caught you. I scheduled a meeting next week for you and I to discuss the rally and banquet being held at the University of Maryland. It's very critical that you do your part with the young voters since they typically don't vote republican," she says. "It's important for them to see that they can relate to you as a . . . well . . . a person who was raised in a blue-collar family."

In other words: poor.

"Tripp's strategist will be joining us as well so he can go over speaking points, your attire, and overall behavior you'll want to exude for this event."

Not wanting to discuss this, I tell her, "That sounds great. I'm actually heading out the door right now, so just send me an invite to my email, and I'll get it on my calendar, but I really do have to run." I end the call and grind my teeth, knowing that she will berate me for my rudeness later. The woman insists on treating me like I'm some imbecile. I'm sick and tired of being the Montgomery's puppet.

They never even ask about anything, they just demand, setting up meetings without even verifying if I'm available. When it comes to their son's political career, I'm expected to be present no matter what. So many times I've had to push my job or my obligations to the side because, to them, I'm the low man on the totem pole.

Not any more.

Sure, I'll play my part for the time being, but it will be a limited act if I can get Emma to help me, which is why I must approach her very delicately.

My palms start to sweat again as I give myself one last look over, tugging at the hem of my navy sweater, which I've paired with jeans and simple slip-on shoes. Second-guessing the pearl earrings, I take them out and set them on my dresser before grabbing my coat and scarf.

The gray sky hangs over the city like a blanket that delivers no comfort. Never did I imagine having to do life on my own, but here I am, taking it in my hands and forging my own path for the very first time. Because this isn't about Tripp or his affairs—this is about me.

When I arrive at my office, my nerves are beyond shot. I'm literally trembling as I sit at my desk, waiting impatiently for Emma to arrive. She's probably wondering why I'm having her meet me at my private practice and not at my office at Georgetown, but I couldn't possibly have this conversation and run the risk of anyone overhearing us. Plus, what if she freaks out? It's too risky to do this at the university—or any public place for that matter.

Maybe this shouldn't be happening at all. Maybe I should leave, tell her something came up and that I have to cancel. Maybe I should—

The sound of the door opening yanks me from my doubts, and suddenly, anxiety rains down on me. My blood runs thin, sending a chill through my body as I walk into the small waiting room.

"Hi, Emma," I greet as calmly as I can, but I can hear the unevenness in my voice. I walk over to the door and lock it. When she shoots me a strange look, I explain, "It's just us. I don't want someone walking in while we're in my office."

She nods and follows me back, taking a seat on my sofa before slipping off her coat.

"How are you doing today?"

"Good," she says. "Is everything okay? We weren't supposed to meet until next week."

"This is . . . umm . . ." Shit. I've rehearsed this a hundred times in my head, planning out exactly what I would say to her, but now I can't remember anything. "I just needed to talk to you about something," I tell her as I drag one of the chairs closer to the couch and take a seat.

"It's okay if you can't continue to see me. I mean, I understand."

"No, no, no. That isn't it at all. I actually . . ." God I can't stop wringing my hands. "I actually needed to talk to *you* for a change."

"Oh," she says, surprised, and as I try to gather my thoughts, she asks, "Is this about the other week at the coffee shop?" She then hesitates. "I'm sorry. I mean—"

"No, it's fine. I know that must've been awkward for you, and I want to apologize if I snapped. As you can imagine, it was just as awkward for me."

As I say this, I glance to where she's twisting her fingers together and fidgeting. At least I'm not alone in my nervousness.

I take a deep breath and do my best to feign calm and control. I have to approach this in the best way possible, and that won't happen if I'm stumbling over my words and can't bring myself to look in her eyes.

Here it goes.

"I see a lot of myself in you, Emma. The way you grew up, your struggles in life, and your determination to fight for what you want."

She huffs. "Didn't get me very far, did it?"

"Maybe I can help you."

She shifts with curiosity in her eyes.

"Maybe we can help each other," I add.

"How so?"

I uncross my legs and lean forward slightly, folding my hands and staring down for a moment, dredging up every bit of courage I can.

God, I can't believe I'm actually doing this.

"Can I talk to you as a friend?"

"Yes."

I take a deep breath and drop my attention to my hands. "My husband is having an affair." She nods uneasily, so I keep going, "And, unfortunately, that puts me in a very difficult situation that I'm struggling to find a way out of."

"What do you mean?"

"You know who my husband is, right? You watch the news?"

"Yeah, I know. He's running for governor."

"I met Tripp when I was a few years older than you are now," I tell her in an attempt to gain her sympathy. "I was so young, and it surprised me when he took an interest in me. He was more than I ever thought I was worthy of. You see, I didn't grow up with a silver spoon in my mouth like he did, as I'm sure you assumed when you first met me. My father walked out on my mom and me after I was born."

"That's horrible," she says softly.

"My mom and I lived in a small apartment, and she did everything she could to make ends meet. I was determined to make something of myself, so I took out student loans and worked hard to put myself through college. Life was never handed to me; I had to fight for it," I explain. "Do you understand now why I see myself in you?"

"I'm sorry. I had no idea."

"It's okay, not many people know the details. But right before my college graduation, my mother lost her battle with cancer. So, I too am parentless."

I watch Emma's eyes tear up, knowing that the wounds of losing her own parents have yet to heal. I grab a tissue from the end table next to the couch and hand it to her.

"I know what it's like to feel lost and alone," I continue. "That was how I felt before I met Tripp and fell in love. He promised me the world, and I trusted him. He knew I didn't come from his world, but he married me even though his parents never approved of me. To them, I only serve to stain their name, but I always had Tripp on my side. He always protected me and fought for me." I then look around the room, saying, "This was my dream, but it took a backseat to the Montgomery dream. I never wanted to work as an academic advisor. I wanted to build this private practice and be a therapist, but that never fit their plan. Hell, now that I think about it, maybe it never fit Tripp's either. Maybe he used his parents as his scapegoat. Either way, I lost myself a long time ago. I take partial blame, of course. I willingly bowed to their pressure and sacrificed my hopes to help him gain his."

"That isn't fair," she says, twisting the tissue around her fingers. "Why do you put up with it? I mean, why don't you stand up for yourself?"

"Because I had Tripp to lean on for support. And because the power of the Montgomery family is immeasurable. And because I loved Tripp."

"Loved?"

I pause, realizing that I'm a little more relaxed talking to her, and admit, "That day at the coffee shop . . . that wasn't the first time I'd seen him with that girl. She actually works on his campaign team. Honestly, I've suspected him of cheating on me for quite some time now."

"Have you said anything to him? Does he know that you know?"

"I have, and the conversation always ends with us fighting and him accusing me of being insecure." I wave my hand. "It's classic deflection.

He doesn't care enough to be honest with me, and it's turned our marriage into a sham."

"So why are you still with him?"

"Because before I married him . . . I signed a prenuptial agreement. If I walk, I get nothing. I'm right back to where I started, but worse. He's in the middle of his campaign. If I divorce him, I'll be left with nothing. Since his parents donate heavily to the school, I'll probably lose my job and my reputation along with it."

"They're really that bad?"

"It's a crazy world I live in. One day you can be on top of the world, and the next? Banished entirely."

She leans back into the cushions, shaking her head with a mumbled, "That's fucked up."

I watch her as she digests everything I just told her as she continues to shake her head in disbelief. Story time is over the moment she asks, "So, why are you telling me all this?"

"I'm telling you because I hope you might be able to help me. In return, I can help you get back into Georgetown."

Her eyes lift. "How?"

Here goes nothing.

"I'm offering you fifty thousand dollars."

Sitting up, she straightens her back with her mouth agape. She doesn't speak, only stares in utter disbelief. Silence stretches between us, and I grow more nervous with each second that ticks by.

Then she asks the fifty-thousand-dollar question.

"What would I have to do?"

Biting my lip with more fear than I've ever felt in my life, I clench my hands together as ice washes through every inch of my body. With my heart slamming into my ribs, I take the hardest breath of my life and answer.

"I want you to seduce my husband."

TEN

Emma

I wait for the punchline to come, but it never does. This woman is dead serious and bat-shit crazy.

Did she seriously just ask me to seduce her husband?

I open my mouth to speak, but I can't find my words. Dropping my eyes from hers to her anxiously bouncing knee, my stomach sinks.

Yeah, she's serious, all right, and clearly scared to death.

"I-I'm sorry. Umm . . . did you say you wanted me to—"

"Seduce my husband."

Holy shit. Has she lost her mind?

"It's my word against his at this point," she says. "I have no proof of his affairs, nothing tangible that I can take to court to nullify the prenup. But if you help me—"

"Wait . . . you want me to have sex with him?" I just really need her to spell this one out.

It takes a moment, but she eventually nods.

With my jaw practically on the floor, I stare at her. A part of me wants to ask if this is some sort of joke, but her demeanor tells me she isn't joking at all.

Her knee stops jumping all over the place, and she draws in a really long breath. "I know you must think I'm crazy, and I shouldn't be asking you what I'm asking. And by no means am I coming to you because I think you're a person of low character. It's quite the opposite, I promise you. I just . . ." She loses her words, dropping her shoulders in defeat, and admits, "You're the only person I have to turn to."

71

"Me?"

"I know you need help, and I thought that maybe we could help each other."

"I need financial help," I blurt out, completely offended. "What you're asking is beyond a simple loan."

"I know."

"You're seriously asking me to sleep with your husband for money? Like a whore? Is that what you think I am? That I value myself so little and am so desperate for money I would fuck your husband?"

"No—I mean—I-I—" she stammers, and when I stand to grab my coat, she urges with desperation in her voice, "Please, Emma. I'm sorry. I just—I don't know what else to do. This is my life on the line."

"Mine's on the line too. Mine's pretty much in the gutter, but I'm not going around asking for handouts. But a handout is a far cry from what you're asking of me." I bite the words out harshly as I shrug on my coat, irritation marking every syllable. "News flash, I'm not for purchase." I'm fuming as I toss my purse over my shoulder and head to the door.

"Wait!"

Turning around, I watch as she moves toward her desk and fumbles with a pen and paper, scribbling quickly.

"Here," she says, holding the scrap of paper out for me.

I debate taking it, but after a second, I snatch it from her fingers to see a phone number scrawled on it.

"It's my cell phone," she says with hesitation. "Please . . . I don't know, just think about it?"

We deadlock on each other. I feel her despair, see it in the restlessness of her eyes, and I want to throw the paper to her feet and storm out. There is a split second where I consider doing just that, but then I find myself giving her a single nod. It isn't one of agreement, which I think she knows. It's one given out of sheer pity, and it's all this woman will ever get from me. There's nothing to think about. It's a hard no for me, so she's going to have to go sniffing for help elsewhere.

A thick haze clouds my head as I drive back to Luca's. I'm

drenched in utter disbelief of what just happened back there. Her proposition was so deranged that I'm starting to question my own sanity, starting to question whether my prim and proper therapist just asked me to sleep with her husband. Could I have misunderstood her?

No.

God, no. She was so clear.

That woman needs a serious dose of therapy for herself. One thing is for sure, I can't continue seeing her for therapy. There's no way we could ever continue with our sessions after that.

I'd be lying if I said that fifty thousand dollars didn't tempt me. It does. For a moment, I thought I'd be willing to do anything for that money. Then she revealed what she wanted from me.

There's an unfamiliar silver car parked in the driveway of Luca's house when I pull up. Inside, I'm greeted with the unpleasant sounds of moaning coming from Luca's bedroom.

Just what I need.

I toss my purse and coat onto the couch as I pass it and then stride right into my room where I kick the door shut. The slamming goes unnoticed, which doesn't surprise me considering the volume at which that chick is expressing her . . . *enjoyment.*

Maybe I should tell Mrs. Montgomery to give *her* a call.

When I can't take it anymore and Luca's grunts become audible, I shove in my earbuds and blast my playlist.

How has this become my life? I love Luca; he's my best friend, but this makes me sick to my stomach. He should come with a warning sign, but they'd probably be too blinded by his wealth and good looks to even notice. I wonder if it was the same for Mrs. Montgomery.

Were there red flags she never saw? I mean, let's face it, her husband is a powerful man and, for his age, very attractive. Was she swept away by all that? By his family name? By his money?

I can't blame her if she was. Any girl would allow herself to be swept away.

Well, any girl other than me. I've never been one to get lost in a guy. I've never even allowed myself to get serious with anyone. My eyes have always been on the future. Goals and ambitions have always ranked above and beyond. In high school, I watched my friends fall in love, only to wind up heartbroken. I never wanted to be the girl crying in the hallway because her boyfriend dumped her for the next girl climbing the rank in popularity.

It's all so superficial.

Hell, it wasn't until my freshman year at Georgetown that I finally lost my virginity. I met the guy at a frat party, and we spent the evening hanging out and playing pool. After a few beers, I whispered in his ear for him to take me to his room. Truth was, I just wanted to get it over with. No one wants to be a virgin in college. So, he took me up to his room, and we had a great time together.

He asked if he could call me.

I told him no.

I've had a few other hookups since then, but they all ended the same way. Luca says I'm icy. Maybe so, but I don't have time to get emotionally caught up with a man. My life has been enough of a roll-ercoaster of emotions without the headache of a boyfriend.

An incoming call interrupts my music, and when I see the call is coming from the facility where my brother lives, I quickly answer, "Hello?"

"Hi, Ms. Ashford?"

"Yes?"

"This is Debra from billing at Valley Crest."

"Oh, hey," I stammer as I jump off the bed. "Can you hold on for just one second?" I head into the living room, grab my coat from the couch, and rush outside before she hears the romping going on in the next room. "Okay, I'm back. Sorry about that."

"No worries. I was calling because I've been trying to run Matthew's housing payment for the month and the credit card we have on file was declined."

Shit.

"Declined? Are you sure?"

"Yes, ma'am. I tried running the card a few times before

calling you. Do you have another card so we can update your billing information?"

"Umm, no. I should probably call the credit card company to see what's going on," I tell her, too humiliated to admit that I'm dirt broke.

Two days ago, my other credit card got declined as well. I couldn't even pay to gas up my car, so I wound up writing a hot check. I felt like such a loser. I mean, who the hell pays with checks these days? Frauds, that's who.

"Yes, of course. Make sure you give me a call back so we can arrange a new method of payment. Just to remind you, we have a ten-day grace period before late fees start accruing."

"How much are the late fees?"

"Twenty-five dollars a day."

"What happens if I can't pay the full amount?" I cringe when I ask this, afraid of what the answer might be.

"After sixty days of non-payment, the patient would be removed from our facility."

"Well, what happens at that point? I mean, I'm not even living in-state."

"You would have to find a facility with an open bed that won't require additional payment beyond what Medicaid pays," she responds. "If you like, I can email you a list of those facilities."

I drop onto the bench on the front porch, sick to my stomach. The frigid air nips at my ears as my bitter cold fingers grip the phone. It's as if someone just sucker punched me, knocking the wind out of my lungs.

Matthew is in a shitty facility as it is, and it costs me beyond what the state and Medicaid will cover. I don't even want to imagine the crap-hole facility that runs solely on Medicaid. Matthew is already miserable, and there is no way in hell I'm going to allow him to suffer more than what he already is.

"No, it's fine. I was just curious. Let me call the credit card company and see what's going on. I recently had to make several purchases for this next semester at school, so I'm sure it's just a precautionary measure," I lie.

"No worries, Ms. Ashford."

"Is it okay if I get back with you tomorrow?"

"Of course," she says. "You have a good afternoon."

Setting the phone on the bench, I drop my head into my open palms as my eyes heat with tears.

"Fuck," I say under my breath as a tear falls to the concrete beneath me.

Why is this happening? Silently, I plead to God, needing to know why he took my parents from me and left me with this mess of a life. Forget about me. Why did He take them from Matthew? Here I am, trying to fill their rolls as his guardian and failing. I fought for it so I could protect him and take care of him, but all I'm doing is letting him down. The thought of turning over responsibility of him makes me even sicker, and I know that I can't. I refuse to put him solely in the hands of the state. He needs me, but I'm so lost. I'm lost and alone, and I'm drowning.

I fight so hard to get to the surface, only to have another wave crash down on me. I've been all over town, putting in applications in hopes of finding a job that will help pull me out of this mess I've created. But there is no out.

I'm fucked.

And if I'm fucked, then so is my brother.

He doesn't deserve any of the shit life has piled on him. He's a kind soul, and he needs me. It's one thing for me to be on my own but not Matthew.

Another tear falls from the tip of my nose.

I've maxed out all my credit cards. I don't even want to know the amount of debt I'm in, but it has to be well over forty thousand dollars. Even if I got a decent full-time job, I would make just enough to pay for Matthew. There probably wouldn't be enough left over to pay off these cards that are racking up late fees with each passing month. I'll never get my head above water. How will I ever afford a place of my own? Food? Gas? Clothing?

The sound of the door opening startles me, and I pop my head up to find a tall blonde step out onto the porch. She looks surprised to see me as she tightens her scarf around her neck.

"Hey," she murmurs, to which I give a subtle nod.

She stares a beat too long as she takes in my splotchy, tear-stained face.

"Are you okay?"

Annoyance strikes like a machete. Rolling my eyes like a total bitch, I grab my phone, walk right past her without a word, and go back inside the house.

"Hey, Em. What's up?" Luca says from the kitchen. His hair is mussed and he isn't in anything but a pair of gym pants.

Hostility, jealousy, and frustration clog my veins, and I snap, "Just leave me alone," as I make a beeline to my room, slamming the door behind me.

Leaning against the door, I heave as my heart pounds violently. I fall to my knees and release an ugly silent cry, but in my head, I'm screaming. Screaming for someone to save me.

Through the ringing in my ears, I hear a knock on my door followed by Luca asking, "Emma, are you okay?"

Mustering up any composure I possibly can, I respond, "Please, just give me some space, okay?"

He doesn't respond, and I hold my breath for fear a wretched sob will break through. As soon as I hear his door close, I let out a slow and uneven exhale. Knowing we share a wall, I curl into myself and quietly cry. If Luca can hear me, he'll just assume either I'm crying over my parents or school.

The tears are for so many more than those two reasons. More than he will ever know because I'm not that girl who dumps her problems on the people who surround her. No one needs to know how fucked up my life is.

After a crappy night, I have to drag myself into my even crappier job. I hate working retail and having to kiss ass just to make a little commission, but until I can find a full-time position elsewhere, I'm stuck.

I make my way to the back room where I shove my coat and purse into my mini locker. As I grab my punch card to clock in, my attention shifts to my boss as he peeks out of his office.

"Emma, can I speak with you before you clock in?" Wesley says.

"Umm, sure." I slip my time card back into its slot.

"Please, have a seat." He's only a couple of years older than I am, but sadly, he prides himself as being the manager of this clothing store catering to high school kids.

"So, what do you want to speak to me about?"

"As you know, business has been on the slow side lately," he starts, and I already know where this is going. "After a long discussion with corporate, I'm forced to make cuts."

"Wes, please," I beg, knowing that having this last thread of hope yanked away will be too much. "I need this job."

"This isn't an easy decision to make. You're a great asset to the store, but this comes down to money."

Everything comes down to money. The one thing I don't have.

"Then get rid of Becky. That girl is always showing up late or calling in sick," I tell him, desperate to change his mind. "The other night when we were closing, she spent the whole time in the break room talking to her boyfriend. She's dead weight."

"She's also full time."

"Then fire her and give me her schedule."

He leans back in his chair with a resigned expression on his face, and I know the decision has already been made. "I'm sorry, but I have to let you go."

I see no point in wasting any more time here, so with an audible huff, I push myself out of the chair, grab my belongings from my locker, and slam it shut.

"Emma," he says when he steps out of his office.

"Just let me be pissed, okay?" I throw the words over my shoulder as I walk out and straight to the parking lot.

As if this week couldn't get any worse.

I sling my purse and coat onto the passenger's seat, shut the door, and drop my head into my palms, completely at the end of my rope.

Here I sit, desolate in my private misery. Without a sound, I beg for a sign. For guidance of any kind. I know it's a pointless effort, but I do it anyway because how many more blows can a person take? I upturn my purse to find my stupid keys, which have undoubtedly sank to the bottom, and a small avalanche of crap spills everywhere. I find them sitting right on top of the small folded piece of paper that Mrs. Montgomery gave me the other day. I pluck it from the mess and unfold it, only to stare at the ink for a moment.

Blinking back tears, I replay everything she told me—everything about her past. Maybe she's just as desperate as I am right now. I wonder if she's sitting alone and crying like I am. If she's pleading with her deceased parents as I am.

Was she really that out of line for coming to me for help? I mean . . . all she's asking for is exactly what I do with guys anyway, only I'm not getting paid. It isn't as if I wear my heart on my sleeve or that I wouldn't know exactly what I was walking in to. It would just be a fleeting moment with a man I'd never have to see again.

Was I truly offended by what she was asking of me, or was I merely pretending to be offended in a subconscious attempt to pretend I was on some moral high ground because society says I should stand there? The one that says having sex for money is distasteful. What about the sanctity of marriage? Society can excuse her husband's disregard for his vows as little more than . . . expected. Why? It's unfair for him to be held to a different standard because he's rich and attractive. Where are the people standing in her corner, willing to have her back when she's been wronged? She asked me to help her oust her husband, and she's willing to help me in return.

So, what's my hang up?

After all, she's offering me a solution. A way out. Fifty thousand dollars would guarantee Matthew wouldn't have to leave the home he's in. It would buy me time to get on my feet and figure out a plan to get back into Georgetown.

Hell, I'd probably do the exact same thing she's doing if I were in her situation.

Looking down at the phone that's now in my hand, I wonder if this is a sign. As screwed up as it is, what if this is my only way out?

It isn't as if she's asking me to kill someone. It's sex.

Simple.

Easy.

Not wanting to think about what I'm about to do for fear I'll talk myself out of it, I plug in her number and type out a quick text.

Me: I'm in. —Emma

ELEVEN

Emma

Merrifield, Virginia—that was where Carly suggested we meet when she texted me back yesterday.

Me: Why Merrifield?

Carly: It's inconspicuous. Can you meet me at 4:00 pm at The Rusted Cup Diner?

Me: Yes.

My head is foggy as I nurse my second cup of coffee. I barely slept last night, and by the circles under Mrs. Montgomery's eyes, I suspect she didn't either.

When my empty stomach growls, I take another sip of my coffee, but it's gone cold.

"Are you sure you don't want anything to eat? And, please, you don't have to continue calling me Mrs. Montgomery. I think we're far past formalities at this point."

I shake my head. "I'm fine."

A young waitress, who stinks of stale cigarettes, comes around with the coffee pot and gives me a much-needed refill.

I'm nervous.

Carly is too.

Neither one of us knows where to begin, so we sit in this rundown diner in the middle of nowhere. Booths with cheap linoleum tabletops line the wall of windows that look out to the parking lot where only a few cars are parked. I start to question my decision to meet her, and the silence between us has turned grating.

"So, what's the plan?" I ask.

Staring down at her cup of coffee, she drags her thumb along the rim, the polish on her nails is almost completely chipped away. "Are you sure you're okay with this?"

I give her a nod, and when I do, she scans the small diner, paranoid someone may be listening, but no one even notices us. The few people that are in here are lost in their newspapers and pancakes.

"He'll be in the city for the next few days," she says quietly. "He's staying at The Jefferson Hotel." She takes a sip of her coffee. "He'll often have a cocktail and work late at Quill, the lounge on the ground floor."

"How do you know for sure?"

"Because Tripp is a creature of habit. He's type-A and predictable."

"So, what do I do?"

"Show up," she says. "You know what he looks like."

"I can't just show up out of the blue. I'll need a room."

"Why?"

Clearly, she hasn't thought this through.

"Because if he asks to come to my room, it would look suspicious if I didn't have one."

I swear to God, I just saw the light bulb turn on inside her head.

"Yeah, you're right," she murmurs. "Okay, then. I'll get you a room for tomorrow night." Her attention stays trained on her hands as she continues to nervously shift around her coffee mug. There's barely any eye contact at all when she continues. "It's a historical luxury hotel. Michelin-starred food. You'll need a nice dress."

"Why a dress?"

Her eyes fall shut for a moment and she fidgets before, almost painfully, saying, "Because legs turn him on." Finally, her eyes lift to meet mine, revealing the slightest hint of tears that well along her bottom lid. "He likes a feminine woman, but a confident one. So, don't be too meek."

When her head drops again, I worry she's doubting this whole plan, but I can't have her wavering because I need this. I need the payout. Reaching my hand across the table, I rest it on top of hers, whispering, "Are you okay?"

She shakes her head, peering up at me. "No . . . no, I'm not okay. None of this is okay."

"But you're right, you know?" I encourage. "You can't let this man rip your whole life apart and get away with it. He's using you, Carly."

Her jaw tightens as she nods. "I know. This is just . . . this is so unlike me."

"You have to take a stand for yourself."

She doesn't respond, and I get the feeling that pushing too hard would be a mistake, so I get back to the plan. "When do you want this to happen?"

She veers away from whatever thoughts are consuming her and takes another sip of coffee. "He has a strategy meeting tonight, so I was thinking tomorrow."

"And you think he'll be that easy?"

She shrugs. "I don't know. It might take a little time, but for now, just do your best to make an impression on him. He can be quiet, you know? It sometimes comes off as rude, but that's just his personality, so don't take it to heart."

"No part of my heart is involved in this," I say, and her head lifts so she can look me in the eyes.

"It's a job, right?"

"Right."

"And the money?" I ask because I'm not doing this for her; I'm doing it for me, and it's imperative that I get the money sooner rather than later.

"Oh, right," she mumbles as she starts digging in her oversized purse. She then pulls out an envelope and discretely slides it across the table. "It's all there. Ten thousand. After the two of you . . . well, you know . . . I'll pay you the rest." She reads my hesitation, and assures, "You have my word."

Pulling the envelope down to my lap, I take a peek inside to see a stack of hundreds bundled together. "And the dress?"

"What about it?"

"I'll need money to buy one," I say as if I don't already have a perfectly appropriate dress hanging in my closet. I might as well get what I can out of her.

"Oh." She seems caught off guard with my request, but if she wants me to play the part, she's going to have to foot the entire bill. Fumbling around in her purse again, she takes out her wallet and pulls out a few bills. "Here. I think two hundred should cover a dress. Make it appropriate. Nothing too skimpy or flashy. Keep it simple."

I take the money and shove it and the envelope into my purse.

"And your hair . . . wear it down."

I take note of her instructions and then ask, "What happens after?"

"After you make contact with him, call me and I'll come meet you. I want to know everything that happens. Every detail."

She turns nervous again.

"Are you okay?"

"You're, um . . ." She clears her throat lightly, and a flush stains her cheeks. "You're clean, right?"

Her insinuation that I'm anything but irks me, but I don't let my irritation show and tell myself that it's a reasonable question nowadays. "Yes, of course I am."

With her eyes downcast, she tosses a few bucks onto the table, slips on her coat, and grabs her purse. Before she stands, she adds, "I'll book you a room under your name for tomorrow." And with that, she turns her back to me and rushes out of the diner, leaving me to myself.

I peer out the foggy window while she gets into her car, clearly unstable as tears slip down her cheeks. The moment she drives away is the moment I empty my lungs with the heaviest sigh of my life.

Hanging my head, I tell myself over and over again that I can do this. That I *have* to do this—for me and for my brother. When I look down and see the manila envelope in my purse, a feeling I haven't felt in a very long time washes over me and my lips lift.

Relief.

My smile grows, and when I gather my things and walk out to my car, I swear a giggle slips out. Heading straight back to DC, my first stop is the bank to deposit the money. After calling my brother's residential facility and paying the bill, I decide to go shopping for a new dress. But shit if I don't feel like treating myself to something special after all the stress I've been under.

Not wanting to fight traffic, I leave my car at the bank and take the Metro, which drops me off near a local boutique I love. I haven't actually been able to shop here, but that has never stopped me from coming in from time to time to browse the latest designers and trends.

Everything costs more than two hundred dollars, but when the sales clerk tells me about the clearance rack in the back of the store, I'm able to find a few dresses to try on. It's been a long time since I've felt the air of levity. I'm so lost in the reprieve as I'm trying on these dresses that I'm not even thinking about the possibility of Carly's husband taking it off me.

No.

I simply enjoy this moment, because who knows when the other shoe is going to drop?

When I think I've found the one, I step out of the fitting room to look at myself in the trifold mirror and smooth my hands along the lush navy fabric. The front of the dress is modest and shows just the right amount of cleavage to still be considered tasteful, but the back boasts a deep plunge. It's a striking dress, tailored to the knees but elegant and proper.

"Wow. Stunning."

In the reflection of the mirror, I spot Olivia from over my shoulder, and I turn and give her a warm smile. "What are you doing here?"

She lifts the necktie she has in her hand. "Tripp spilled coffee on his tie this morning, and he has an important meeting tonight, so here I am."

A part of me wants to pick her brain about everything Tripp, but I refrain and give her a quick and discreet once over. She is the woman

he's cheating on Carly with, so I want to make sure I bear resemblance
to her.

"What's the occasion?"

"Oh, um . . . it's for a Cystic Fibrosis Charity Gala back home in
Tennessee." The lie comes quick and easy, simply rolling off my tongue.

"What a wonderful cause," she remarks, to which I smile in agreement. "I'm sorry I never called you after the New Year's Eve party. Things
have just been so busy."

"No worries. I've been pretty tied up myself. What does your schedule
look like later this week? You free for lunch?" I ask, even though I have
no desire to get to know her better. Hell, maybe she'll open up to me
about Tripp. At this point, with the position I'm in, I should probably
keep this girl close to me.

She scrolls through her phone, saying, "How about Thursday?
Sometime in the afternoon?"

Since I have no job and I'm no longer in school, I don't even have
to check my calendar. "Yeah. Thursday sounds great. You still have my
number?"

"Yes. I'll pick a spot to meet and text you."

"Great. I'm looking forward to it." It isn't a total fib, but it also isn't
the truth.

While she heads toward the register to purchase the tie, I slip back
into the dressing room to change.

"Did any of those work for you?" the sales associate asks when I
step out.

"I think I'll take this one," I say, handing her the dress.

"Perfect choice."

Relaxed, I hand over my bank card without fear of it being declined.
When she zips the dress up in a hanging bag, I smile as I take it from her.

Happiness is an old friend I haven't seen in over a year, and I embrace it. Sure, it's a bit dented and sinister, but I'm not trying to dissect
what I've been longing to feel.

When I arrive back home, Luca is watching television in the living
room.

"Where have you been?" he asks, eyeing the garment bag draped over my arm.

"Shopping. I needed a new dress for interviews."

"I still can't believe you got fired."

I head to my room, and Luca follows, stopping at the door.

"Is everything okay?"

I hang the dress in the closet and tell him from over my shoulder, "Yeah, I'm fine. Yesterday was a crappy day. No big deal. Sorry I snapped at you."

Leaning against the doorjamb, he stares at me with concern.

"I promise, Luca," I try to assure. "I'm fine."

"I worry about you."

"Don't."

"I just know that whatever you're going though is a lot and that you probably aren't talking about it with anyone."

"I talk to Mrs. Montgomery," I defend.

"You know what I mean."

"Well, if it makes you happy, I just so happen to have a coffee date later this week with Olivia."

"Olivia?" he groans as he strolls across the room and sits on the edge of my bed. "Just do me favor and try not to bring her around. She's a clinger."

"You're so full of yourself." I laugh. "You really think she's still hung up on you? You guys hooked up a couple of years ago."

"Hey, what can I say. I leave a lasting impression."

"You need an ego check."

"You wouldn't be saying that if you'd give me a chance," he teases with a cocked brow.

I roll my eyes, and he shoots me a smirk.

"Just sayin'."

When he stands to leave, I stop him with a quick, "Oh hey, I'm going to be making a quick trip back home tomorrow, but I'll be back the following day."

"What's going on back home?"

"My niece has a school performance, and I promised her at Christmas that I would attend."

"Cool. I'll see you when you get back," he responds, not even batting an eyelash at my deceit.

The rest of the day passes with ease. I even call Matthew to check in and see how he's doing. He's agitated, and his audible ticks have become more frequent, which is a sign of anxiety. I promise myself that I'm going to find him a better home once I get back on my feet.

Luca and I camp out on the couch, eating Chinese takeout and watching a movie until we both fall asleep.

It isn't until I wake up that the boulder in the pit of my stomach returns. The gloom hovering above me has returned, and I've been a bundle of nerves all day. I go to The Jefferson in the afternoon to check in and pick up my room key, and then I walk around the prestigious hotel, familiarizing myself with the space, making sure to peek my head into Quill.

When I go up to see the room Carly booked for me, I am blown away by the opulence and end up hanging out there for a while. If only my mind weren't spinning in a million different directions, I could enjoy it. But it is, so I can't, and I end up going back home.

Luca isn't here. He has an evening class tonight and he always goes out to a local bar with his buddies afterward, so I don't have to worry about him seeing me when I'm supposed to be in Tennessee.

Jittery hands make it difficult to apply my mascara, but when I take a step back from the mirror in my bedroom, you would never know the level of anxiety I'm under. I'm also freaking out because, if Olivia is with him, I'm screwed, and not in the good way.

"Pull yourself together," I murmur as I slip on my nude heels.

Wearing my long blonde hair down, just like Carly instructed, I look at the con I'm about to become, sheathed in a designer dress and about to seduce a well-respected politician.

I feel like a cliché of sorts, but I keep my eye on the endgame, which is the paycheck. I need this money. Ten thousand isn't nearly enough, but the full fifty will be a good start.

I check the clock.

It's game time.

The drive to the hotel is short, but I forgo the expensive valet and park a block down in a garage. With my umbrella in hand and my wool coat wrapped around me, I make my way down the street.

Snow has given way to rain, which is already starting to freeze in small patches. My heart beats wildly, and I do my best to slow its tempo to match the clicking of my heels against the pavement, but it's a failed feat.

When I approach the hotel, the windows are fogged over, making it difficult to see in, but I know he's there. That thought alone releases a swarm of bees within my stomach.

"You can do this," I whisper before opening the door and stepping inside.

"Evening, Miss," a gentleman greets when I make my way into the lounge. "May I?"

With a polite nod, I allow him to help me with my coat. "Thank you." I then hand him my umbrella before he rushes off to check them.

My eyes skitter across the lavish lounge, rich in mahogany and deep-brown leather. It's nearly empty, but he's here.

Holy shit, there he is.

Something inside me dip-dives as I watch him from across the room. He sits at the bar with an open briefcase to one side and an almost empty tumbler in front to the other. Carly was right—he's hard at work. His suit jacket is draped over the back of his chair and the sleeves of his dress shirt are rolled up.

After a silent pep talk, I remind myself of what Carly told me earlier and the demeanor I should have. More than anything, I think of my brother and how I can't fail him. He needs me, so I have to do this.

I approach the bar and notice him rubbing his forehead after he slips off his glasses that he never wears when he's on television.

"May I?" I question as I take the seat next to him, thankful that this man is sharply handsome and not some ogre.

"Um, of course . . . yes."

He seems flustered, or maybe he's just tired. Eyeing his open briefcase with papers scattered about, I ask, "Working off the clock?"

He looks over to me, smelling of spiced cologne and scotch. "In my line of work, there are no clocks."

"What can I get for you?" the bartender inquires as he sets a cocktail napkin in front of me.

"Grey Goose martini, up, stirred, with a twist."

I've never tasted the drink before, but it's what Luca's mother drinks so I figured I couldn't go wrong.

When I turn my attention back to my target, he's wearing a slight smirk, and oddly enough, it eases my tension.

"So, no clocks," I state. "How do you know when to stop?"

The clink of the martini glass being set in front of me sounds at the same moment his eyes land on my cleavage.

"I'm not a man who likes to stop."

TWELVE

Carly

Alone at the dining table with an empty bottle of wine.

How has this become my life?

The rain gave way to snow a few hours ago, and it feels like a reflection of my soul. A metamorphosis seemingly beyond my control.

Only, I am in control. It is by my hand that I sit here, in the early hours of the morning, turning my blood into alcohol as I wait for the call. My eyes burn from lack of sleep and the many tears that have slipped out of them today.

Salt eating flesh.

Thoughts tormenting me.

It's after three in the morning, and I can't stop torturing myself with thoughts of what the two of them are doing that's preventing her from calling.

What have I done?

I'm second-guessing this plan in its entirety, but there's no turning back. At least I know that Emma is on my side, and she'll tell me everything I need to know. It's the other women I have to worry about—the wild cards who are looking for their ticket to advance in social standing. Or maybe it's the thrill of the forbidden that drives them to married men.

Yet, here I sit, a desperate wife, doing what she can to regain control of her life. When I walk away from this marriage, I'll be damned if my head isn't held high.

The wine acts to medicate me, putting me to sleep right here at the table with my head resting upon my folded arms.

When the chiming on my phone wakes me, I raise my head and squint against the morning sun that's pouring into the room. My head spins, and when I pick up the phone to read the text, it takes a moment for my vision to clear from the haze.

Emma: Tripp just left my room to go to work. The coast is clear.

Putrid gurgling from my gut makes me flee from the table. Sour bile rises as I run to the kitchen sink because there's no way I'll make it to the restroom. With my hands braced on the edge of the glazed lava stone countertop, I vomit the burning remnants of last night's wine into the sink. My stomach bubbles in disgust as another round barrels its way up my throat.

Flicking on the faucet, I hang my head as the tears fall.

He spent the entire night with her.

I swish my mouth out with water and then soak a paper towel and press it along the back of my neck. The effort to right myself is for naught. All I can hear is the echo of Margot's words in my head.

"Without hard evidence to back your accusations, you're disposable—not him."

"Get it together, Carly," I tell myself because I need to hear the words. I need them to give me strength because I have to become an armored shield when I see Emma and listen to what she has to tell me.

I let my mind go straight to the very thoughts I typically try so hard to bury—Tripp in bed with these women. I think of the sounds they make, the words they speak, their writhing bodies. The visions that play in my head infuriate me, and before I know it, my hands are fisted so tightly they're shaking. I remind myself of the life my husband stole from me—and for what? For a tryst?

Straightening my spine. I go back to the dining table and pick up my cell.

Me: I missed you last night. How is your morning so far?

I'm surprised by how quickly he responds.

Tripp: Late night working. I'm in the office but about to walk into a meeting. Talk later?
Me: Talk later. Love you.

Now that I have the clear that he isn't at the hotel, I tap on Emma's name and send her a text in return.

Me: I'll be there in 2 hrs.

A weird sense of anticipation comes over me, and I move quickly as I toss the empty bottle of wine and set the glass in the sink. I then rush upstairs, take a shower, throw on some makeup, and get dressed. Before I know it, I'm in the car and heading to the city.

The hour-and-a-half long drive tests my patience. One minute, I'm angry, white-knuckling the steering wheel, and the next minute, I'm fighting back tears. Shuffled in between are moments of pure numbness. I savor the numb; it's where I feel the safest. No thoughts, no feelings—just emptiness.

After I drop my car off with the valet, I take the elevator up to the sixth floor. When she answers the door, she's wearing a pair of jeans and a burgundy sweater with her hair tied back. She's pulled together, which is encouraging, and when I step in, I spot a food cart draped in white linen. I turn cold when I see the two cups of half-drunk coffee and a messy bed.

I don't say anything at first as I wander over to the set of chairs positioned by the windows and take a seat. She joins me. It's so quiet in this room that it amplifies the chaos inside my head.

"What happened?" I finally ask. "Was he here?"

"Yes," she breathes.

"And you two . . ."

"No."

"I want to know everything."

She pulls her legs up, tucking them in close with her arms wrapped around them. "I showed up at Quill around ten o'clock, and he was there, just like you said he would be." She speaks slowly and cautiously. "He was sitting at the bar, and I joined him. We talked for a while and had a couple of drinks. When the lounge was about to close, I invited him up here for a nightcap, and he accepted."

My hands twist as I listen to her, but in a way, I'm detached, as if it isn't Tripp she's talking about.

"When we got to the room, he poured us both drinks and we talked for a bit."

"Did you sit here?" I ask, eyeing the chairs we're in, and she shakes her head.

"He kicked off his shoes and sat on the bed. I joined him. He seemed comfortable but also uneasy. He turned on the television," she says and then shrugs. "He turned it to some old movie; a comedy. We drank and laughed, chitchatting all along."

"What did you talk about?"

"He asked about me. I lied, saying I'd just graduated from the University of Pennsylvania. He laughed, when I told him."

"Laughed?"

"He said something like . . . '*Leges sine moribus vanae.*' Said it was Latin for—"

"Laws without morals are useless." I smile tightly as Emma lets out a breathy laugh.

"Yeah, that's what he said. Ironic, huh? Apparently, it's the university's motto."

"So, you just talked?"

"We kissed," she reveals. "Nothing intense. No touching or anything. Just kissing. Like I said, he came off confident, but there was a hint of uneasiness. It was him who pulled away first, but then he asked if he could stay the night."

"He slept in bed with you?"

She nods. You'd think I'd be irate to know they kissed, but I'm not. It doesn't even feel real.

"We both had a little too much to drink, so that's all that happened. We talked, kissed, and then fell asleep."

"And this morning?"

"He was up and had ordered room service before I was even awake. He seemed rushed, but he asked if he could see me again tonight."

"That's um . . . that's good."

"Can you rent the room for an extra night?"

Flustered, I rub my brows. I don't know what I was expecting. I mean . . . I sort of figured this would be a one-and-done, but that was stupid of me to assume. "Um, sure. Yeah, I'll extend the reservation on my way out."

Emma reaches over, lays her hand over mine, and with a gentle tone, says, "If you don't want me to meet him tonight, I don't have to."

"No," I blurt a little too quickly. "It's fine."

"I'm on your side," she assures.

"I know. It's just . . ."

"Yeah, I know."

I take in a deep breath before letting it go and standing. "So, that's it?"

Looking up at me from where she still sits, she responds, "That was it. Aside from the kissing, it was harmless."

I stare into her eyes, knowing everything she's been through this past year, and I get an overwhelming urge to protect her. It's stupid of me. How can I possibly protect her when I've thrown her into this situation? But the feeling is there in spite of what I've done.

"Are you okay?"

She hesitates for just a moment. "I'm fine. Like I said, he was harmless. Actually, he was pretty gentlemanlike, all things considered."

"Yeah, he's a man of chivalry, all right," I condescend, to which she chuckles.

She then stands with an air of lightness to her. "You know what I mean."

I smile before asking once more, "Are you sure you're okay?"

She nods, adding, "So, is the routine the same? I should text you after I see him tonight?"

"Yes."

I pick up my purse, take one last look at the bed, and then turn for the door before she stops me, saying, "Oh, he said he wanted to have dinner at Plume."

I turn back to her, and she lifts her shoulders.

"He said it was a Michelin-starred restaurant. I don't have anything nice enough to wear."

Her eyes are bashful, and I feel bad that she's having to ask for more help when I know how much she hates it.

"It's okay," I tell her as I pull out my wallet and slip a few hundreds from it. "Here. This should be enough." She takes the money, and before I walk out the door, I remind her, "If you need me, I'm here."

Her only response is a slight smile that I mirror in return before leaving.

THIRTEEN

Carly

Groundhog Day. It's what I woke up to.

The same unease remains, the same pit in my stomach, the same restlessness in my hands. It's a litany of side effects that torment me. I couldn't sit at home any longer, so I came into the office first thing this morning even though I don't have any students scheduled for today.

I've been rifling through paperwork, updating files, and doing anything I can to keep myself busy, but there's no reprieve for my head and heart. No. Those two are webbed in a labyrinth of anguish.

"I'm running out to grab a sandwich," Jenny says from my doorway. "You want anything?"

"Lunch already?" I look down at my watch, surprised to see it's already half-past noon.

"Yeah. You've been buried in here for hours," she notes.

I shove a file back into the drawer and slide the cabinet closed.

"You hungry?"

"No, I'm fine. Thank you, though."

When she heads out, my stomach grumbles—not with hunger but with anxiety. I look at my cell to see I have no missed texts or calls and then double-check to make sure my ringer is turned up.

Are the two of them still together?

Spinning around in my chair, I retrieve another file to keep myself busy, and about an hour later, my phone finally chimes.

Emma: He just left for work. Coast is clear.

Me: Be there in 20 min.

One foot in front of the other pulls me out to the parking lot and to my car. Chilly hands navigate my car down each busy street, leading me over to The Jefferson. Before I know it, I'm ditching my car with the valet and stepping onto the elevator. In a repetition of yesterday, I knock on the door, but this time, when Emma answers, I know our conversation will be a stark contrast to yesterday's.

She's freshly showered with wet hair, and she's wearing a hotel bathrobe. Her eyes don't meet mine as she widens the door.

I step inside, and Emma hesitantly walks over to the chairs we sat in fewer than twenty-four hours ago, but I don't follow. It's too close to the tangled sheets. Too close to where her dress and panties are strewn on the floor. Instead, I lean against the dresser that's across from where Emma sits, twisting her hands anxiously.

Lines that etch her youthful face expose guilt. But she shouldn't feel guilty. She did nothing wrong, only what I asked of her. It's me that should feel guilty. I'm the one who put this innocent girl in this situation.

"Are you okay?" I eventually ask, but her eyes remain downcast when she gives me a nod. I look to the nightstand where there's an open bottle of vodka. Walking over, I pick it up and pour some in one of the glasses that's on the room service cart with two plates of half-eaten breakfast and a pitcher of orange juice. After adding a splash of the juice into the vodka, I hand it to Emma. "Here."

Reluctantly, she accepts it, staring into the glass for just a moment before taking a gulp. "Thanks."

I move back over to the dresser and try to keep my voice steady and un-accusatory when I ask, "So, what happened?"

Her eyes skitter around the room and eventually land on the bed. "Exactly what you wanted to happen."

Tense, I lick my lips. My stomach barrels into itself, and I'm forced to brace my hands along the edge of the dresser. "How?"

Slowly, she looks up at me, finally showing me the confusion and apprehension and guilt that stain her cheeks.

"Start from the beginning," I prompt. "Start with dinner."

She takes another swallow of the vodka, seeming to relax a little when she begins. "When I got to Plume," she says, her voice timid, "he was already at a table, drinking a glass of scotch. He seemed tired, but he was probably just hungry because after we ate our dinner, he became livelier. We talked about my family . . . of course, I lied, telling him I was the youngest of two brothers and that my parents were still alive and well. He laughed when I recalled fictitious stories of my childhood."

"And what about him? What things did he tell you?"

"Not much," she admits. "He was more interested in getting to know me rather than me getting to know him." She pauses for a second. "I asked him about you."

My eyes widen in surprise. "And?"

"He dodged the topic. Said that things were complicated."

Exhaling an annoyed breath, I push forward. "What happened after dinner?"

"He asked if I was tired, and I told him no. I invited him up here, and as soon as we got into the room, he kissed me," she tells me. I know she's nervous to see how I'll react, so I stay as poised as I possibly can. "I think he was nervous."

"What made you think that?"

"I don't know. He just wasn't as relaxed as he'd been in the restaurant. He seemed anxious when we got up here. It was different from the time before."

"How so?"

With trepidation, she bites her lip and drops her head.

"It's okay, Emma. I just need you to be honest with me."

She runs her fingers along her brow, takes the last sip, and glances at me. "As soon as we got up here, he kissed me."

I'm unmoving, unbelieving, but *believing*.

"There was a sense of urgency that he didn't have the night before."

My chest constricts as I flash back to memories. Memories of that very same urgency. As if he couldn't get enough of me. Those moments feel like ages ago. "I want to know *everything*," I stress, hoping she'll feed my sick desire to know every detail, every touch, every word spoken.

"Like I said, as soon as the door closed, he was kissing me. We stumbled over to the bed, and I was kissing him back, pulling at his tie while he was tugging down the straps of my dress. He stopped when he saw I wasn't wearing a bra and lowered his mouth to my chest."

My knees weaken as a cool stream of shock swims through my veins. I wonder where the white-hot anger is because it's absent. It should be roiling inside me, but all I can grasp on to is the curiosity to know more. She continues to talk as my vision swims out of focus, and when I glance over to the mussed-up bed, I see myself with Tripp as we play out the events Emma is describing.

"He pulled my dress down to my waist, and I started fumbling with his belt, but . . ."

I shift my focus back to her. "But what?"

"He was still soft," she admits. "He was frustrated, and that was when he told me to call down for a bottle of vodka. I pulled my dress back up, and when the bottle came, we both started drinking. He sat on the edge of the bed, and I kneeled between his legs. I opened his pants as he took another shot of vodka. He was still soft, so I went down on him."

My heart double thumps, and I don't know how to feel as my lids fall shut.

As she goes on, I drop my head, getting lost in her voice. "He grew hard in my mouth, and I could tell he wanted to come, so I backed off. He watched as I slipped my dress off, and when I was naked, he stood, grabbed my hips, spun me around, and bent me over the bed."

Warmth pools low in my belly as I hang on to each of her words. I lose myself in them, painting my face over hers in an effort to feel closer to my husband. It's like a magnet of desperation, the yearning to go back to what we once were. A beacon illuminating just how long I've been deprived.

I miss him.

I miss my husband.

"He kicked my legs open, knelt behind me, and jerked me back toward his face. He licked me until my knees gave way."

There's a faint sizzle that begins to spread through my core, and when I notice that she isn't talking anymore, I open my eyes and clear my throat. "Was there any talking at all?"

"He said that I tasted like sin."

"Like sin," I repeat under my breath. "Anything else?"

"He made a few comments about my body. He said I was beautiful, and when . . . when he finally pushed himself inside me, he told me that . . ."

She drifts off, and her face flushes as her eyes avoid me. "Go on," I implore.

"He said my tight pussy felt amazing."

My breath tangles in my throat, and my hands grip the edge of the dresser even tighter. I shouldn't be this turned on, but I am. I miss the connection we used to have. The raw passion that made me irresistible to him. The way he would talk dirty for me. I can't remember the last time he spoke to me that way. Crude and intimate and loving. Words would slip from his lips, and I would completely lose myself to him.

"Are you okay?"

Her voice flitters through the thoughts that cast a cloud over my sanity. "I'm sorry, I'm just . . ." I shift in my stance, but I feel uneasy on my feet. "I'm fine . . . go on."

"Are you sure?"

"I want to know how it happened—the details." I tell her this with a bashfulness I hope she can't hear. It would make this so much worse if she knew how eager I was to feel even a shred of closeness to Tripp.

"It started out with him taking me from behind. He then laid on the bed, and I got on top of him. He used his hands to maneuver my hips, and I could sense he wanted to take control, so I went with it when he flipped us over and got on top of me. He spread me wide, pushing my knees down into the mattress. I could feel him growing inside me," she says, and as the two of us lock eyes, she adds, "As soon as I orgasmed, he pulled out of me, ripped the condom off, and started jerking himself off. I must've gotten carried away because I pushed his hand aside and finished him off with my mouth."

"Did . . . did he . . ." I mutter, finding it hard to spit out the question.

"Did he come in my mouth?"

I nod.

"Yes."

I hang my head, trying my best to temper my arousal when aroused should be the last thing I feel. I should be heartbroken or furious, but those emotions are so far away. Instead, I'm hung up on desire and need, wanting to know even more, wishing for my senses to be consumed with their sounds, their smell, their taste. As twisted as it is, I feel a connection with Tripp that I haven't felt in a while. It's disturbing, but also thrilling.

What's wrong with me?

Clearing my throat again, I glance back to the bed, wondering what the sheets would feel like against my bare skin. I'm ripe with lust. With my skin tingling in erotic delight, my head sways for a moment before I right myself. Pushing off the dresser, I walk over to the credenza and grab a bottle of water that's sitting out. It's nothing more than a distraction, and when I screw the lid back on and turn to face Emma, she apologizes.

"I'm sorry. I didn't mean to upset you, but you said you wanted—"

"No. It's fine. You didn't upset me, it's just not that easy to hear."

That isn't exactly the truth. Surprisingly, it was easy to hear, and even more to my surprise, I want more, and I'm not exactly sure why. One thing I do know is that I have to get out of here because there's no chance of me collecting my thoughts while I'm swimming in the wake of their sex.

Going back to the dresser where my purse sits, I pull out the envelope that holds the promise I made to her when she agreed to do this. The forty thousand dollars that my mother left me when she died is now hers. I never spent the money because I know how hard she worked for every penny she earned, and for some reason, I just couldn't touch it, so I hesitate to hand it over.

But it isn't the only reason I hesitate.

It's a sadistic feeling of wanting more—needing more. I want to keep this connection to my husband alive just a little longer before he's gone from my life for good. So, when I hold out the envelope, I ask, "Do you think he'll want to see you again?"

"He asked for my number."

"You gave it to him?"

"I didn't want to. I mean, it didn't seem right, but I felt it would've looked suspicious if I didn't," she admits. "Why?"

"Maybe . . ." I second-guess myself, but I need this. I don't even know why, but maybe the why isn't what's important. I throw all attempts at rationalization out the window and continue, "Maybe it would be best to really cover our bases."

There's confusion within her gaze. "Are you asking me to sleep with him again?"

"I'll pay you," I offer quickly.

"How much?"

She's too quick to ask the question, and it hints at her willingness to agree. Knowing that she's already established a connection with him, it'll be an easy feat this time around. "Ten thousand."

FOURTEEN

Emma

I shove the envelope Carly gave me under my mattress and then sit on the edge of my bed. After she left the hotel room this afternoon, I was soaring above cloud nine. I got dressed, threw on some makeup, and packed my bag. When I got into my car, I blasted the stereo and drove. There was no plan, no destination, and no time limit—I simply drove. For a moment, my shoulders were free from the weight that had been pressing down on them.

I smiled.

I actually smiled, and it was so genuine that I felt its mirth from between my ribs.

There's finally a light at the end of this dark tunnel I've been trapped in this past year. I filled up my gas tank without the worry of my bankcard being declined. I even treated myself to a coffee that was way over-priced because I could. Sometimes, it's the little things that have the biggest effect on us. That coffee perched me on top of the world. It made me feel powerful and alive.

Eventually, the drive led me back home. Luca's still in class, and now that I've unpacked, there's a sudden shift.

The world eclipses, casting darkness upon me once again. But this time, it breeds panic instead of defeat.

Dropping my head, my breathing shallows when I consider the possible repercussions, which I should have already thought about. How much can I trust Carly?

What if, aside from her attorney, other people find out?

What if it somehow gets leaked to the press?

It'll be my face all over the news, not theirs. I'll be the college slut. The whore. They'll paint me as the next Lewinski while everyone else will get away with their reputations at least somewhat intact.

Too anxious to sit still, I stand and begin pacing. The only way I'll be able to mitigate any possible damage is if I never tell a soul. No one can ever know. Frantically, I twist my hands, all the while reminding myself that I'm doing this for my brother, for myself, and for our future that's solely dependent on me.

It was why I agreed when Carly asked me to go through with it one more time. When she told me how much she would pay, I didn't even hesitate. All I could see was the money I so desperately need. Although sixty grand isn't even close to the amount I need to get myself back on my feet, it's a start.

My cell phone chimes with a text.

Luca: Just got out of class. Heading to The Tombs with some friends. You should come.

The thought of getting wasted is insanely appealing right now, but I just don't have it in me to be in a crowed bar filled with college goers.

Me: Thanks, but the drive back from Tennessee drained me. I think I'm going to call it a night.

Luca: Are you sure. I haven't seen you in a few days. Missing my girl.

His words put a smile on my face.

Me: Yeah, I'm sure. Have fun. I'll see you in the morning.

Tossing the phone aside, I flop down onto my bed, still feeling the low burning embers of panic when I think about how badly this could all end. I've always known DC was filled with all sorts of corruption.

That awareness has turned from being distant and removed to something that fills my field of vision and drenches my hands in filth.

The sun gave way hours ago as I lie here, staring out the window. Snow clouds hang heavy in the sky as flurries float down. Reaching up, I drag my finger along the foggy glass, slowly drawing the shape of a small heart. As I run my finger through the middle, the condensation builds, and soon the droplets of water skitter down like tiny teardrops.

How poetic.

A bleeding heart.

I think about my mother and the way she would hold me at night when I'd be scared of the shadows in the dark. I'd find my way into her room, where she would pull back the blankets for me so I could snuggle between her and my dad. We'd giggle when he'd let out a snore. It's amazing how one person's embrace has the power to chase away the monsters.

I wish she were here.

I wish so badly for her arms to hold me again.

For her to tell me that everything will be okay.

A tear creeps out from the corner of my eye, and when I wipe it away, I hear Luca come home, followed by the sound of his bedroom door closing. I roll onto my side and tuck my knees against my chest. My fog heart still weeps, sending tiny streams down the icy glass.

I'm scared.

Scared of what will happen to me, of what my future holds, about the choices I'm making. Most of all, I'm scared for my brother. What will happen if I fail him? The burden is almost too much for me to carry, and when I see my heart chilling once more, fogging over and fading away, I slide from my bed and go in search of comfort.

I knock on Luca's door.

"Come in."

He's sitting up against the headboard when I step inside.

"Everything okay?"

I give him a slight shake of my head and can't stop the tiny wobble in my bottom lip as I fight back emotions. Memories of my parents and the fear of my world imploding lodge in my throat, making it difficult to speak without crying. I try so hard to keep it together, not to crack under the pressure and show my true emotions. To always put up a brave front because, when people look at me, I want them to see strength and not the fragile girl I hide deep inside myself.

Just like my mom used to do, Luca pulls the sheets back, and without a second thought, I go straight to him. His arms are warm as they band around me, and his bare skin smells of liquor and cologne.

His fingers run through my hair. "Talk to me," he whispers.

"I don't know what to say."

"I hate this—this distance you insist on having."

"I'm not distant."

"You are," he tells me. "This past year . . . especially since you left school, you haven't been the same."

"How can I be the same when my world isn't the same?"

He lifts my chin so that I'm forced to look at him and whispers, "You're hiding something."

My brows cinch. "What makes you think that?"

"Because you aren't you. It's as if you avoid me every opportunity you get."

"I'm not avoiding you now."

His arms tighten around me. "You may be in my bed, but you're still hiding from me."

"I'm not hiding." Damn it if I don't have to bite my lip to stop it from giving me away.

"Then tell me why you're knocking on my door in the middle of the night? Why are you in my arms?"

I'm forced to look away from him when I feel the tears start to build. Resting my cheek back on his chest, I silently scold myself when I blink and one of them slips out, dripping onto his bare chest, which he can surely feel.

"Please, Emma. Just talk to me."

I know I should talk to him about what is going on, but I don't want him to worry or snoop around and possibly find something that will send him running. God, if he ever finds out what I've been doing these past few days, he'll be disgusted with me. He'll never look at me the same way again. Hell, he might even kick me out of his house. After all, people in this city don't want to be associated with a disgrace like me.

I love Luca, and I don't know what I would do if I ever lost him. So, I decide it's best to feed him a truth instead of a lie.

"I feel really alone." My words break on their way out, and he hugs me tighter.

"Babe, you are not alone," he stresses, but he's clueless to my truth. "It kills me to hear you crying in the middle of the night. I want to come to you every time."

"Why don't you?"

"Because you'll push me away or lie and say that nothing is wrong. Tell me everything's okay when we both know it isn't."

"My life is a mess right now."

"You're right, it is a mess. But, like you said, it's only a mess for right now. It won't always be this way. You're a fighter, and soon you'll be back on your feet."

"What if that doesn't happen?"

His eyes drop to mine as I look up at him, and with fervency, he promises, "It will. I will never let you fall, but you have to be willing to let me help you."

He then drops a kiss in my hair and tucks my head beneath his chin. In the warmth of his bed, my anxiety begins to settle. Silence spans between us as we hold each other, and I think about what he's telling me. He's right. I shouldn't be pushing away the one person I have to depend on. Maybe I am creating my own prison of loneliness.

"Can I ask you about something and have you be honest with me?" he eventually asks, breaking the stillness. Before I can answer, he shifts enough to reach his nightstand and picks up a white envelope. "This came in the mail for you yesterday."

I take it from him and sit up, reading the return address: Valley Crest Home for the Mentally Disabled

"You're snooping through my mail?" I chastise harshly.

"I didn't open it. And, no, I'm not snooping. Like I said, it came in the mail," he says. "Are you going to tell me why that would come for you?"

I cross my legs and drop my head, worried about him being angry with me when he finds out I've been lying to him about Matthew. Of all my lies, this is one I can own up to. "It's about my brother. It's where he lives."

His eyes narrow. "What are you talking about?"

Releasing a defeated sigh, I tell him, "My brother isn't married, and he doesn't have any kids."

The confusion and anger and disappointment on his face stings, so I go ahead and come completely clean.

"Matthew is low-functioning autistic. He can't take care of himself, so when my parents died, he had to go into a facility for the mentally disabled."

"Why didn't you tell me? Why lie?"

I shrug. "Because I've always lied about him. It's just the way it was in our family."

"I don't understand."

"My mother never wanted the judgment of others. She didn't want people looking down on him for being different. It was her way of protecting us—of protecting him. So, we kept Matthew private so that he'd never have to be under the scrutiny of others or fear bullies. My mom did her best to homeschool him and devoted her life to taking care of him." Finally, his expression softens. "We never told people that he was autistic or different, so when you asked about my family, I didn't even think of it as a lie even though it was."

"So, what were you doing these past few days?"

"The same thing I do every time I visit him. I check him out of the facility and we go to a hotel."

"Were you in a hotel for Christmas?"

I nod.

"Jesus, Emma." He pushes out a deep breath. "I wish I would've known."

"Why?"

"Because I would've made sure the two of you weren't all alone in a hotel. I would've had you two come with me to my parents'. They would never judge your brother, I can promise you that."

Another tear finds its way down my cheek, and Luca wipes it away before I can.

"It isn't as easy as you make it sound."

"It is. The truth is, you don't want people judging you or your brother, but you're the one judging everyone else around you, assuming the worst in them." He takes the envelope and sets it aside and then holds my hands in his. "It's me, Emma. And I'm telling you that you'd have a fucking hard time finding anyone else on this planet who loves you as much as I do."

"I'm sorry," I whisper. "It's really hard for me, you know? I don't trust that easily."

"I know," he soothes. "And that's fine when it comes to other people but not with me, okay?"

I nod, and this time, when he pulls me into his arms, I feel safe enough to let out a couple more tears before stifling them and eventually falling asleep.

FIFTEEN

Emma

When I open my eyes again, Luca is already up, sitting next to me in bed and watching television.

"Finally," he says when he looks down at me with a smirk. "I was about to check your pulse."

I roll my eyes as I shift to sit up next to him. "How long have you been awake?"

"Long enough to be working on my second cup," he tells me before taking a sip of his coffee. "You've been out like a rock."

It isn't surprising that I slept in since I've barely gotten any sleep over the past few nights. A deep yawn presses out of me, and when I look to the nightstand, I grin a little when I see a bagel resting on a plate.

"Figured you'd be hungry."

It might not seem like much, but coming from Luca, it is. Despite his playboy, rich-kid reputation, he has a soft side that would surprise most.

"Thanks." I slide the plate onto my lap and rip off a piece of the blueberry bagel before he hands over his coffee to share with me.

"I was thinking that, if you don't have any plans for today, we could hang out. My first class isn't until two o'clock."

After our conversation last night, I would feel terrible if I didn't accept his offer. After all, he was right when he said we've been growing distant. We used to be inseparable. "What did you have in mind?"

"Would you want to hang out at Gravelly Point?"

Handing the coffee back to him, I agree and then tear off another bite of the bagel.

"Maybe we can grab a bite before heading back."

When he suggests this, I scrunch my nose. "I can't. I actually have a coffee date with a friend at one thirty."

He arches a brow. "What friend?"

"Olivia. I told you about it earlier this week."

"You're seriously ditching me for that chick?"

"Oh please." I huff. "Now look who's being clingy."

"Uh-uh. Don't you dare compare me to her."

We both laugh before I ask, "How do you two know each other anyway?"

"Our families are close, so I've known her since we were kids."

"And do you make it a habit to sleep with all your life-long friends?"

"That was a mistake. Long story short, we got drunk one night after finals week and hooked up. That's all. Next thing I knew, she wouldn't stop calling or texting."

"And that happened your freshman year?" I am trying to remember him telling me about it, but I come up empty.

"Yeah, something like that," he mumbles before chugging the last of the coffee.

"Hog."

"Hey, I was nice enough to get you a bagel," he quips. "Go brew your own coffee."

I smile at my friend, realizing how much I've actually been missing his company.

"Come on. Get ready so we can get out of here."

Grabbing my bagel, I head into my room and jump in the shower. It doesn't take me long to pull myself together, and when I walk into the living room, Luca is waiting on me.

"I already have the camping chairs and blankets in my trunk."

I go to the kitchen and pull down a coffee thermos. "I'm going to make a cup to go. Want one?"

"Nah, I'm good."

The drive takes about thirty minutes down to Gravelly Point Park, and I watch the scenery pass through the passenger's side window. Luca was the one who told me about this place, and I've loved it from the very first time he brought me here. Today, the park has a different feel to it. It's the middle of winter and only the two of us are crazy enough to come out here, but we don't care.

We walk along the snow-covered grounds and situate ourselves in our favorite spot. Luca pulls his chair right next to mine, and with my hands snug around the warm thermos, we sink down in our seats, snuggle under our blankets, and tilt our heads back so we can watch the sky.

We're less than half a mile from Reagan National Airport, and the planes take off and come in for landing right over this park. It's loud and windy when they fly overhead, creating a vivacious rumbling in the ground. When the weather is nice, Luca and I will lie on the grassy knoll just to feel the earth vibrate beneath us.

"I see one in the distance," he says, pointing straight ahead.

As the plane draws in closer, the engines become louder and louder until eventually, they are so loud that you can't even hear yourself talk. A huge smile grows on my face as the ground rumbles under our feet, and before I know it, the plane is right on top of us, whipping my hair into a nest of disarray. The plane feels much closer than what it actually is, so much so that it seems as if I could reach my arm up and touch the belly of the magnificent aircraft.

The moment it passes, laughter erupts from my chest like a child who just stepped off a wild roller coaster. It's an incredible feeling, which is why I love it here so much. A few seconds pass, and when the engine's noise fades, I turn to Luca with an ecstatic, "That was awesome!"

He laughs at my excitement and then slips his arm around me, tucking me in his blanket as he does. My coffee warms me up when I take a sip, but too soon, Luca takes it from my hands and starts drinking.

"That's mine," I playfully scold.

"Your point?"

I soften into him as he continues to drink my coffee and then laugh when he complains, "Shit, how much cream did you dump in this?"

Snatching it out of his hand, I swallow another gulp before handing it back to him. We relax into each other in an attempt to stay as warm as possible, and ten minutes later, another plane zooms over us, sparking another barrel of laughter from me. Again, a few seconds is all it takes for the roar of the engines to subside, and when they do, I tilt my head to rest it on his shoulder.

As I stare off into the distance, I whisper a soft, "Matthew would love this."

His arm strengthens around my shoulders. "Will you tell me about him?"

His question catches me a little by surprise. No one has ever asked me about him before, at least, no one I would tell the truth to has.

"He's like a six-year-old stuck in a grown man's body. He's fun and playful, but he struggles to communicate properly. He likes routine and is very literal. In his world, there is no room for error."

"How so?"

"If you say you're going to be somewhere at a certain time and you're either one minute early or one minute late, it disrupts something inside him. It's nearly impossible for him to be flexible, and he won't let it go."

"Sounds like most women I know," he teases, which earns him a nudge in the ribs.

"He's obsessed with planes. And when I say obsessed, I mean *obsessed*. Ask him anything, and he's going to know the answer. He's like a vault filled with so much knowledge that it's staggering to think about."

"So, he'd kick our asses at *Jeopardy?*"

We both chuckle. "No doubt. He'd humiliate us, for sure," I

tell him. "He's sensitive, yet stubborn. He likes what he likes, and he doesn't do well with change."

"How has he been handling your parents' death?"

I shrug. "He's confused. He's a smart guy, but he struggles to fully comprehend death, like any child would. When I call him, sometimes he talks about them as if they're still alive, and he asks me why they haven't visited him yet. Those conversations are the worst because I have to talk him through it and help him understand that death is final." I take in a slow breath to steady my emotions. "It just brings everything to the surface again."

The way he's looking at me with complete understanding makes it a little easier to breathe. "I used to be really close to my grandfather when he was alive. He had a place right on the water. When I was little, we'd sit on the edge of the dock and he'd help me catch crabs," he reminisces. "He'd tie a long piece of twine around a nail he'd hammered into the planks and then knot a piece of chicken neck with a heavy washer onto the end and drop it in the water. We'd sit together, and when that twine would start to move out, he would slowly pull the string, bringing the crab to the surface while I waited with the wired net to scoop it up. We would spend hours out on his dock catching crabs."

I smile at his memory even though I can't really relate to it.

"He died of a stroke when I was in the second grade. I kept asking my parents when he would be coming back, as if real life was just like the video games I played. You die, but you always have more lives."

His analogy is spot on, and I nod in agreement. "That's exactly what it's like for Matthew. It's hard for him to grasp that you only get one life and when it's gone, it's really gone."

"We should take a road trip to Tennessee sometime. I'd like to meet him."

I turn to look at Luca, shocked that those words just came out of his mouth. "Why?"

"Why not?" he counters. "He's an important part of your life. Plus, he sounds like a cool guy."

"He isn't . . . I mean, he isn't like other people." I stumble over my words, nervous about the thought of introducing Luca to my brother.

"I get that, but there's no reason to hide him, right? Don't you think it would be good for him to meet the people in your life?"

I stew on what he's saying, and I suppose he has a point. I wonder if Matthew, in his own way, feels excluded from my life. I mean . . . he's never been a part of my life outside of our home and our family. Sure, I visit him and take him places, but it's always just the two of us.

"You'd really do that? You'd come home with me?"

"Why do you act so surprised?"

"I don't know, I just . . ."

"I wish you'd put yourself out there more," he adds, and I respond with a smirk, "I am. I'm meeting up with Olivia later."

With a dramatic roll of his eyes, he grumbles, "Fuck me."

"Maybe you should stop sleeping around so much. You're depleting my pool of possible friends."

"So now this is my fault?"

"You said it," I tease as another plane soars our way.

The ground starts vibrating under my feet, and I reach up as if I'm really going to touch it. Closing my eyes, I tilt my head back and relish the gust of wind that coils around me.

SIXTEEN

Emma

"**Y**ou look a mess."

As I take a seat at the table where Olivia has been waiting for me, I comb my fingers through my tangled hair only for them to get caught in the knots. "Sorry I'm late. I took the train straight from Gravelly Point."

"What were you doing there? It's freezing outside."

"Luca and I were watching the planes."

"And he made you take the Metro here?"

Immediately regretting even mentioning it, I take a swallow from the glass of ice water that's in front of me.

"Is he avoiding me?"

"No," I lie. "We lost track of time and he had to rush back to campus to make it to his class."

The waiter stops by, and when I see that Olivia is already working on a glass of white wine, I tease, "So much for a coffee date," and order a glass of rosé.

She grins, lifting her hands to mimic the balancing of a scale. "Coffee? Chardonnay? Coffee? Chardonnay?" before picking up her wine glass. "Chardonnay wins every time."

I smile and pick up the menu, scan it, and settle on a Caesar salad with fresh anchovies.

"So, how was the gala?" she asks, catching me a little off guard.

Right. The fake gala I told her about.

"Oh, it was wonderful. It was great to go back home and reconnect."

"Have you ladies made your selections?" the waiter inquires as he sets my wine down.

We place our orders, and when he excuses himself, she says, "So, how is it living with Luca? You must see a lot of interesting things."

"If by things, you mean girls, then yes." I stifle a slight chuckle when I take a sip of my wine.

"I see he hasn't changed much. Has he mentioned me at all?"

"Just that you two are old family friends," I respond, feeling too uncomfortable to mention my awareness of their hookup. "Why?"

"Oh, we had a brief fling a few years back. It's been a bit awkward ever since."

"That's too bad considering how long the two of you have known each other."

She shrugs. "I should've known better, but with our history, I figured it would've turned out differently."

If I didn't know better, I'd assume this girl was still hung up on Luca.

"I tried calling him after we ran into each other at his parents' New Year's Eve party." She shakes her head slightly, adding, "I'm not even sure why I called in the first place. My life is a bit of a disaster right now."

I can only assume she referring to the affair she's having with Tripp, which I seriously doubt she would ever reveal to me, a girl whom she met a few weeks ago, but I pry anyway.

"I'm told I'm a good listener if it's anything you want to talk about."

"You really want me to dump my baggage on you?"

"What else are we going to talk about?" I say lightly, hoping she'll grab the bait, and to my surprise, she does.

"Okay, but I owe you!"

"Deal, when my life falls off the hinges, I'll be calling you."

We both laugh, and after she takes another sip of her wine, she lays it out there for me. "My fiancé just left me."

"Oh my God. What happened?"

"Just over a year ago, Tripp gave me my first real job since graduating. He was still the attorney general, and I had just signed the one-year contract to replace his assistant, who had just resigned. A week before my first day, my girlfriends and I thought it would be fun to take a celebratory vacation to Manhattan. The first night, we got all dressed up and went out dancing. That's when I met Court Rothman." She says his name as if she's in dreamland, and I have to hold back a snicker at how douchey that name sounds. "He's an investment banker on Wall Street. We caught eyes, he bought me a drink, and we wound up dancing all night. The following day, he took me to brunch and we went for a walk in Central Park." She smiles. "I know it all sounds like some corny Hallmark movie, but he really did sweep me off my feet. For the next few days, if I wasn't with my friends, I was with Court."

"It sounds like a fairy tale," I remark.

"It really was. By the time we were boarding the plane to come back to DC, I swear I had already fallen in love with him. Every weekend thereafter, either I was flying to New York or he was flying to DC. I was a few months out from the end of the contract with Tripp and had already made the decision to pack my bags and move to New York so that Court and I could be together. It was during that time when Court flew me out to his parents' vacation house in the Hamptons and proposed." She stops and takes another drink. "Anyway, Tripp ended up making me an offer to work on his campaign team, and I couldn't refuse. When I dropped that bomb on Court, that's when things started falling part, and he ended things two months ago."

She tells me all this, as if I'm really supposed to care, but I'm not here to build a friendship with this girl. "That had to be hard. To chose between Court and your job."

"It was. All the announcements had already been sent out so that people could save the date. When he called it off, I was humiliated. I could hardly function, and I kept dropping the ball at work. I was so scared Tripp was going to fire me. I mean, this is my dream job, and the experience I'm getting is priceless."

"Are things better at work and with Tripp?"

"They are. I ended up telling Tripp about what was going on and he was totally understanding, which wasn't at all what I was expecting. Even though he's so busy and being pulled in every direction possible, he's been there for me in a way I never expected. He's truly an amazing man."

I bet.

"You're so lucky to have a boss who's so understanding," I say while thinking that Tripp must've viewed her as an easy lay with how vulnerable she must've been at that point. No wonder she started sleeping with him. She strikes me as the type of girl who can't be without a man's attention.

Her smile grows. "Maryland is going to be so lucky when he wins this election."

It takes everything inside me to keep from rolling my eyes. Sure, Tripp is a shoo-in for governor. Hell, there's even whispers of him running for president in the next election, but this girl has some serious hero worship going on.

Interesting that not once did I see her at The Jefferson during my stay there.

"So, are there any perks to the job? Do you get to travel with him? Stay at the same hotels as him? I can only imagine the luxury."

"It really depends on the schedule and the events he's attending. He often stays overnight here in the city, but since I'm right down the street in Bethesda, I just go home. Enough about me. I'm sure you don't want to be bored with campaign talk."

"It's actually fascinating. I mean . . . it's my dream as well to work on a campaign such as Tripp's. I think it's an amazing opportunity that will help you move forward in your career," I boast on her behalf, and she eats it right up. "And between you and me, I think you made the right decision by staying in DC. You shouldn't let go of your dreams and ambitions for a guy, and if he couldn't understand that, you're better off. He would only serve to hold you back."

Our food arrives, and when the plates are set, she places her napkin onto the table, saying, "You're absolutely right. I'm really glad we're getting to know each other." She then scoots her chair out. "Now, if you'll excuse me, I need to use the ladies' room."

She heads to the restroom, and I stab my fork into a crisp romaine leaf. As I'm chewing, I notice Olivia's cell phone lying facedown on table. Casting my eyes over toward the restrooms, I consider all the information I could find on the device she so carelessly left behind.

My next heart's beat is filled with a dose of adrenaline.

Olivia is Tripp's scheduler, which means that her calendar should be a mirror image of his. With fast hands, I reach across the table, and I'm shocked to see it isn't locked with a password or anything.

What a moron.

I skip past the calendar and go straight for her texts. Tripp's name is third from the top, and I quickly scroll through the messages, trying to find anything—anything that doesn't involve work.

There's nothing obvious, so I close out the app and pull up her calendar as I fish around in my purse for my own phone.

I start tapping on each day to get a detailed view of her schedule, which is pretty much Tripp's schedule. With time being my enemy, I can't waste any more. I use my phone and snap pictures of as many days as I can. My jittery fingers keep me from moving as fast as I want to, but I do as best as I can while keeping my eye on the door to the restroom.

When I've collected a little over two weeks' worth of information, I close down her calendar app, go back to her home screen, and exit out before sliding the phone back across the table.

Nervously, I look around the room, paranoid that someone may be watching me and my peculiar behavior, but no one seems to be. So, I drop my cell back into my purse and then take a gulp of my rosé to quell my nerves.

Peering out of the corner of my eye, I spot Olivia heading back my way.

Shit, that was close.

"I was just thinking," she says as she takes her seat and picks up her fork. "A few of my girlfriends and I have a girls' night once a month. You should totally join us for the next one. I think you'd really like them."

I smile my plastic smile. "That sounds like fun."

"Great! We're getting together next weekend."

"Perfect."

For the next forty-five minutes, we eat our food while continuing to chit chat. I keep the focus on her since there isn't much about my life I care to share with this girl. She goes on about what it was like for her growing up in DC, occasionally dropping a story here and there that involves Luca.

Yeah, she definitely still has lingering feelings for him.

Once we've paid the bill, Olivia has to rush to get back to the office. She offers to drop me off at the Metro station, but I politely decline, lying about wanting to do a little shopping before heading home. Truth is, I need a break to settle the tension inside me. Never have I lied and deceived so much in my life, but this situation I've gotten myself into has me behaving so out of character that I barely recognize myself. I know Carly is crazy. Hell, when I was describing my time with Tripp, I thought she was going to orgasm right then and there. When I arrive home, get into my car, and plug the address I found in Olivia's phone into my GPS, I begin to question my own sanity.

I pause with my hand on the gearshift, but before I second-guess myself, I throw it into reverse and back out of the driveway.

Turn by turn leads me closer to the broken home of the Montgomery's. And nearly an hour and a half later, I'm pulling down the long stretch of road that leads to their massive property on the Eastern Bay.

I know Tripp is in the city, but I have no clue if Carly is as well, so I hesitate to stop, to get out of my car, and to peek in the windows just to get a glimpse of the opulent life Carly wants to run away from.

If I lived this kind of life, I'm not sure I'd be so quick to walk away from it. Hell, she has it made, and with the name she carries and the money behind it, she'd never have to work another day in her life. With as much as her husband is away, she could easily find her own sidepiece to keep her company and fill the void without having to give all this up.

I would never actually say that to her because the path she has chosen benefits me. If it takes her ruining a good thing for me to better my situation, then so be it. I won't feel guilty for doing what I have to do to survive. I just wonder if *she* will.

SEVENTEEN

Carly

I crunch on an ice cube from my glass of water as if the coolness will snuff the flame under my heated skin. It's a worthless attempt, but at least it soothes my dry throat.

"Did anything else happen?"

Emma, who sits across from me, is pulled together with her golden hair in loose waves, her perfect makeup, and her flawless, tight body. No wonder Tripp can't keep his hands off her. It's only natural for me to feel the torment of jealousy.

It took almost a week, but this morning, she called me to let me know that she would be meeting up with Tripp today. And now, here we sit at the same roadside diner in Virginia we met at after she agreed to help me out. She just finished telling me all about their encounter today, explaining that he was pressed for time, which I know to be true. His schedule was pretty full today before he added in an extra appointment to meet and fuck a girl young enough to be his daughter.

She described it as quick and passionate, saying that Tripp was eager and hard when he met her at an old, abandoned lighthouse and fucked her against a wall. It's too reminiscent of when Tripp made love to me against the wall of the greenhouse the day he asked me to marry him.

For every detail she gives me, I'm able to find a memory of my own.

"That was pretty much it. We had sex and then he had to rush off." She fingers one of her earrings before adding, "He asked if he could call me again."

"What did you say?"

"I didn't know what to say. I didn't want to come off as a bitch and tell him no, so I flirted and told him I wasn't a beck-and-call type of girl."

"What did he say when you said that?"

"He laughed and then took my wrist and pressed my hand against his dick, which was getting hard again. He told me I was the only one who could do that to him."

Beneath the table, my hands fist so tightly my nails feel like they might break skin. At the same time, I have to cross my legs and squeeze, create a little friction just to release the tension that's building between my thighs.

"If he calls, I don't want you to answer."

She nods. "Okay. So, that's it? That's all you need from me?"

"That's all," I confirm, unsure of what to say to the girl I paid to fuck my husband—twice. There's an awkwardness that hangs over the two of us, so I go with the obvious, confessing, "I don't even know what to say . . . thank you?"

Emma chuckles uneasily under her breath. "You're welcome . . . I guess?" She shakes her head in plight. "I'm sorry. I don't know what to say either."

"It's okay." I then pull out the envelope of cash I promised her and slide it across the table. "I don't think any less of you, by the way. I just . . . I felt you should know that."

She drops her head and nods, and I worry that I just made her feel like a prostitute, a slut, a whore. That wasn't my intention at all, so I lay my hand over hers and add, "You're a strong woman, Emma. Much stronger than I could ever be."

"Thank you," she whispers when she lifts her chin.

"If you ever need anything, you know how to find me." I give her an endearing smile before grabbing my purse and heading out.

Once in my car, I watch Emma through the foggy windows. She sits there, staring down into her coffee, which must be cold by now, and I'm concerned about the damage I might've possibly inflicted on her by dragging her into this situation. Guilt loops around my conscience like a snare for taking advantage of this girl while she's at her lowest. I feel like a snake, but at the same time, I'm not sure any help or guidance from me would be welcome. She already told me that she didn't think it would be wise for her to continue seeking therapy from me, and I agreed. But that doesn't mean that I don't still care for her well-being.

The moment I see her stand from the booth, I start my car, pull out of the parking lot, and head back to my office. Traffic around campus is heavier than normal, causing me to run late for a student advisory meeting. When I finally arrive, I run into the building and find a few students already waiting.

"Sorry I'm late. Traffic was a little crazy," I say to Jenny as I walk past her desk and into my office.

She trails behind me, rattling off my schedule for the day. "Your three o'clock cancelled."

"Who are those students here to see?"

"Mr. Wilkenson," she says about the other counselor whose office is on the opposite from where Jenny's desk is. "But you have a new student who made an appointment while you were out for four o'clock. He's a freshman who needs help declaring a major. I emailed you all his information already."

"Thanks. Would you mind shutting the door on your way out?"

When she leaves, I rest my elbows on my desk and drop my head into my hands. With a heavy breath, I allow my muscles to slacken and close my eyes. Emma's voice is still echoing softly in my ears, and it doesn't take but a second for the ache to return from between my legs.

"We practically stumbled into the lighthouse, and when he kicked the door shut, he couldn't strip me out of my top fast enough, pulling and tugging at the fabric."

My neck heats as I recall her words, each one sending a frisson down my spine where it pools in my belly.

"He sucked my nipple into his mouth, licking it fervently while he shoved his hand down my pants and into my panties, thrusting his finger inside of me."

Looking up, I do a quick scan of the room before walking over to the window and closing the blinds. I then go to the door and press my ear against it. When I hear Jenny chatting with the students who are waiting for their appointments, I turn the little knob and lock the door.

Sitting back at my desk, heart pounding in my ears, I hike my pencil skirt up around my thighs and slip my hand under my panties. With my back turned toward the door, I relax and close my eyes as I drift back to the diner. It's a perverse desire to connect with my husband that drives me to touch myself, and I'm shocked at how aroused my body already is.

"He yanked my pants down, slipping them off one of my legs. Then he dropped to his knees and put his mouth on me."

My breathing grows heavy as my fingers roll over my tender flesh. In my head, it's *my* pussy he's licking. It's the taste of *me* that has him moaning for more. It's his vehement desire to have *me* that sets his hunger ablaze.

"I didn't even get a chance to return the favor before he hoisted me against the wall and started fucking me. I clung my arms around his shoulders and hung on."

Sweat beads along my hairline as my body begins to stagger.

"Everything about this time was different from the last. He was eager—rapturous, really. Like each grind of his hips came with purpose as the concrete wall bit into the skin on the back of my hips, scraping them up as he buried himself inside me."

My skin dampens as I begin to falter, tensing as my orgasm draws nearer.

"He moved with so much intensity that I came quickly. It wasn't long after when he couldn't hold on anymore. He grunted my name as he bucked into me, coming hard."

My thighs shutter as my body clenches, causing me to lose my rhythm as a fierce orgasm pulses through my entire being. With my free hand clutched onto the armrest of my chair, my nails bite into the soft leather as I ride out my pleasure. I do my best to stifle the breathless pants that force their way out of me, but they're still audible and completely beyond my control.

Suddenly, there's a knock on my door, and I startle, yanking my hand out of my panties.

"Mrs. Montgomery?"

"Just one second," I call out, frantically pulling my skirt down and praying that my office doesn't smell of my own sex.

Still flushed and hot, my jittery hands fumble with the lock, and when it finally opens, I'm practically breathless, my orgasm still lingering between my legs.

"Everything okay?"

"Yeah. The door must've jammed or something." Her eyes carry a hint of doubt, so I ask, "What do you need, Jenny?"

"Oh." She holds out a file. "This needs your signature."

I take the file from her, needing her to leave so I can catch my breath. "Anything else?"

"That's all."

When she steps back, I close the door, bracing my hand against it as I take in a deep breath. My heart races wildly as I try to tame desire and panic.

What am I doing?

Emma has me in a million shades of delirium right now. Stammering back over to my desk, I fall into my chair and close my eyes, because to look at myself would be to look at a stranger.

What the hell am I doing?

I don't recognize this woman. The one who just masturbated in her university office with students a few feet away.

Pull yourself together.

I jump again when my cell phone chimes.

Tripp: I had an unexpected meeting today that's thrown me off schedule. I'm going to be a little late getting home tonight.

EIGHTEEN

Carly

"Would you like something to drink? A glass of wine, or, perhaps, a hot tea?"

"No, thank you," I respond to Margot as I follow her into the sitting room of her historical DC home. "I really appreciate you rearranging your schedule so that I could stop by. It means a lot."

She takes a seat in one of the wingback chairs that's close to the grand fireplace. Nothing in this home is out of place, and the same can be said about her poised appearance—her black hair is sleek, hitting along her jawline with a simple strand of pearls that dips over the neck of her taupe cashmere sweater. "Don't be silly, I'm the one who should be thanking you. You got me out of going to the Ladies of the Senate luncheon."

I take a seat on the couch across from her, snickering at her refusal to call the organization by its new name. "You don't call it that when you're with the other members, do you?"

"Heavens, no! Well, at least not around the younger members. I can't stand all their new-age ideas." She brushes her hand down the fabric of her ivory slacks. "Senate Spouses," she grumbles as if the words taste foul in her mouth. "Why do we all have to be clumped together? I mean, call me a traditionalist, but I don't want to lunch with men. It changes the whole dynamic of what the organization should be. You would think the feminists would want it to be strictly women, the way it used to be in the past, but, as always, the rules have to be changed so that nobody feels left out . . . *pansies.*"

I laugh at her flair of honesty. She speaks her mind, not caring what others might think of her opinions. With a legacy such as hers, a person would be stupid to cross her in any way. She's a viper, which is why I'm so lucky we are friends. I wouldn't dare want to be on her bad side.

"So, what was so urgent that you needed to see me on such short notice?"

"Do you remember the conversation we had over lunch the other week?" She nods, so I continue, "I took your advice."

"And which piece of advice was it that you took?"

"To keep my hands clean." The corner of her mouth lifts ever so slightly. "I paid a woman to help me."

"What exactly did you pay her to do?"

Looking into the eyes of the one person who I can talk to about this, a woman who is just as deeply rooted in this political world as my husband, I reveal, "I paid her to sleep with Tripp."

The other corner lifts, morphing her lips into a complete smile as she shakes her head slowly in disbelief. "Damn, girl. You've got some balls in those panties."

"I don't know about that," I admit. "But I had to do something. I can't sit around being his doormat anymore." I tell her this, but it gets caught in the strings of confliction. Hell, it was only a couple of days ago that I was getting off to the thought of him with her, wishing it were me. In this attempt to take control, I feel like I've lost more than what I've gained. All this has done is make me miss my husband and what we used to have even more.

"So, what's next?"

With a shrug, I say, "I'm not exactly sure, which is why I'm here. You're the only person I can trust to help me." And it's true even though I feel like our friendship is on borrowed time. If Tripp wins this election, which many say he will, he will be on the same political path as Conrad, Margot's husband.

Conrad is currently a fourth-year US Senator and has his eyes on the presidency. We are two years into the current presidential term, which means that around this time next year, our husbands will be announcing their run for the White House. I'm not quite sure what this means for my and Margot's friendship since all campaigns involve some level of smearing, whether public or private.

"You know I'm here for you, right?"

"Sometimes I worry," I confess.

"About?"

"Our husbands. Their goals are the same, so that will likely put us at odds. I don't want that to happen."

"Dear, you worry for nothing," she says before crossing her legs and leaning forward. "You speak as if you didn't just pay someone to screw your husband so that you could take half when you divorce the poor bastard. When it's time for him to announce his run for president, you'll no longer be the woman on his arm."

That felt like ice water being thrown in my face, and in an attempt to hide my thoughts, I allow my eyes to drift over to the crackling fire. Why did I let myself assume that I'd be in the mix of that campaign? Denial that this is even happening? Perhaps. That particular emotion is just as useless as my fear of us being at odds.

"You're right. I don't know what I was thinking."

Margot stands and walks over, taking a seat next to me on the couch. "So, let's plot our next step, shall we." I give her an agreeing nod before she asks, "Show me what you have on him?"

"He fell for her instantly. I knew he would. She's young and vibrant, a close reflection of myself when I was that age, the age Tripp fell in love with me."

"And?"

"He slept with her . . . twice."

With an evil smirk, she quips, "That filthy pig," before adding, "Good for you for catching him with his pants down—literally. Let me see what you have on him?"

"What do you mean?"

Her brows cinch in puzzlement. "You did get proof, right?"

My muscles tense, and I fear I've made a huge screw-up in my plan.

"Carly, please tell me you have photos, emails, texts, recordings, *something*."

Shit.

Margot releases a disappointing sigh. "You're kidding. Please, tell me you're kidding."

I should've known better than to think I could pull this off. I've never really been a deceitful person before this, my mind doesn't operate like that.

"How could you be so stupid?" she chastises as I slump my shoulders, silently scolding myself for being exactly that—stupid. "My god, Carly, you're a politician's wife; use your brain. Obviously, you need to get proof. Otherwise, it's just your word against his—now, it's worse. It's your word against her word against his word. You've just made this whole situation worse. I mean, what a disaster. You have three people who are going to have three very different stories. No one will take any of these claims seriously. It'll be a media joke if they ever get wind of this."

What little confidence I had about this situation capsizes. "You think this will find its way into the press?"

"With all the missteps you've made? I think it's a question of when not if. Come on, how often have you watched news coverage of a politician being caught with his pants down because his mistress went to the press? And why shouldn't they when these media outlets dump money at their feet in exchange for just a snippet of the juicy details?"

"I can't believe this." After paying Emma sixty thousand dollars, I'll be damned if I let that happen. I can't let this all be for nothing.

"Listen, you need to talk to the girl you paid. At the very least, I would assume they've been texting each other, so ask her for her phone records before she realizes what they are worth."

I'm freaking out, wondering what other mistakes I've made, and then my stomach knots and my eyes widen.

"What is it?"

"I've been texting her. If I can get the paper trail that connects Tripp to her, what does it matter when there's a paper trail connecting *me* to her as well?"

Margot stands and paces a few steps away from me before turning back. "Christ," she breathes. "You really know how to screw yourself."

This whole plan to walk away from this failed marriage with a sense of dignity and money in the bank to start my new life is a joke. "What if I bow out of the plan to leave Tripp so this doesn't come to bite me in the ass?"

"You can't do that," she refutes. "You're in way too deep. How much do you even trust this girl you paid off? Is she going to keep her mouth shut since you probably never even thought to have her sign an NDA?"

"Without a doubt. I'm safe with her, which is why I chose her."

"Wait, you knew her before?"

"Yeah, her parents passed away a year ago and she's been coming to me for therapy ever since. I trust her."

"Then talk to her, ask her for whatever proof she has, and then give her whatever she wants in order to keep her mouth shut," Margot insists. "Damage control should be your priority right now."

With fear swimming in my stomach, I thank Margot for her help before rushing out, feeling like I have no time to waste.

Once I'm in my car, I call Emma, cursing each ring until she answers as I drive to my private practice office.

"Hello?"

"Emma, hi. It's Carly. Do you have a moment to talk?"

"Um, sure," she says hesitantly.

"I've been getting everything in place, but I need one more thing from you. I need any texts or emails that you and my husband have sent to each other to ensure the terms of the prenup have been compromised."

My request is met with silence on her end, rankling my stress even more.

"Emma? Are you still there?"

"Yeah."

"Can you get those for me? I'll be at my office off campus for the rest of the day."

"I don't . . ." She's apprehensive. "I don't know if that's a good idea."

"Why? There are messages that you have between the two of you, right?"

"I mean, yeah, but . . ."

"Emma, I need those."

"I can't give them to you," she tells me, and my hands are shaking so badly that I'm forced to pull off onto the side of the road.

"What do you mean?"

"I mean, those messages will be traced back to me."

"The only person I'll be showing them to is my attorney, I thought you knew that. I promise you they will remain private. You trust me, right?"

"You know as well as I do that nothing is private. What if they get leaked? Because chances are, they will." Her voice grows uneven, a sign that she's starting to freak out. "I'll be the villain, and you'll be the victim. And Tripp . . . well, he'll just be another politician, one of so many others who strayed. The media and public will destroy me, my name, my future—"

"No, Emma. I would never let that happen."

"It wouldn't even be in your control. Just look at the Clinton's, look what happened to Lewinski. It was the media and public that persecuted her. I'll have no voice. No one will believe anything I say because all they will see is a slut that ruined your marriage. Or even worse, if they ever find out about the money you paid me, I'll be nothing more than a prostitute—a whore!"

"Emma, please."

"No way. I can't risk the crucifixion. I just can't. I'm sorry, but no." And just like that, she ends the call.

"Damn it!" Slamming my palms against the steering wheel, I scream out, hating myself for being so stupid, hating Tripp for ripping us apart, and hating Emma when I don't even have a true reason to hate her. Her concern is valid, and truth is, it's what is likely to happen.

So, what was all this for?

What have I done?

NINETEEN

Emma

The bass of the music thumps heavily, rattling the dance floor and sending its vibrations through my body, which is halfway to numb. With my arms in the air, I lean my head back as the guy I'm dancing with moves in closer from behind me. Lights strobe throughout the club, and Olivia's laughter echoes from nearby.

Where?

I'm not sure.

I've drowned my anxiety in liquor to the point of freedom. Freedom from my financial burdens, freedom from Carly calling me the other day and stressing me the fuck out, freedom from just about everything.

One shot, two shot, three shot, blasted is what I am.

Hot Guy pillows my head with his broad shoulder as he moves in perfect time with the music. He told me his name, but that was after my blood dissolved into alcohol, and I don't remember what it is. With his hands low on my hips, he turns me around when the DJ shifts into another song with the same beat. I slip my arms around his shoulders to keep my balance, and when one of Olivia's friends holds out another shot for me, Hot Guy takes it and pours it into my mouth as they all cheer me on.

There's no flavor.

No burn.

No anything as I dance the night away.

My head spins, taking me on a wild tilt-a-whirl, and when I open my eyes, I find myself on a small leather couch in the back of the club. Hot Guy is nowhere in sight, but Olivia is stumbling up the two steps to where I'm sitting. She flops down next to me in a fit of giggles as the rest of her girlfriends follow up the steps, equally amused by whatever the hell they find to be so funny.

"Are you having fun?" she yells over the music, to which I give a lazy nod. "Are you wasted?"

Again, another nod. I'm not sure how to get my muscles to move in order to talk.

Girls' night. When the day rolled around, I was already regretting my choice to join them. It's one thing for me to hit a local campus bar with Luca and have a few drinks, but this is the nonsense I try to avoid. Yet, here I am, in the throngs of desperate, horny drunk people who are looking for their next lay.

I'm blinded when the lights flash on, and then someone announces, "Last call!"

"Shit," I groan, slinging my arm over my eyes.

The music lowers in volume, and a few people flock to the bar to get their last drink before calling it a night.

"I need a taxi," I slur to anyone who's paying attention. "Can someone call me a ride?"

"I'll be your ride," Olivia chirps. "I'm not tossing you in some skeezy taxi."

My eyes fall shut as the girls continue to squeal and laugh. My hands have finally lost all feeling, causing me to grin. At least, I think I'm grinning. It isn't until Olivia and one of her friends pull me to my feet that I realize my legs are numb too.

With the three of us clinging together, we pass by Hot Guy on the way out to the parking lot. He shoves something into the pocket of my pants and follows it up with a hard slap to my ass.

Somehow, I'm able to feel its sting.

"Was he hot or am I just drunk?" I ask to anyone who cares.

"No, girl. He's definitely hot," one of them answers. "Who is he?"

"I dunno."

Frigid air nips my skin when we make it outside. I'm doing the best I can to carry my weight as they help me to Olivia's car, but I'm on my way to blacking out when a parking curb takes me down. Tripping, I fall onto my knees as my shins slam hard against the block.

"Fucking hell!" I seethe in pain.

"Are you okay?"

The two of them pull me back up to my unstable feet, and thank God her car is only a few more steps away. They help me into the passenger seat, and somehow, I manage to fasten the seatbelt. Fumbling, I find the button to recline back, and before I know it, the car is moving and I'm fading.

A sensation of movement dizzies me before my eyes open. The weight of boulders on me makes it difficult to move, but I eventually get my eyelids to flutter open. Blades of sunlight stab my vision, and I slam my eyes closed again. My muscles ache when I roll onto my belly, and this time, I don't rush as I slowly open my eyes, taking in the morning light in fractions.

"Kill me now," I mumble into my pillow.

The room spins and so does my head. I can't recall the last time I felt this hungover. I vaguely remember dancing with some guy for most of the night while I also consumed far too much alcohol. The details are static, and I can't remember how I even got home last night or who put me in my bed.

Lifting the covers, I see I'm still in the same clothes, and I reek of cigarette smoke while the aftertaste of vodka lingers in my mouth. I grow nauseated, and when my stomach gurgles, I bolt to the bathroom, expelling god knows what into the toilet. Gripping the seat, another expulsion bubbles in my gut before I hurl again. Tears fall as I rest my cheek against the cold porcelain and attempt to take in a deep breath.

I curse myself for getting as drunk as I did because this hangover is already something fierce. My hand is dead weight when I reach up to flush all that remains from last night. Closing the lid, I pull myself up and sit with my head hanging between my knees to ward off my light-headedness. Once my vision clears, I drag myself over to the shower, turn on the water, and strip out of my clothes.

About thirty minutes later, I'm dressed in fresh pajamas with the hint of toothpaste still on my tongue. As much as I want to go back to bed, I want coffee even more.

While I'm in the kitchen waiting for my coffee to finish brewing, I riffle through the fridge to find a decent flavor of creamer. It's as I'm closing the door that I hear Luca coming out of his room. When I turn to ask him if he wants coffee too, I'm taken aback when I see Olivia instead, looking sloppy with a terrible case of bedhead.

She stops in her step when she catches eyes with me, and neither of us speak as we stare at each other.

I feel like I'm going to be sick again.

"Hey," she says meekly as she makes her way over to the island bar top where her purse sits.

There's no need to ask why she's here, and no, it doesn't irk the shit out of me in the same way it usually does when a random girl stumbles out of his room. This is a different level of annoyance. It's scathing.

As much crap as Luca talks about this girl, why the hell would he even go there with her . . . again?

I don't say a word, and next thing I know, Luca is walking out of his room in nothing but his boxer briefs. His eyes lock on to mine, causing an eruption from somewhere deep inside me.

I'm angry when I have no reason to be, so the emotion is confusing.

"I'll call you later?" Olivia asks, and all I can give her is a feeble, "Whatever."

I dump the creamer into my coffee, the front door closes, and I take my mug back to my room.

"Emma—"

The door slams behind me, cutting him off. Setting my coffee on the nightstand, I crawl back into bed as my emotions stir from beneath the surface.

I feel like crying, and I'm not entirely sure why. A big part of me wants to lie to myself and say it's because of everything that I've been dealing with lately, but, damn it, if there isn't a pit of jealousy in my gut.

There's a light tap on my door, and before I can even speak, he opens it and steps inside.

I should have remembered the lock.

He holds a glass of water as he walks over to my bed. "Here. You should take these." He then opens his palm, dropping a few pills next to my cup of coffee before setting the water next to it.

I want to thank him, but even more, I want to yell at him and tell him to stop fucking everything with a pulse.

"You were completely passed out last night. I had to carry you in from the car," he explains. "You shouldn't drink that much."

"What are you now? My dad?" My words come with fangs meant to bite, and I can see their infliction within his expression.

His eyes fall from mine, and he opens his mouth to speak, but nothing comes out. He's clearly uncomfortable, and even though a part of me wants to soothe him, I don't because I'm too confused. The moment he lifts his head is the same moment I look away to avoid him.

"I'm sorry." It's all he leaves me with before walking out and closing my door.

Turning onto my side, I peer out the window and stare into nothingness.

His words echo in my head.

I'm sorry.

It isn't the words I hone in on, it's how he said them. His tone, his inflection, his meaning behind them. Something about his apology tells me it wasn't about him intruding into my personal space.

No.

His sorry was for something else, but I'm too hungover to dissect it.

Sighing, I roll over and swallow the pills, secretly wishing I had the whole bottle just so I could be with my parents again. Instead, I close my eyes and pray I find them in my dreams.

TWENTY

Emma

Waking up to darkness, the world is no longer spinning, but I'm so thirsty. I pick up the glass of water that's next to the untouched cup of coffee and swallow it in large gulps. It's close to nine in the evening, and I can't believe I slept the day away.

My stomach growls, begging for food, so I sling the covers off me and head out to the kitchen. Walking past the living room I notice a slew of beer bottles on the coffee table and a half-smoked joint in an ashtray, none of which were there this morning.

Luca's door is closed, and by the looks of it, he's probably been here all day.

Something is wrong.

It takes me a moment to realize that my anger from earlier has dissipated, and I let go of whatever it was that had me so bitchy and knock on his door. When there's no answer, I let myself in to find him slouched on the loveseat that sits by the large windows. More beer bottles are scattered about, and he has me worried when he doesn't look up.

"Is everything okay?" I ask softly, and when I do, he finally looks up with bloodshot eyes. "Luca?" I go to him, taking the bottle that's dangling from his fingers and sit next to him. "You're scaring me."

He leans back, resting his head on the cushion and staring up to the ceiling. "You're scaring *me*."

"What's that supposed to mean?"

He shakes his head, remaining silent, but his behavior right now ... it isn't like him.

"I'm serious, Luca. Why do you say I'm scaring you?"

His head tilts to face me, and his eyes are both bloodshot and glassy. "Because you're *you*," he says, pausing for a beat before adding, "And because I'm me."

"We're who we've always been."

"Exactly."

I pivot so that I'm facing him dead on, not understanding anything he's saying. Sure, he's been drinking all day, but I can tell he isn't totally wasted, just a little drunk; he's simply running off the remaining fumes of what he's consumed, so I push him to explain and ask, "What's wrong with who I am?"

"Nothing." He sighs. "That's the problem ... you're perfect."

"I'm not."

Sitting up, he props his forearms on his knees, refuting, "You are. You always have been."

"So, what's wrong with who you are?"

"Everything." He drops his head. "Which is why we'll never work."

His words come out of leftfield, catching me completely off guard. Did he just admit to having feelings for me?

"I don't know why I even let my head go there with you."

"Go where exactly?" I ask, needing not to misconstrue whatever it is he's trying to say. When he doesn't answer, I press on. "Just be honest with me."

It isn't until I lay my hand on his knee to get his attention that he turns to me. It takes him a moment, and I can see he's struggling before he says, "I love you."

My lips part in complete shock, but my thoughts run rampant, silencing me.

"I didn't want to fall for you because I knew it would never work between us, but I fell anyway, and now ... now it hurts to look at you. It hurts to be around you because I want more than that."

"Luca—"

"I already know what you're going to say. I already know I'm no good, which is why I've never told you. I've been fighting it for a while now."

"Fighting what?"

"To not give in to what I've been feeling for you. To not touch you in ways I never have. To not kiss you when I hear you crying, because I want to."

His hand comes straight to my cheek and slides back into my hair. A touch that's too tender for him.

"I know better than to ever cross that line with you. I care too much, and I know I would probably wind up hurting you."

My heart softens, and I can't deny the jealousy I felt when I found out he slept with Olivia. And even though he's making his confessions, I'm too terrified to make my own. To admit that I might be feeling more than what I should for him.

While he's completely wrong about him not being good enough, he's right when he says that he would most likely wind up hurting me, and I can't risk hurting any more than what I already am. The pain I carry from losing my parents is a pain I wouldn't wish on anyone, but as much as I want to protect myself, I want to protect him too. It isn't easy seeing Luca like this. Distraught to the point he had to drink himself into being honest with me.

"I want you to get everything this world took from you, and I want to be the guy who gives it to you. I just don't know if I could ever be faithful."

And I fear that too.

"You deserve so much more than what I am, but it's becoming impossible to keep this all buried."

His hand falls away, and the loss of his touch chips at my heart. I want to tell him something—anything—because I know it took a lot for him to tell me all of this, but I'm so confused. God, I'm confused about everything in my life. I've been drowning for what seems like an eternity with nothing to grab on to.

If I were being honest, there've been moments when I just wanted to grab on to Luca. Everything I know about him suggests that he might just be the only one strong enough to pull me out of this madness. Then his flaws remind me of why I can't go there. Why I can't lean on him the way I crave to. More than anything, I fear losing him, losing my only real friend.

How do I ignore that pang of jealousy from this morning though?

What do I do with that?

Where does it go?

Taking a leap of faith, I give him what he deserves. "I was mad at you this morning."

"You mean disappointed?"

Shaking my head, I give him what I want to hide, because that's what I'm good at—hiding. "No. I was mad."

The lines in his forehead deepen, and I dig further, giving him more when it feels so foreign to me. It worries me because I should be doing everything to protect myself, instead I'm doing the opposite. I'm exposing myself, opening up in a way I'm not sure I should, but I do it anyway.

"I was jealous."

"Jealous?"

Bashfully, I nod.

"You have no reason to be jealous. You don't want what I give those girls." He moves in closer, taking my now jittery hand. "They only get the worst of me. The parts I hate."

Squeezing my fingers around his hand, I hesitantly murmur, "This scares me."

"What does?"

"*This*," I stress.

He tugs my hand and pulls me into his arms, hugging me. "It scares me too."

My arms tighten around him, and no other words are spoken as we hold each other in a cloud of fear and confusion. Luca is my best friend, and I doubt I am willing to risk losing him just because I've had moments where thoughts of wanting more with him have crept in.

That thought is chased by another.

What if I've spent so much time despising his crude behavior with women as a way of convincing myself that he's all wrong for me, like a shield to protect against the inevitable. In turn, I could've been focusing on all the great qualities about him, the million reasons to adore him.

Reasons that far outweigh this one negative.

But, just like him, I've never been in love.

I've never committed myself to anyone.

I've never even considered opening myself up to having something like that in my life.

I'm not even sure I can.

In this moment, all we do is hold on to each other as I try to keep myself together, because what the hell are we doing? I'm not even sure I want to go down this road with him—or with anyone, for that matter.

After a while, we trade the couch for the bed, and even though we've spent a few nights sleeping next to each other, tonight feels like the first.

Despite having slept the whole day away, I'm eventually able to fall asleep in his arms.

As always, the morning comes all too soon. The ringing of my cell phone from the other room pulls me from my dream, and as I begin to rise, my movement stirs Luca. Slipping out of bed, I shiver against the chill in the air as I make my way to my room. When I see I have a missed call from Valley Crest, I quickly call back.

"Valley Crest. How may I help you?"

"Hi, this is Emma Ashford. Someone just called me."

"Just one moment."

She puts me on hold, and when I peer out the door, I see Luca getting a pot of coffee going.

"Ms. Ashford?"

"Hi. I saw that I just missed a call."

"Yes. This is Dr. Lopez, I'm the new resident psychiatrist here at Valley Crest. I'm calling in regards to Matthew."

"Is everything okay?"

"Your brother got a new roommate a couple of weeks ago," he tells me, but I already knew that because Matthew called me the day after, complaining about the guy. "This has been a difficult adjustment for him. I've been able to meet with him to discuss coping skills, but there was an altercation—nobody was hurt—but your brother has been very upset ever since. My concern is his well-being at this point."

"His well-being?"

"Apart from him trashing his room and kicking a hole in the wall, Matthew has been refusing to eat. He's demanding we move his roommate."

"Well, move his roommate."

"It isn't that simple, Ms. Ashford. We have no empty beds, and moving him would just cause more chaos among the other residents who also respond to change in similar ways as Matthew does."

"When was the last time he ate?" I ask as Luca walks into my room, watching me with curiosity.

"Three days ago. We tried giving him a PediaSure when he woke up this morning, but he refused and became even more agitated. Ever since, he's been demanding to see his parents."

My heart slips a few ribs down, and I hate myself for leaving him alone and still confused about Mom and Dad.

"I know you're in DC, but if there's a way you could come . . . it's just turning into an urgent situation that's causing a disturbance among the other residents."

"No, I understand," I say. "I'll pack a bag and head out now. It's about a ten-hour drive for me, but I'll get there as quickly as I can."

"What's going on?" Luca asks when I end the call and drop the phone onto my bed.

Rushing over to the closet, I get my suitcase. "I have to go back home. My brother needs me."

"Is everything okay?"

I pull clothes from their hangers and toss them onto the bed. "He's upset about his roommate and refuses to eat. They can't seem to calm him down." Grabbing a few more items from the dresser, I add, "They said he won't stop asking to see our parents." The words tangle in my throat, balling up in a lump of emotion, but I don't stop moving as I go into the bathroom and start gathering toiletries.

"Let me come with you," he says when I walk back to the suitcase and dump everything in.

"What? No. I'll be fine. It isn't the first time this has happened."

Luca grabs my wrist, forcing me to stop and pay attention to him. "Let me come. Just let me be there for you." His tone borders on need. "Please."

I want to push back and tell him no, but there's something deep inside me whispering yes.

"Are you sure?"

"I'm sure," he asserts. "Whatever you're worried about, don't be."

"It's just that . . . Matthew isn't—"

"The only one who's uncomfortable here is you, not me, okay?" he states with an encouraging nod, and when I find myself nodding with him, he smiles.

"Just hurry because it's a long drive."

TWENTY-ONE

Emma

It's almost eight o'clock when we arrive at Valley Crest. The car hasn't even come to a complete stop when I open the door. Luca doesn't try to tame my eagerness, in fact, he's only a few steps behind me as I rush for the door.

I stop by the front desk and ask to see my brother. I'm unable to sit still as we wait. My knee bounces as I stare impatiently at the door, waiting for one of the nurses to come get me. I'm consumed with irritation that they didn't call me sooner. Along with the irritation lies the guilt. I know it isn't my fault that he's in this place, but he's depending on me to get him out. If I had the means, I would pull him out of this place and find him the best home there is. I'm broke, though, and that sixty grand Carly has given me will only get the two of us by for a little while before it dries up.

When Luca's hand lands on my knee that won't stop bouncing, I give him a weak smile—so weak I doubt he can see it.

"Emma, hi," Maggie, one of the nurses I've come to know, greets. "Sorry if I kept you waiting."

I stand. "It's fine." I turn back to Luca, worried about how he will react if I take him back to where Matthew is, fearing the other residents will freak him out, and ask, "Do you mind waiting here while I go get him?"

"Are you sure?"

"Yeah. Just give me a few minutes."

Maggie directs me through the secured double doors and down the hallway that leads to the housing unit.

147

"How has he been?" I ask, knowing I'll get the honest truth from her. She's close to my age and has a genuine heart for this job, unlike most of the other people who work here who let things fall through the cracks.

"Not good. He's been very irritable and upset, but I spent some time with him earlier, and he kicked my butt at checkers more times than I can count. He seemed to enjoy the distraction," she tells me. "He was excited when he found out you were coming. His bag is already packed."

"It's quieter than normal," I note when we enter the residential wing.

"It's movie night. Everyone is in the rec room." When we reach his room, she gives a quick knock on the open door as we step inside. "Matthew, look who's here."

He stands from the small desk and nearly knocks me over when he hugs me. "Hey, buddy. I heard you are being a trouble maker," I tease.

"He broke my Legos." When he steps back, he's visibly upset. "He touches all my things!"

"They said you kicked a hole in the wall."

"It was his fault. I came back from playing outside, and he had broken the Lego airplane I had just finished building."

"Did you have fun building it?"

"Yeah, but now it's destroyed," he fumes.

"True. But now you can build it again and have more fun," I say, trying to add a silver lining.

"Ugh! You don't get it!"

"Okay. I'm sorry." I give up trying to defuse him. "What do you say we get out of here?"

"What if he touches more of my things?"

"Don't you worry about that, dear," Maggie tells him. "I'll keep my eye out." She grabs his duffle bag and hands it to him. "You go and have fun with your sister. Don't worry about what's happening here, okay?"

"But—"

"No buts. You heard the woman," I say as I hold out my hand for him to take. "Come on, let's go. I have a surprise waiting for you up front."

"What surprise?"

"Let's go and find out."

When we step into the lobby, Luca stands. My hand still holds Matthew's, and I feel a tinge of protectiveness when I introduce them, having never exposed anyone to my brother so honestly.

"Matthew, this is my good friend and roommate, Luca."

"Hey, Matthew."

Matthew doesn't respond, which isn't unusual. He's always very awkward around strangers and doesn't fully understand social cues, so I have to help him out. "Can you say 'hi' to my friend?"

"Hi." He then turns to me and says loud enough for Luca to hear, "He has a hole in his jeans. Poor people have holes in their clothes."

I stifle a laugh because Luca is far from poor, but Luca doesn't miss a beat when he responds, "It's the style. You buy them like that. It's called distressed."

Matthew twists his face, and the expression is priceless. "It's weird."

"It isn't weird," Luca defends. "We'll take you to the mall while we're here and prove it to you."

"Come on. Let's go to the hotel."

"His hair looks hard," Matthew says, again, not understanding that he shouldn't talk about people right in front of them.

"Be nice," I tell him before Luca adds from over his shoulder, "You're deflating my ego, Matthew."

"Can I touch it?" he asks, reaching out when we get to the car, but before I can swat his hand away from Luca, it's too late. Matthew laughs. "It's crunchy. Emma, feel it. It's crunchy."

"It's hair gel. It's supposed to do that," I say as we pile into Luca's car and head to the hotel.

Luca and I took turns driving, and when we stopped to grab

lunch, he booked us a room at a hotel that's much nicer than the ones I stay in when I come home. Guilt tugged me beneath the surface, but he insisted on taking care of the room.

When we are in the elevator, Luca looks over to Matthew, saying, "Your sister told me you're into airplanes."

Matthew immediately perks up but turns to me instead of Luca. "Can we go to the airport while you're here? You didn't take me last time."

"Why didn't you take him last time?"

"Because we were busy," I tell Luca before saying to Matthew, "We're only here for a couple of days. I don't know if we'll have time."

"Don't listen to her," Luca says when the elevator doors slide open and we step off. "I'll take you to the airport."

"Really? Can we go tomorrow? Do you think we will see any pilots?"

"If we don't see any pilots, I'm sure we'll see some cute flight attendants."

Matthew breaks out in a nervous chuckle.

When Luca opens the door to our room, I'm surprised to see he booked us a suite. Matthew rushes in with total awe as Luca strolls over to the sitting area with nonchalance.

"This place is huge," he exclaims with a beaming smile. "Look, Emma, there's a balcony, and not one of the fake ones. You can actually go out on it!"

Matthew opens the doors to the balcony and goes outside.

"Be careful and don't lean over the railing." Setting my purse on the coffee table, I tell Luca, "You didn't have to get us this big room."

"There are three of us. No point in being cramped." He pulls out the room service menu from the desk and starts flipping through the pages. "Where do you normally stay?"

"Greenfield Motel," Matthew hollers from outside, and when Luca's eyes shoot up to mine, heat creeps up my neck and I'm forced to look away. "The towels smell like cheese there."

"No, they don't," I say to Matthew as he comes back inside, but they do, in fact, smell like cheese.

Luca hands my brother the menu. "Here, tell me what you want for dinner."

Matthew sits on the couch next to me and starts reading through the options. "You can't tell them that I ate. I'm on a hunger strike."

"Your secret's safe with us," Luca responds. "Anything look good?"

"Can I have the shrimp fettuccini with no shrimp, no mushrooms, no shallots, and no sauce?"

The look on Luca's face is *everything*, and it takes a lot of effort to hold back my laughter.

"You're shitting me, right?"

"Oooooh, you shouldn't say that word."

Luca holds his hands up. "Sorry. My bad."

I take the menu from Matthew before he gets up and starts exploring the rest of the suite. When Luca takes a seat next to me, I say, "He just wants buttered pasta."

"And what about you?"

"I'll just have the turkey wrap."

After Luca places the order, he turns on the television and starts flipping through the channels. It's awkward to have him here, hanging out with me and my brother. That feeling only amplifies when he asks, "Is that where you spent your Christmas? At that motel?"

"Not all of us were born with a silver spoon." My reaction is defensive.

He doesn't respond, and I instantly regret being so rude.

"I'm sorry. I shouldn't have said that."

"No worries."

"Emma," Matthews says as he peeks out from one of the rooms. "There are two beds in here; can Luca room with me?"

"You don't want to share a room with me?"

"I always share a room with you."

"Luca probably wants his own space."

"No, it's cool." Luca smiles, telling Matthew, "But only if you tell me some embarrassing stories about your sister."

Matthew's smile grows. "I've got a ton of them!"

"Don't you dare tell him anything."

Matthew just laughs as he plops down into a chair and kicks his feet up onto the ottoman. He's lost in his tablet, no doubt watching videos about airplanes. I sit back with Luca as he finds a random movie to watch. Even though there's so much unsettled between the two of us, I'm grateful to have him here. There's always a dark gloom when I come back home, but right now, Matthew seems content, which is all that matters.

After room service drops off our food, we devour our meals, especially my brother, who hasn't eaten in days.

"So, about your hunger strike," I start. "You can't just not eat."

"Says who?"

"Says me," I stress. "I worry about you."

"I need a new roommate."

"Buddy, they can't move him to another room. You're going to have to be more flexible. I know it isn't what you want, but this isn't forever. As soon as another bed opens, I will do everything I can to have him moved, but for the time being, can't you just ignore him?"

"He eats glue."

Rolling my eyes, I say, "Yeah, well, you used to eat rollie pollies, but I never made Mom find you a new place to live."

His face falls when I was hoping to make him smile.

"What is it, buddy?"

"Do you think we'll ever see them again?" He looks into my eyes with so much sadness.

I open my mouth to speak, but nothing comes out because there are times I wonder the same thing. It's completely irrational, I know, but sometimes, the misery of losing them becomes too much, and I trick myself into thinking that maybe, in some unexplainable way, they'll come back.

"Of course, you'll see them again," Luca tells him when I'm silent for too long.

I'm too upset to mutter a word for fear I'll cry, but I also can't watch him as he talks to my brother because it hurts too much.

"I'll be right back," I murmur as I excuse myself to the restroom to get a moment of reprieve.

After locking the door, I sit on the edge of the bathtub and try to breathe through the barrage of emotions. Everything has become so unstable, but it's in moments like these that I want to grab on to the people I love and never let them go. Never let them out of my sight for fear I'll lose them too. It's neurotic, I know, but it's overwhelming at the same time.

When I finally come out of the bathroom, Matthew is already in bed and Luca is in the room with him, digging through his suitcase.

"I think I'm going to call it a night," I tell them as I head to the other room with a single king bed.

I pull out a pair of pajamas but don't have it in me to change as I stare blankly out the window.

"Hey."

When I turn around, Luca steps into the room, closing the door behind him.

"Are you okay?"

Yeah, I'm fine. I'm just tired.

It's my automatic response, and the words are on my tongue, yet I don't say them. This time, I don't push Luca away. With my heart in shreds, I shake my head.

I'm not okay, and I don't know if I can go another day pretending that I am.

TWENTY-TWO

Emma

These past two days in Tennessee have been great. Luca held true to his word with Matthew, taking him to the airport where my brother got to meet a pilot who had just finished a twelve-hour shift. Luca slipped the man some money on the sly to visit with my brother. The four of us sat at a coffee shop next to the security entrance while Matthew chatted the man's ear off. The pilot even gave Matthew the real wings from his uniform. When I told him that the plastic ones would be just fine, he insisted, saying that he had a few extras for backup.

We even went to the mall so Luca could buy Matthew a pair of jeans with holes in them. He wore them out of the store, and I laughed at the two of them, walking around in their matching jeans, twinning like it was the coolest thing. It's comforting to see my brother bonding with my best friend, and I'm so grateful that I didn't push Luca away when he asked to come on this trip. Because he was right all along; I do need to involve Matthew in my life more. After watching the two of them these past few days, I hope they will continue to keep in touch after we go back to DC.

Since Luca cannot miss his classes tomorrow, we have to wake up and hit the road early in the morning. My brother doesn't do well in the mornings, so we decided that instead of battling to wake him up in the middle of the night to drop him off, we would just say our goodbyes and take him back to Valley Crest tonight.

But my peace about the situation quickly vanished during lunch when Matthew started to insist that I take him to go to our parents' gravesite. Neither one of us have been there since the day of the funeral. As many times as I've come back to see Matthew over the past year, I've never gone, and if he brought it up, I was always quick to make an excuse as to why we couldn't go. This time, my rebuttals are shot down when Luca agrees before I can stop him.

Now I sit in Luca's car, my stomach in knots as I stare out the window and into the sea of headstones. This is the last thing I want to be doing, and I just want it to be over with.

"Come on, Matthew," I say as I open my car door.

Luca looks over his shoulder at me as I get out of the backseat. "I'll wait here for you guys."

My brother and I step out of the car, and it takes me a moment to conjure the courage to move my feet. All too soon, they move, leading us over to the plot my mom and dad share.

Matthew spots it first. "Ashford! There it is!"

His enthusiasm contradicts my misery, and I slowly trail behind him as he rushes over to the headstone that wasn't here when they were buried. Seeing it for the first time knocks the wind out of my lungs, preventing me from taking another step closer.

"Look, Emma. It has their names on it," Matthew calls out as he traces his fingers along the etched letters.

I take a few steps more, crunching snow beneath my feet as I do.

Matthew turns to me with glassy eyes. "Where are they, Emma?"

His question steals the breath from my lungs, and I realize that he truly expected to see them. I want to protect him, tell him a lie so that I don't have to hurt him with the truth.

But there is no lie to tell.

They're dead.

"They're buried," I force around the knot in my throat, but it does nothing for the confusion that remains in his eyes.

"Where?"

My chin begins to quiver, and I wish I were the one who was confused, who didn't fully understand, because living in complete awareness of the unvarnished truth is agonizingly painful.

He sees grief at its purest trembling through me. "Why are you sad?"

"Because I miss them," I weep as tears fill his eyes.

"Where are they?"

With a voice that is reduced to crumbles, I try to be as clear as possible when I say, "They're in the ground. They are right underneath you."

His head drops, and he stares at his feet as his breathing grows thicker. With each passing second, he becomes more upset. Tears spill from his eyes, and when he begins to whimper, he falls to his knees. I want to go to him and console him, but I can't. I'm stuck in my own hell of anguish as I stand here on weak legs.

"Why are in they in the ground?" he cries, rocking back and forth. "Why are they in the dirt, Emma?"

"Because . . ."

"Why?"

"Because they're dead," I choke out. "Because when you die, you don't come back."

"But I want to see them." His words are nothing but sobs.

Seeing my brother so broken fractures something inside me. Matthew cries like a little boy while staring up at me as if I have the power to fix this situation.

But I can't.

Life doesn't grant us the power he childishly believes I have.

"I want to see them."

"I do too, but we can't."

His cries amplify, echoing through the bare trees. "It isn't fair."

"I know."

My brother is falling apart. I want to go to him and hold him, but I'm afraid of what that would do to me. I'm not strong enough to feel this—to actually endure the agony of this situation. Something in my subconscious holds me hostage, rooting me in this very spot, and all I can do is watch as tears stream down his face. From the corner of my eyes, I see Luca a second before he passes me and falls to his knees next to my brother. With Luca's hand on his shoulder, my brother continues to cry out, "It isn't fair."

"It's okay, man." Luca says before helping him to his feet. As Luca takes him back to the car, I remain. I should go with them, but for some reason, I don't. Instead, I move closer until I'm right in front of their headstone. Reaching my hand out, I lay it on the icy-cold monument. The touch is profound, knocking me straight to my knees, and I shatter—I shatter into a thousand pieces of sheer heartbreak. No one would know it from the outside because it's caged inside me.

Burning tears cut me from the inside, never finding their way down my cheeks. No matter how hard I try to fight the agony, deep down, I'm just as juvenile as my brother. I'm a little girl lost, screaming and crying for her parents. It's been over a year, and I'm still not ready to be without them. I still need them.

Wrapping my arms around myself, I wonder what they must think of me and all my deception.

"I'm so sorry," I whisper, feeling the full weight of shame for the choices I've been making. "I never wanted to disappoint you."

I say these words, hoping they find their way to them. They raised me with faith and morals, but in their absence, I've shot that all to hell. I know they would be so disappointed in me.

I press my hands into the snow until they meet the earth. The frozen tips of my fingers sink into the dirt that leads to the both of them. It's a closeness I don't think I'm ready for, but I'm also not ready to walk away. So, I don't. I stay, the wet ground seeping through the knees of my pants as time sunders into something so abstract it becomes unrecognizable.

As I bleed from the inside, I make infinite wishes, tossing them up, only to have them crash back down on top of me, reminding me over and over that they're gone. Nothing could've prepared me for this type of loss. A loss so severe and excruciating that it changes the very fiber of my being.

I'm so abandoned, left on my own, and entirely mangled.

Warmth touches my back and then wraps around me wholly. I fall into Luca willingly, allowing his embrace because I'm too weak to push him away. And even though I'm already so broken, my pieces find a way to splinter even more, disintegrating into dust. Somehow, I'm able to wrap my arms around him and hold on until this torrential anguish subsides, leaving me thoroughly drained.

He doesn't say a single word as he helps me to my feet and walks me to the car. When I see that Matthew is sitting up front, completely focused on his tablet, unaware of the world outside of this car, I slip into the backseat.

As we drive away, the onslaught of a headache makes its presence known, and I rest my head against the cold window in an attempt to alleviate the throbbing. Matthew talks about the airplane Lego set Luca bought for him at the mall yesterday as if we didn't just leave our parents' grave. Sometimes, I'm jealous of his autism. I know it sounds horrible, but at least he doesn't have to endure the full weight of this misery. He gets it in fragments whereas I get it in its entirety—all the time. It's unbearable.

When we arrive at Valley Crest, I shove down my emotions and put on a brave face for my brother's sake. He says his goodbye to Luca before I take him inside. I hug him longer than what he's comfortable with, but I do it anyway. Eventually, he maneuvers out of my hold, saying, "Too much."

Once he's settled and I'm back in the car, I let go of a heavy breath. When my eyes fall shut, Luca's hand slips into mine. It's a touch I didn't know I even needed until right now, and I'm so thankful to have it. He holds my hand all the way back to the hotel.

When we make it up to the room, I'm too tired to feel the embarrassment I probably should. Instead, I'm just empty.

"Are you hungry at all?" he asks, and I can't believe I didn't even notice the dark sky until now.

I shake my head.

"Are you okay?"

"I have a really bad headache," I tell him.

"I think I have some medicine in my bag."

He goes into the room he was sharing with Matthew, and I head to my own. Kicking off my shoes, I crawl into bed and close my eyes, wishing this day into extinction. Like ripping a scab off an old wound, everything from a year ago comes crashing back with a compounded force I wasn't ready for.

"Hey."

Opening my sore eyes, I sit up and take the pills from Luca's hand, along with the bottle of water he's holding out for me. He waits while I swallow the medicine, and when I hand the water back to him, he turns off the lamp and heads out.

I stop him when he reaches the door. "Luca?"

He turns around.

"Will you stay?"

Without a word, he walks through the darkened room, kicking off his shoes and shrugging out of his shirt before he slips into bed with me. I go to him freely, resting my head on the pillow next to him as his arms come around me.

Staring into each other's eyes, there's a peace within the pain. Words dance along my tongue, words I'll never speak.

Help me.

Save me.

Don't ever leave me.

Words of desperation and fear. A hundred pleas. All of them dying in my mouth.

His hand comes to my face, brushing along my forehead as he pushes a few strands of my hair aside, and when a tear falls, he catches it.

"It's going to be okay. *You're* going to be okay."

Those words are exactly what I've been longing to hear. For someone—anyone—to scoop me up and assure me that I'm going to be all right. That this world won't destroy me. That I'm not alone.

"I'm scared." The words slip out on a whisper.

"Of what?"

"Everything."

"Tell me."

With a slow blink, I confess, "Of not knowing how to help my brother and the responsibility of looking after him. I'm scared of failing him."

"I wish I would've known about him and what you've been dealing with. I can't imagine how hard this has been on you."

"I didn't mean to lie—"

"I know," he assures. "But you're doing everything you can for him."

"What if it isn't enough?"

"You can't do this to yourself. Your brother is lucky to have you, and I don't doubt that you're doing everything possible to take care of him."

"I'm all he has."

"He has me too."

My lips lift ever so slightly. It's the mere fact that he would even make a statement like that affects me in a way I can't explain. "You mean that?"

"I wouldn't have said it if I didn't," he says before adding, "What else are you scared of?"

Looking into his sincere eyes, I grab on to a shred of courage and reveal timidly, "You."

"Me?" His hand slides along my cheek, threading his fingers into my hair. "Why?"

"I'm afraid of losing you."

As soon as I say it, he pulls me in, resting his forehead against mine. Closing my eyes, I feel my heart as it ricochets in my chest, and I'm terrified I've said too much.

"I could never leave you," he murmurs, and his lips press against mine before I can deny his words.

When Luca kisses me for the first time, it's terrifying yet comforting. My pulse races in a way that doesn't beat at all. I want to push him away and pull him closer all at the same time. Happiness and confusion collide, and somewhere within the space separating my heart's faltering beats, I kiss him back.

He holds me with a strength I didn't know he had as my hands cling to him, wrapping around his shoulders. I hold on tightly, fearing that, if I let go, I'll never find my way back.

Luca's arms constrict around me tighter, his body pressing against me as his tongue caresses mine. My head spirals out of control. Selfishly, I want to take the comfort he's giving me, but I know all too well how quickly life can change, how in a slip of a second, you can lose everything.

His lips leave mine, taking my breath with them as he drags kisses down my neck. Our bodies begin to move, and I feel myself falling.

But I can't.

Because this is Luca.

He takes my breast in his hand, squeezing me gently as his lips find mine again, and suddenly, I panic.

I'm too exposed, too vulnerable, too fearful.

"Wait." I breathe, ripping my lips away from his.

"Are you okay?"

"I-I don't know if I can do this," I admit.

"Because you're afraid?" he says, echoing my earlier words, and I nod bashfully. He takes my face in both of his hands. "Tell me what you're thinking."

I hesitate because I'm too nervous to say anything.

"It's just me," he assures. "Don't shy away. Tell me what you're thinking because I need to know."

There's something in his voice that tells me he's just as scared as I am. It's a vulnerability that reflects my own. So, I give him what I know he needs—honesty. "I'm starting to fall for you."

Exhaling heavily, he closes his eyes before pressing his head against mine.

"I just . . . I've never done this before, and I'm scared."

He nods, completely understanding what I'm saying. We've both kept ourselves closed off from relationships, and we are figuring out how to give each other what we've been too terrified to give to anyone else.

"I'm scared too," he admits. "Scared I'm going to fuck this up, but I want you. You're all I want."

I run my thumb along his brow, revealing, "You're all I want too."

TWENTY-THREE

Carly

After talking to Emma about the texts and emails, I've been reconsidering everything. With her unwillingness to provide what evidence she has, I'm back at square one and sixty grand in the hole. Agonizing over this whole ordeal, I've come to the conclusion that staying in this marriage is going to be much easier than walking away from it. The destruction the Montgomery's are capable of terrifies me, and without anything to back my allegations, I'm nothing more than a dead man walking.

I guess this is why, in this political world, women keep their mouths shut while their husbands do whatever they want. I once thought they were weak doormats, but now I understand. Those women just know the effort of leaving isn't worth it.

Standing at my dresser, I pick up the scissors and clip the tags off the new bra and panty set I bought earlier today. I lay the delicate lace garments out in hopes that Tripp will find them just as sexy as I do. It's been a long time since I've bought lingerie—too long—but if I'm going to attempt to make our marriage work, I need to do everything I can to remind him of the young girl he fell in love with. The vibrancy and youth he still seeks out and desires. I may not be as young and green as Emma or the other women he's fallen into bed with, I may have wrinkles and a few stray gray hairs, but I'm still a Montgomery. I'm still the woman who wears his ring on her finger.

It's been nearly a week since I last spoke to Emma. I tried contacting her a couple of days ago, but the call went to voice mail. I think I scared her when I asked her about the texts and emails. Looking back at how I've handled this whole situation, I could kick myself for not being smarter, for not covering all my bases. But what's done is done, and I don't know how to move forward without any solid evidence. So, this is what I'm left with—sexy lingerie and Tripp's favorite perfume of mine to help me in my quest to save our marriage. To make him see me in the same desirable light he sees the girls that so freely sleep with him.

I need to remind him that I'm still the same girl he couldn't keep his hands off of. If he needs me to ramp it up in the bedroom, then I will.

I called Tripp earlier today, and he assured me he wouldn't be working late, so after I slip into my new purchases and crawl onto the bed, he proves a man of his word when I hear him walk into the house. Of course, it crosses my mind that he might turn me down, which I should be used to at this point, but I'm a woman determined.

"Carly, I'm home," he calls out from downstairs.

"I'm in the bedroom."

With nothing but the silvery glow of the moon illuminating the room, I sit up on my knees, shove my hand in my bra, and give the girls one last much-needed boost before he appears in the doorway.

His brows lift in astonishment. "What are you doing?"

"Waiting for you."

He drops his briefcase to the floor and tugs on his tie, surprising me when he walks right to me.

When I take over removing his tie, he murmurs, "Stunning," before gripping my hips.

I kiss him passionately as I begin to unfasten the buttons on his dress shirt, and I do my best to shut out the voice inside my head that's telling me to sniff his collar. It's something I do quite often just to check if I can smell the traces of the other women. Instead, I throw myself into Tripp, ripping his shirt off and eagerly pulling him down on top of me. His lips spill over the lace of my bra, sucking my nipple into his mouth through the delicate fabric.

We move in a way we haven't in years, and that alone is enough to muffle those taunting voices. His deft hand trails up my inner thigh, and I cry out in pleasure when his fingers slip inside my panties and find their way into my body. The room spins, forcing me to close my eyes when euphoria takes over. Without missing a beat, he continues to pump his fingers at the same time as he rips my panties off. When his hot mouth covers my most intimate parts, my hands fist the sheets, and I wonder where this man has been for the past few years. Because this is the man I fell in love with. The man who, on our wedding day, snuck up to the room I was getting ready in and fucked me wildly while hundreds of guests mingled on the back lawn below, right on the other side of the window. But Tripp didn't care. And with the attention he's giving me, I doubt I would stop him if those people were standing in this very room.

His tongue abandons me, and when I open my eyes, he stands over me as he unbuckles his belt and shoves his pants down.

"Where has this Carly been hiding?"

Short on breath, I respond, "I've been here all along."

He looks so powerful, standing in front of me bold and naked when he says, "Tell me how you want it."

"However *you* want it."

The corner of his mouth lifts in a pleasing smirk, and I gasp when he abruptly flips me onto my belly, grabs my hips, and yanks my ass up in the air. On my hands and knees, my vision blurs when he licks through my seam. It's a gentle touch that he doesn't let me get used to before he pulls away, only to return with rapture. He thrusts into me hard, jolting my body forward and ripping a moan of pleasure from my throat.

Tripp unhooks my bra, and it slips down my arms, falling around my wrists. When he palms me roughly, everything inside my body swims in voracity while his hips drive into me over and over. Reaching behind, I clutch my hand around the back of his neck. He drops one of his hands from my breast to between my legs, sending me over the edge much quicker than expected. I explode as he buries himself deeper, my body shuddering as pulses of ecstasy radiate through my entire being. My vision blurs, and in the next second, Tripp grunts loudly as he comes. His chest sweats against my back as we both lose ourselves, and the room fills with the sounds of our orgasms—wild and raw.

Arching back into him as he drives into me a few more times, he drains himself inside me before pulling out. A moment later, we collapse onto the bed—breathless and sated.

"Shit," he pants, and I smile.

And this—this right here—is what I want him to remember when he thinks of me, not the nagging housewife who's grown old and stale. I want to bring that excitement back into our marriage so he doesn't have to seek it elsewhere. With that very thought, I do something unexpected when I crawl between his parted legs and take him into my mouth, licking him clean as he stares down at me in shock, proving he's far more agile than his age when he grows hard again.

"Fuck," he breathes.

I crawl on top of him and take control. Straddling him, I roll my hips and savor this feeling I've been missing—the feeling of my husband inside me. I ride him, and it only takes half the amount of time as our last round before we are both ripping apart at the seams in our ferocious orgasms.

Falling on top of him, head over heart, I listen to the *thump, thump, thump* as my own beats slow. My body softens against his, relishing what we should have never let fall apart. How did we become so strained? At what point did we decide to drift? I never knew how difficult this life would be when I chose to marry Tripp. This political world is filled with fabulists and monsters, but they're disguised as the good guys to fool the public into believing they're honest, believing that they're fighting for the good of all of us.

Lifting my head, I stare down at Tripp and wonder when he became one of them. As I look into his eyes, I refuse to accept that the man I fell in love with is no longer there. Beneath the grime, I want to believe his goodness still exists. I can't ignore that he is the man who took my side and stood up for me when his parents were so against us getting married. He didn't let the opinions of others sway him. No. He stood strong for what he believed in. Maybe he still does. Maybe he hasn't changed as much as I've led myself to believe.

"That was unexpected," he says, running his fingers through my hair. "What got into you tonight?"

I smile with a shrug. "I've just missed you, that's all."

"So, this is what I get when I work too much?" he teases. "Maybe I should work even harder."

"Don't even think about it." I chuckle as I slide off him and lie on my back, my skin still dewy.

I watch as Tripp walks into the bathroom, admiring his naked, fit body, and wonder if we can get back on track with our relationship. I want to be hopeful, but I don't know where his head is at—where it's been—and for how long. For some time, it's as if I'm on the outside looking in.

When Tripp reemerges wearing a pair of athletic pants and a T-shirt, he gives me a tender kiss on my forehead. He then bends and picks up the thong I bought just for him. It dangles from his finger as he looks at me with sinful eyes.

I smile.

"I'll call in dinner," he says before shoving the panties into his pocket and heading downstairs.

Butterflies.

That's what he just gave me, and my smile grows even bigger. Maybe this is our turning point. Maybe the reminder of what we are when we're together was what we needed.

"Is Italian okay?" he hollers from downstairs.

"Sounds perfect," I respond as I pick up my phone to see it's past nine o'clock and I have a missed text from a few hours ago. I must've been so distracted with shopping and getting ready that I never even heard my phone buzz. I swipe the screen to see the message came from Emma.

Emma: Tripp called me today. We need to talk.

TWENTY-FOUR

Carly

My stomach hollows as I stare at the text, wondering if she even took the call, and if she did, what did they talk about? I told her I no longer wanted her involved with my husband and to cut all ties with him, but what if she didn't? And even worse, what if she doesn't want to?

Tripp is a charming man, one who I easily fell in love with, so who's to say she didn't allow herself to develop feelings for him as well?

No.

I shake that thought right out of my head. After all, they've only known each other for a couple of weeks.

Still naked, I walk over to the door to hear Tripp on the phone placing our dinner order before tiptoeing into the bathroom. Closing the door, I grab the robe that's hanging behind it and slip it on. Curiosity gets the better of me, and I know I won't be able to wait until tomorrow to talk to her. I tap on her name, and when the phone begins ringing, I step over to the tub and sit on the edge.

"Hello?"

"Emma, hi," I say in a hushed voice. "I just got your text. You said we needed to talk."

"Are you okay? You sound—"

"No, I'm fine. It's just that Tripp is downstairs, so we need to be quick," I tell her.

"Like I said, he called me earlier today and wanted to know if we could get together and talk after his lunch with Senator McAvoy."

167

"You took his call? I told you not to answer or reply to his texts anymore."

"I'm sorry, I know. But I was out with friends and was distracted. I honestly didn't even look to see who was calling before I answered."

Knowing I'm pinched for time, I rush her. "It's fine. What happened?"

"All he said was that he needed to talk. I know you don't want me interacting with him, but he sounded . . . I don't know . . . *off*. I figured what harm would it do to just talk, so I met up with him. Turned out that he didn't want to talk at all . . ."

She leaves her words hanging, and suddenly, my appetite vanishes. "What happened?"

"We had sex."

Blood drains from my head, and I'm forced to drop it between my knees so I don't pass out. My fingers clench the phone when I ask, "Where?"

"In the parking garage at his office. We were in the back seat of his SUV," she explains, stammering a little. "I don't know. It all happened so fast, and I guess I got carried away."

Knowing he was having sex with her while I was getting ready for him to come home has the bile in my stomach turning sour. The truth twists around my gut, and when I sit up, I snap my words beneath my breath, "I told you to stay away from him!"

"I know, and I said I was sorry."

"Sorry? You slept with my husband after I made it clear to you that—"

"You're kidding, right?" Her tone is sharp, surprising me because she's normally so even keel. "You're the one who put me in this mess. This wouldn't have even happened if it weren't for you."

"This wouldn't have happened if you would've done what I told you to do."

"Well, I'm sorry, but it happened, and I thought you should know." She pauses, and I'm certain she can hear my angered breathing on her end. "Look, I didn't mean to upset you, but we need to figure out how we should handle this."

"Handle what?"

"The money."

"What money?"

Again, another stretch of silence before she says, "For sleeping with him."

"I didn't tell you to sleep with him."

"Carly?" I hear Tripp call out.

Rushing across the bathroom, I crack open the door. "Yes?"

"I'm in my office," he says from down the hall. "I want to talk to you about an event at Georgetown that I've just been invited to speak at."

"Give me a second, I'll be right there." Shutting the door, I bring the cell back to my ear. "Look, I can't talk right now. How about we meet at the diner tomorrow, say ten o'clock?"

"Fine," she replies with an annoyed huff before hanging up.

Leaning my back against the door, I close my eyes and fight to keep the tears at bay, but it's useless.

They fall anyway.

Ten minutes ago, I was completely found in the arms of my husband, and now I'm lost. He's down the hall, two rooms away, and I'm not sure who I'm more upset with, him or her. Or maybe it's myself. I was the one who stupidly thought I could outsmart my way from this marriage only to have lost over sixty thousand dollars plus whatever else she might demand. And for what? For hearsay evidence that won't benefit me whatsoever?

She's been no help at all and refuses to hand over any sort of hard proof that will invalidate the prenup, so this is what I'm left with. A sham of a marriage and crying alone in a bathroom with my heart in tatters wondering what it is about me that makes me not enough for him to want to be faithful to.

"Carly?" he calls again, and I quickly wipe the tears from my cheeks.

"Coming."

I splash my face with water, but my skin is blotchy from the few stray tears. It's nothing a small lie won't cover if he should ask.

With a deep breath and my mangled emotions, I head down to Tripp's office to find him sitting behind his laptop. At first glance, the burn of bitterness tangles around my heart, and before he can say a word, I feed into that very bitterness.

"Where were you today?"

His head pops up. "What?"

"This afternoon . . . where were you?"

"At lunch with Jim McAvoy. Why?"

If there were any doubt about what Emma told me, he just vanquished it. There's no way she would've known about this if it weren't for Tripp telling her.

"And after lunch?"

He rolls back in his chair and crosses his arms over his chest. "So, we're back to this? The distrust and accusations . . . really, Carly?"

"Just answer me."

"Why? For what reason?" he says, growing agitated with me. "Apparently, you already have your mind made up about my whereabouts."

"I just want you to be honest?"

Shaking his head, he refutes, "No, you don't."

I take a step into the room.

"I'm always giving you the truth, but it's never enough, is it? You're so set on painting me out to be this piece-of-shit husband, but guess what, maybe you're the piece of shit who can't find it in her heart to trust and love her husband."

"I do love you," I exclaim. "If I didn't, I wouldn't care that you're out screwing around on me."

He stands abruptly and slams his hands down onto his desk, leaning on them as he shouts. "When the fuck would I even find the time to screw around on you? I am busting my goddamn ass, jumping from meeting to meeting, from rally to rally. Interviews and press conferences. I can barely keep my head on straight, and you think I have time to fuck other women when I barely have time to fuck you!"

Words are weapons meant to injure, and I fight back. "Oh, so what was that, huh?" I lash out, pointing in the direction of our bedroom. "Was that just a quick fuck to you?"

"You tell me."

"God, you are such an asshole!"

Stepping away from his desk, he pinches the bridge of his nose and loses a heavy sigh. "I'm the asshole? Really?" He drops his hand. "Sometimes I wonder if you're trying to force me out because you don't have the guts to end this yourself."

"You think I want to lose you?" I question defensively as I step closer to him. "All I want is to keep you forever." It's the ugly truth that's hard for me to admit—even to myself. No matter how furious I am with him, no matter how much he tears at my heart, deep down, I love him. I always have. Maybe that's the reason I simply can't walk away. It isn't the money or the pride holding me here, it's my love for him that keeps me from leaving.

The day I said "I do" is the day I promised for better or worse. Now, here we are, in the deep-end of worse. I can't help but wonder if we have enough fight left in us to get back to the shallows, to get back to the better we spent so many years living in.

Even though I have hope that we can save this, there's still a possibility we won't.

And then what?

Are we left in a marriage of convenience like Margot and Conrad? What if I can't find a way to be happy with Tripp? What then? Do I find my own side piece just as he has done? The thing is, I chose a life with Tripp—any life as long as it was with him. Maybe I was foolish to believe that, in this adulterated political world of corruption, we were different. For so long, I allowed myself to believe Tripp when he assured me we would never turn into the very people we've become.

Unfortunately, this is the life we wound up with.

I can't walk away, but who's to say I won't find someone else on the side to make me happy one day. I never thought I would wind up in a marriage like this, that I would ever consider having a forbidden relationship within the one I have with Tripp. Truth be told, I don't know if I ever could because I still desperately want Tripp, want what I know is buried beneath all the wreckage.

"I can't believe you're pulling this shit again," he grits, rounding the desk and walking right past me.

"Tripp, I'm sorry." I reach for his arm as he makes his way out of the office, but he easily yanks it out of my grip. I rush behind him down the stairs, cursing myself for stirring the pot the way I just did. If only I could learn to keep my mouth shut and emotions under control. "Where are you going?"

He grabs his wallet and keys from the kitchen island. "What does it matter?"

"Please, just stay," I beg. "I'm sorry I accused you of being unfaithful. I didn't—I didn't want to fight."

Shrugging on his coat, he yells, "What the fuck, Carly? Did you really think you could, once again, accuse me of cheating on you and that I wouldn't get angry?"

"No. I mean yes. I-I—"

Stepping up to me, he gets in my face and seethes, "Don't worry about where I'm going. Don't worry about me at all."

"Tripp—"

He grips my jaw painfully, and I'm wide-eyed petrified at his fury. "The only thing you need to worry about is yourself because I'm this close to leaving your nagging ass."

He lets go of me with force, causing me to stumble back. I'm shaken to my core as I watch him swim out of focus behind the tears filling my eyes. Watercolors blur as he slams the front door behind him, leaving me in a hurricane of wretched shock.

TWENTY-FIVE

Emma

"Hey, I'm running out with some buddies to grab dinner," Luca says when he peeks into my bedroom. "Want to come?"

"I'm not hungry. Thanks anyway."

"You sure?"

"Yeah," I tell him. "I think I'm going to turn in early; I'm pretty tired."

When he leaves, I walk over to the dresser and pull out a pair of pajamas to change into. Things have been a little awkward between Luca and me ever since we returned from Tennessee. It's a weird gray area we are stuck in. We've both let our feelings be known to the other, but it isn't as if we're dating or anything; not at all. And not much affection has been shown aside from some light necking the other night when I slept in his bed.

I don't know.

If I were to be forced to label our relationship, it would be: *It's complicated.*

To be fair, my complications run deeper than Luca's. I hung up with Carly a little while ago, and the conversation was tense and ended with her wanting to meet me tomorrow morning.

After I'm changed, I hop into bed and grab my phone. I swipe through the pictures I took of Olivia's calendar, but there's nothing that puts Tripp in DC over the next few days.

As I think about what I'm going to do, I mindlessly flip through

173

my photos until I come across the selfie I took of Luca, Matthew, and me while we were at the airport. I zoom in on my brother, whose smile is so full and genuine as he stands between Luca and me.

I miss him.

Ever since returning from Tennessee, I've been thinking about the possibility of moving him here to be closer. The cost would be substantial, and I'm not sure I would even be able to find him a bed at a facility that's close to me. The idea is so new that, I haven't even mentioned it to Luca yet. I know he will jump on it and push me to make the move happen. I wouldn't put it past him to try to fund it, and I want to make sure I have the money to do this on my own.

The ringing of my phone pulls me from my thoughts. When I see Olivia's name appear on the screen, I roll my eyes, sit up, and take the call.

"Hey, Olivia."

"Hi! Do you have time to talk for a second?"

"Sure. What's up?"

"Nothing really. Just mulling around my apartment," she says. "I wanted to call to make sure that everything's okay with us."

"Yeah, everything is fine. Why?"

"I don't know. I've been feeling a little weird about last week," she admits before adding, "You know . . . my hooking up with Luca. I just want to make sure that you and I are cool."

"Oh, totally. What you choose to do is none of my business, so don't feel weird at all. Sorry if I was a bitch. I hadn't had a hangover like that in a while," I say. "So, what's going on between the two of you?"

"Nothing. I haven't heard from him since, but that's Luca for you. One and done, you know?"

I do. I think it's that very notion that has us both stalling. We have feelings for each other, but we're both so unsure about moving forward that we can't take that first step.

"Are you okay?" I ask, not that I actually care.

"Yeah. I knew exactly what I was getting into when I made that choice. No big deal. And it isn't as if I'm waiting around for him." She pauses for a beat. "It was a one and done for me too."

I don't know if this is a fact or her trying to convince herself of it.

"Oh, can you hold on? I have another call."

Before I can respond, she's already clicked over, leaving me alone with tendrils of jealousy I'm trying desperately to squash. I don't want to think about him fucking Olivia—or any girl, for that matter.

After a minute, Olivia comes back on the line. "Are you there?"

"Yeah."

"Sorry, but I have to go."

"Is everything okay?"

"Yeah, Tripp is heading back into the city and needs to get a hotel room for the night, so I have to hurry and get one booked for him."

I tuck her words into my back pocket. "Okay, no worries."

"I'll call you tomorrow," she says. "Let's try to grab lunch this next week!"

"Sounds great."

There's nothing left of this evening, so I turn in early, only to wake the next morning still groggy and slow to start. I drag myself out of bed and get ready for the day. Luca has already left for school by the time I'm put together and emerge from my bedroom.

He was nice enough to leave the coffee on for me, and I grab myself a tumbler so I don't have to drink the coffee at that shitty diner where Carly always wants to meet. It really does taste like an old ashtray.

The morning is gloomy, and I'm anxious for spring. Winter has been unrelenting this year, and I'm ready to welcome back the warm sun. Barren trees, rimmed in layers of ice, line the streets as I make my way to the diner. As usual, I park my car under the dilapidated sign that I doubt even lights up at night. Carly's car is already here. I sit for a moment and remind myself of all the reasons why I have to keep pressing on. There's too much on the line, so I'll do whatever it takes in order to keep her wallet open.

She sticks out like a sore thumb when I enter the diner, wearing a silk blouse and a pair of Chanel earrings, which are tacky as hell with their in-your-face double c's.

"I ordered you a coffee," she says, as if it's some favor to me.

"Thanks."

I sit across from her, and she watches as I slide the cup and saucer to the side. I'm still irritated with how she treated me on the phone last night. I expected her to be pissed, but it still pinched a nerve in me. I don't know this woman very well, but from what I have figured out, she makes very rash decisions and doesn't appear to have a firm grasp of what she's trying to accomplish. That's okay because it makes it possible for me to take advantage of the situation, and that's why I agreed to meet her this morning.

"Look, I'm not sure where to start, but when I told you that this was done and over with, I meant it," she says. "I need you to cut off all contact with my husband."

"It isn't that easy."

She shakes her head, confused. "Why not?"

"Because he's the one who keeps calling. He even called me late last night. I sent it straight to voice mail, but that didn't stop him from showing up at my front door."

Her eyes widen just slightly as her lips part in shock.

"He said he was under a lot of stress and that he's been having a hard time dealing with everything that's on his plate. We talked for a bit on my front porch, but he was insistent that I come with him to the hotel he was staying at."

Her hands are talons, twisting the napkin she has a death grip on. It's how I know I have her.

"My roommate was home, and I worried that he would raise his voice or get upset if I told him that I couldn't go with him, so I went."

"You did what?"

"I went with him," I repeat.

"I can't believe you."

"*Me?* You can't believe *me?* What about your husband? At what point are you going to stop looking at me the way you are right now?

As if I'm the bad guy." The tension becomes too much, and her napkin rips. "In case you forgot, I'm here because of you. Because *you* needed *my* help, so why are you treating me as if I'm the enemy?"

"Because you keep pushing and this needs to stop. Right now." Her words are sharp, stabbing each syllable with fervency. "Stay away from him. Understood?"

Being scolded like a child makes me want to push back and abrades my patience with this woman. Instead of fanning her flame, I comply. "Understood."

Without another word, she slips the strap of her purse onto her shoulder and begins scooting out of the booth.

"Wait."

She stops.

"What about yesterday? The money?"

She leans across the table, getting close to my face, and in a hushed voice, tells me, "I told you the plan was done the last time we met. We were done as soon as you refused to give me the texts and emails. There is no money."

"You're shitting me, right?"

"*Shitting* you? No. I told you not to see him again, so what happened yesterday is on you," she says before slipping out of the booth and standing.

When she tosses a few dollars onto the table, I grab her wrist, and her eyes fly open in shock. "Do you realize the damage I could do to you, both you and your husband?"

Her jaw locks.

"If I don't get paid, I'll release the texts."

She yanks her arm free of my grip as her eyes dart around the empty diner. Carly sees the young, knocked-up waitress watching us, and choses to take her seat again instead of making a bigger scene. "You wouldn't."

I stare her down in hopes of intimidating her, and after a handful of uncomfortable seconds pass, she rebuttals my threat.

"What about your reputation that you've been so fearful of damaging?"

"I'm not talking about the texts between Tripp and me."

It takes her only a breath of time for her to read between the lines and realize that she, not her husband, would be my target.

I smile. "None of the texts I ever sent you incriminate me. You'd never be able to prove that I slept with him, and I seriously doubt Tripp would come to your defense and admit his affair."

"I don't have any more money to give you," she seethes under her breath. "If I pull out more cash, he'll notice. I've already given you all the money from my private accounts."

"That isn't my problem."

"Think about what you're asking of me."

It's laughable that she's still making herself out to be the victim. "And think about what you're asking of *me*. I'm not out here fucking your husband for free."

"I told you not—"

"I get it. But it happened, and if you think I'm simply going to chalk yesterday up to *taking one for the team*, you're wrong."

She takes a hard swallow, her neck flexing as she does.

Yeah, it's a jagged pill I just forced her to swallow.

"Fine," she bites. "I'm going to need a little time to get the money."

"How much time?"

Flustered, she stammers over her words as she slides out of the booth. "Three . . . maybe four days."

"Ten thousand. Same as last time."

"Are you insane?" she whisper-shouts. "I'll pay you five and not a penny more. After that, you leave my husband and me alone. I want you to stay away from us, got it?"

"Whatever you say."

TWENTY-SIX

Emma

My stomach has been tangled between anxiety and elation ever since I left the diner. Never had I felt like such a badass as I did in that moment, taking this situation in my own hands. When she drove away, I released the biggest breath of my life. There was no questioning whether she bought my threats, hell, I even convinced myself that I would go to any length to ensure she pays me. My heart rate is still through the roof as I drive back home.

In a way, my ability to be that conniving alarms me but also excites me, to realize how strong I could be when pushed against a wall. But there's also fear woven between these emotions, the fear that, after she hands over the measly five grand, that will really be it. I've been able to bank sixty-five thousand dollars, which helps, but only a little. It still isn't enough to get myself through my last few semesters of college after I pay for Matthew's expenses and pay down some of my debt. I'm still short . . . by a lot.

I need a new angle to keep her checkbook open.

When I contemplate my options, thoughts begin to flit in and out of my head. Some I dismiss because there's no way to make them work, but one sticks. It also terrifies me because I would have to involve someone else.

Traffic slows as I make it back into the city, but it allows me more time to break apart this idea in order to find its flaws, of which there are few. Yet, it still seems too risky on too many levels, so I put it out of my head for the time being, knowing I'll have to figure something out eventually.

Arriving home, I see Luca's car parked in the driveway. When I step inside, he's sitting in the living room, laughing at whatever the person he's on the phone with is saying. With remnants of adrenaline still lingering, I grab one of Luca's beers from the fridge, pop the cap, and take a long pull. I stroll into the living room and take a seat next to him on the couch, swiping the remote from his hand and changing the channel.

"Dude, your sister just got home and turned off the show."

You're talking to Matthew? I mouth.

He nods while continuing, "No worries, man. It's saved to the DVR, so I'll watch it later and call you back."

I'm surprised to find the two of them talking on the phone, but it settles my adrenaline and puts me right at ease.

Holding my hand out, I whisper, "Let me talk to him."

"Hey, Emma wants to say hi," he says into his cell phone. "Have fun today, and I'll check in with you tomorrow, okay?"

With a grin, Luca hands me the phone, and I smile back.

"Hey, buddy," I greet my brother. "What is it that you're doing today?"

"Bingo at lunch. They are even ordering pizzas!"

The fact that he's this excited about eating delivery pizza bothers me. It also confirms that I need to be doing what I can to get him closer to me so that he can eat delivery pizza whenever he wants. "That sounds like fun," I respond, my chipper tone completely feigned.

"But I have to go so I can get a good seat up front."

"I miss you and love you."

"Okay, bye," he says quickly before hanging up.

"You're drinking early," Luca teases when I hand him back his cell.

"Since when do you and my brother talk on the phone?"

"Since the day we got back from Tennessee," he answers.

It's things like this, things that may seem insignificant to most but are monumental in my eyes, that make me appreciate Luca. It amazes me that he would take it upon himself to forge a friendship with my brother, but it also scares me that he's embedding himself even deeper into my life than he already was.

"Is that okay with you?"

It takes a moment because I'm still a little stunned, but I eventually nod and tell him, "I've been thinking about moving him here to be closer to me."

"You should. It would be good for the both of you."

But it isn't simple when money is an issue. If I allow Carly to be done with me, I'll never be able to get stable enough to afford to move him here, let alone pay for a private facility. And even though I've been trying to find another job, I still don't have one. I'm not convinced that, even if I did, I would make enough to scrape by and be able to pay for school. These thoughts snuff out all the good I was just feeling, turning one emotion into another like the flip of a switch, and suddenly, the overwhelming stress returns.

Dropping my head, I wring my hands as I go back to the thoughts I was having on the drive from the diner. Bricks slam down into the pit of my stomach. It's one thing to have certain thoughts, and it's another to actually voice them to the person who's become a cornerstone in my life. Still, my love for my brother and the drive within me to provide the best possible life for him outweighs the fear I have of losing Luca.

"Is everything okay?"

I look up to my best friend, scared as shit to make this needed confession. I just don't see any other way around this. I never thought I'd be able to scheme the way I have been, but when life offers you no other choice, you do what you have to do. With a slow breath, I hope to God that Luca will see it the same as I do.

He takes my fidgety hand in his, and with worriment etched in the lines of his forehead, he asks once more, "Emma, what's wrong?"

I wonder how long it's going to take him to let go of my hand when he realizes just how manipulative I've become beneath the surface.

"I'm in trouble, Luca." I say in a voice I hardly recognize. Slowly, my eyes lift to meet his.

"What kind of trouble?"

"It's bad . . . and the last thing I want to do is involve you, but . . . but I need help."

He tightens his hand around mine, but it doesn't alleviate the rampant fear coursing through me. I pull back, needing a little space between us, and he watches me intently when I pick up the bottle of beer from the coffee table and take a long drink, nearly draining the entire thing.

"Are you going to tell me what's going on?"

Setting the bottle down, I try to swallow my unease, but it gets hung up in my throat.

"Tell me what's going on, Emma," Luca pushes with a tinge of sternness.

"I've been hiding something from you," I say. "I've gotten myself into a situation, but I'm in over my head, and I need help. I really thought I could handle this on my own."

"Handle what?"

I hesitate, and when he reaches to take my hand again, I pull away. "I don't think you're going to want to touch me after I tell you."

"You need to start talking because you're freaking me out."

It's now or never.

"You know how I've been seeing Mrs. Montgomery since my parents passed away?"

He nods.

"About a month ago, she came to me for help. We met up, and she explained to me how her marriage was in shambles. That her husband has been cheating on her, but because of a prenup, she wouldn't be able to leave him without being left with no money. She also feared that his family would retaliate against her."

"What does this have to do with you?"

"She needed proof that he was cheating, so . . ." My words fall short, and I'm too cowardly to reveal my role in the collusion, but I have to. I have to allow Luca to form whatever opinion about me that he wants in order for me to keep my and Matthew's world from turning to shit. "So, she's been paying me to have an affair with him."

Luca's face falls, and it takes a moment for him to register what I've just said, and he's in utter disbelief when he questions, "You mean William Montgomery? The man running for governor?"

I nod.

"Are you fucking crazy?"

I flinch at his tone and then straighten my shoulders. I knew his reaction would be bad, and I need not to shy away from it. "No, I'm not crazy."

"You've been sleeping with him?"

"You don't understand. It's complicated."

"Then uncomplicate it for me, because if this ever gets out, you'll be ruined, you know that, right?"

"Of course I know the consequences; I'm not an idiot, but I needed the money."

His face pinches in disgust. "That's bullshit."

"Why else would I involve myself in this if I weren't absolutely desperate?"

"I've offered to help you out with money time and again, and you always have some weak-ass excuse as to why you refuse. You won't take money from me, but you'll fuck this woman's husband for money?"

"I've told you that I can't take that type of money from you."

"Yes, you can. Whatever you need, you know I'll help. If I don't have enough, I know my parents wouldn't think twice about helping you, but you have to remove yourself from this situation," he stresses. "That man is on television every week. If this ever leaked, it would be all over the news."

"You think I don't know that? God, Luca, I'm well aware of the destruction this could cause."

With force, he takes my hand, refusing to let me pull away again. "I'm fucking serious. You have to cut all ties with these people. They are powerful, Emma. There's no way you would ever have a fighting chance against them, and they will make certain that you, and only you, are the one who takes the ultimate fall."

"You aren't telling me anything that I don't already know," I say around the emotions that are beginning to surface. "It's the constant fear of this getting out, of me being exposed and ripped to shreds by not only the media but also the most influential political powerhouses in the country that keeps me up at night. My god, Tripp is only two years out from announcing his run for the President of the United States, and everyone knows it. I'm pretty much a dead man walking, which is why I need your help."

Luca doesn't initially respond. He's lost in his thoughts, ones I'm not sure I want to be privy to. His eyes bore into mine, and all I can do is pray that he isn't seeing me as the very thing painted before him—a whore. And then, out of nowhere, he grits, "That bitch has completely taken advantage of you."

She didn't. If anything, it is the other way around, but . . . yeah, I'm not going to tell him that. Not with the way he's already looking at me.

"I met with her today. She doesn't want me anywhere near her or her husband, which means no more money."

"Fuck the money. I'll go to my parents."

"No."

"Why are you so prideful?"

"I don't think you understand the amount of debt I'm in," I tell him before explaining, "I didn't have the money to pay for Matthew's living expenses, so I took out a few credit cards, but they're all maxed out at this point, and I now have collectors calling me constantly. I have no way to continue paying for him, but it's an expense that's my responsibility for the rest of my life. There's no way I can afford taking care of myself and him as well unless I can graduate and get a real job, and even then, I'll still be scraping by, but at least he'll be taken care of. In order to do that, I need to finish my degree, which will cost over a hundred grand, not including all my books." I tell him and wait for him to finally understand the seriousness of my situation. "If it were a few thousand dollars that I needed, sure, go to your parents, but it isn't. It's more like one hundred thousand, and I could never take that amount of money from them because I would never be able to pay it back, and I can't have that weighing on my conscience."

He releases a heavy sigh, breathing a winded, "Fuck," as he does.

"I never would've gotten myself wrapped up with the Montgomery's if I weren't desperate, but I am. It was the only way I could see a way out for myself."

"But it's over, right? She's done with you?"

"That's what she says, but the thing is, I can't let her be done with me." I go on to explain how Carly doesn't have any hard evidence on Tripp because of my refusal to provide it, but that we could get evidence on her that will keep her wallet open for my benefit.

"You mean you want to blackmail her?"

"Exactly. They're loaded," I say. "The amount I need is barely even a fraction of what they have. I mean, you should see the house they live in."

"You've been there?"

"I've only driven by out of curiosity," I admit.

"This is crazy, you know that, right?"

"You don't understand," I tell him. "She makes rash decisions without thinking them through. What's to stop her from becoming so desperate that she turns her back on me and outs my affair? Because she easily could."

"So, tell me," he says, pushing a stressed hand through his thick hair. "What are you going to do?"

Shrugging, I admit, "I don't know, but I have to do something."

Luca's eyes drift from mine as I begin biting anxiously on the inside of my cheek. When his hand lets go of mine and he stands, I doubt my decision to tell him all of this. My eyes follow as he walks into the kitchen, opens the fridge, and grabs a bottle of beer. Popping the cap, he chugs it quickly before grabbing another two bottles. When he returns, he hands me one and takes his seat next to me.

Nerves wreak havoc on me as I wait for him to say something. He takes another draw from his beer before setting it down. "I'll sleep with her."

My jaw drops. "What?"

"I'll get her to sleep with me," he repeats. "And you'll get photos to blackmail her with."

Staring into his eyes that reflect his hesitation, I tell him, "I can't ask you to do that. I can't allow you to get involved and risk—"

"You aren't asking. I'm offering."

A multitude of hesitations crash overhead, and I cannot believe what he's offering to do. "Do you have any clue how insane this is?"

He takes another sip and then sets the bottle down. "Yeah, I do. Allowing her to continue to hold all the power is insane."

He shifts away from me and leans forward, bracing his elbows on his knees as his head hangs. He stews in his thoughts for longer than I'm comfortable with, but I'm too shocked to say anything. It wasn't that long ago that Luca confessed his feelings for me, and now here he is, offering to have sex with another woman so I can blackmail her. It's beyond screwed up, but so am I.

My whole life is a disaster, and it isn't an easy thing for me to look in the mirror and see the person I've become—a liar and a schemer and a fraud. If only my parents were alive, I would never have found myself in this predicament and everything that has led me to this point never would have happened.

When he finally lifts his head, he turns to look at me with pain-filled eyes. "I don't want to lose you."

Shaking my head, I reach out and take his hand, promising, "You won't." Because what he is offering is more than I ever would've expected from him. In a way, it's evidence of his feelings for me, and in this moment, I feel so incredibly undeserving.

"My love for you has always scared me, but now . . . now it terrifies me because I realize there isn't anything I wouldn't do for you."

After taking a shallow inhale, I hold my breath, and when I exhale, a slight whimper slips out from my heart. Exalted in gratefulness, I wrap my arms around his neck and hug him. I'm a barrage of emotions. I hate myself for dragging him into this. Hate myself for all the turmoil I'm causing when I know how sincere he is when he says he really wants to try to have a relationship with me. Hate myself for not being entirely honest with him, but there is no person in this world that I would ever tell the whole truth to. There's too much at risk.

TWENTY-SEVEN

Early

Sitting at my desk in my private practice office, I open my newest client's file to review before he shows up for his appointment. It was nearly two weeks ago when he called to inquire about receiving services. After our first appointment, he asked if he could see me for another session in a few days, admitting that he didn't think he could wait a solid week to come back.

Those first two sessions were intense—*he* was intense, but last week, he seemed calmer, which isn't abnormal. Typically, people new to therapy can be tightly wound at first, but that generally wanes over time and they become more comfortable talking about their feelings.

Luca Sadler, twenty-three years old, exhibiting signs of depression.

His case is one I can relate to. He had been considering proposing to his long-time girlfriend, only to be blindsided when he discovered she had been cheating on him for the past year.

The break up has been difficult, affecting not only his mood but also his grades. During our last session, he opened up about how isolated he's felt recently, and it took everything I had to keep my composure. The heat of tears burned the backs of my eyes when his words hit too close to home, practically mirroring my own despair. As hard as our sessions are, they're helping me in a convoluted way. It's as if his words could be my own, and as I help him navigate his way through the emotions, I feed off my own advice. In a weird way, my treating him feels as if I'm treating myself.

I've kept so much inside for so long that I hadn't even realized it has been stifling me. When he left after our last appointment, I sat at my desk and cried. Somehow, through our shared trauma, he exposes my wounds when he exposes his own. For that reason, selfishly, I've been looking forward to our appointments.

There's a loud knock, but when I step out of my office, it isn't Luca who stands outside. It's a deliveryman holding a big vase of red and white roses.

Unlocking the door, the gentleman says, "I'm looking for Carly Montgomery."

"That's me."

He hands me a clipboard, and I sign next to my printed name before he hands over the crystal vase.

"Have a good afternoon, ma'am."

"Thank you."

Carrying the flowers back to my office, I take a seat and open the card.

Life has been crazy, I know, but you're still the one I choose to share it with. You'll always be the one I choose.

—Love Always, Tripp

I read the card again. It should soothe, but instead, it scathes, scraping all the tender wounds he's inflicted upon me. Before I know what I'm doing, I've crumpled the card and tossed it onto my desk next to the roses.

He's become a master at trying to manipulate me into believing he isn't the man he clearly is. He flushed his vows and promises of fidelity down the toilet and has the audacity to think a bouquet of flowers will wipe his slate clean. I may have decided to stay in this marriage, but I don't need him belittling my integrity with his worthless tokens of fake affection.

Getting up from my desk to refill my coffee in the small kitchenette, I glance outside toward the parking lot to see Luca's black sports car pulling in.

"Good to see you," I greet when I meet him at the door, locking it behind him since it's drawing into the evening and I have no receptionist.

He responds with a passing, "Hey," as he makes his way down to my office, taking his usual seat on the couch. Closing his file, I grab my notepad and situate myself in the chair that's directly across from him.

"So, how have you been?" I ask as he removes his coat and tosses it over the arm of the sofa.

"I ran into her this morning."

My brows lift in surprise. "What was that like for you?"

"Fucked up."

"How so?"

He leans forward, clasping his hands together. "Because I used to be able to look into her eyes and see everything. Now, all I see is a stranger. I didn't even know what to say to her. It was as if I don't know her at all."

I continue to ask questions about their interaction earlier today. We then shift into discussing how he's been handling school, and I suggest a few coping skills he should try, which I can tell he isn't on board with—*stubborn*. But as a circle story would go, we wind up at the beginning again, further discussing his ex.

"Have you ever been cheated on?" he asks, catching me off guard.

This happens all the time. Clients will often ask me personal questions. It's only natural for them to want me to open up to them because they spend so much time opening themselves up to me. This particular question coming from this particular kid strikes a chord deep within me. I should keep the focus on him, guide the conversation better, but I stall. He stares at me, wanting some sort of confirmation that he isn't alone in this.

It almost feels unfair to deprive him of the same thing I'm greedily taking from him. I second-guess and then triple-guess myself before giving him a subtle nod.

"You know what's weird?"

"Hmm?"

"When I saw her this morning, as much as I fucking hate her, I still wanted her. For a moment, I questioned if I would be able to turn a blind eye to her shit just so we could be together again. That's pretty fucked up, huh?"

I know exactly how he feels because it's what I feel with Tripp. No matter how angry I am at him, I still want him. I can't seem to detach myself from the love that's still inside me.

"Did you ever feel that way?"

Setting the notepad aside, I cross my legs and lean my elbow against the armrest. "Sometimes, the hardest part of healing is learning how to unlove the person who hurt you."

"How long did it take you?"

"It took a while," I admit, regretting my words the moment I speak them. I shouldn't have told him that, but at the same time, I want to tell him so that he knows this isn't something that can be fixed overnight. It also feels good to finally talk about this. Even though it's only a version of the truth, it's cathartic to say some of these things aloud.

"How long ago did this happen?"

"When I was in college," I lie.

He nods in a slow understanding. "Were you guys together for very long?"

While I'm telling him another lie that sways him to believe that this is far back in my past, he reaches inside his coat and pulls out a vape pen.

"You mind?"

"No, it's fine." He did this during our last session too. When our conversation became deeper, he took a couple hits off his pen to help him relax.

"Did you ever go back to him?"

"In moments of weakness, I did. It was far from a clean break."

He then holds the pen out, offering it to me as he did during our last two sessions. I stare at the pen in his hand, knowing how unethical this is becoming, but in a world where I've committed so many wrongs, what's just one more? I take the pen, push the button, and take a long pull. Inhaling the vapor deep into my lungs, I hold it, allowing the chemicals to breathe tranquility into me. When I let go and blow out the remaining fumes, my head already feels lighter.

When I hand the pen back, he smiles and then takes another hit.

"My husband would kill me if he ever found out."

"Then it's our secret," he says with a loose grin, setting the pen next to the tissue box on the small table next to him. "I have to run to the bathroom. Be right back."

The moment he shuts the door behind him, I grab the pen and take a second hit. Last time I smoked weed was when I was in college—back when it was still illegal. It's been a while, but, man, this makes me feel so good—light and free. Sinking back into my chair, I close my eyes and find myself swimming in negative space. There's no fear in the dark water as I kick easily, propelling myself deeper into the abyss.

"You're blasted."

Opening my eyes, I right myself in my chair as Luca resumes his spot on the couch.

"Maybe just a little bit."

"No maybe about it. You're gone."

"Like it's such a bad thing to be gone," I say, and I can't tell if the words are actually coming out as slowly as they seem to be or if it's just in my head.

"What do you want to be gone from?"

With all walls down and no more inhibitions, I latch on to his question as if the more I think about it, the more sober I'll become. But he's right, I'm entirely stoned and that thought alone makes me laugh. "This is so not me."

"What? You getting blasted?"

"You do realize I could probably lose my license for this. At least, I think. I mean . . . I don't really know, but it seems plausible," I ramble, wondering if I'm making any sense.

He then picks up the pen with a huge smile on his face and holds it back out for me to take. "What's one more hit then?"

I reach out, but he pulls it back, teasing me, and when I lift my bottom up off the seat to get closer, he pulls it back again. His playfulness causes me to laugh and stumble over my feet. He's quick to move, grabbing my arms and guiding my fall so I land next to him on the couch. Giggles erupt out of me, and I'm not just stoned—I'm stupid stoned.

When I look over at Luca, he wears a straight face, and it silences my laughter as I meet his mood. "Why so serious?"

"Because I'm waiting for you to answer me."

One of his hands is still on my arm as he slides it down to my wrist. The touch should feel awkward, but, truth is, it doesn't. "What was the question?"

"What do you want to be gone from?"

I lose myself in his gentle voice, and give him the honesty that only sobriety has the power to keep secret. "Everything—life . . . the campaign . . ."

"You seem sad, and I'm not just talking about now. Every time I come here to talk to you, I feel like I make you sad."

I look into his eyes and wonder if I'm really that transparent or if he's just that intuitive. No longer able to poise myself, I freely admit, "Life is hard right now, and I doubt anyone would understand. It's just . . . I feel really alone."

"Do I make you feel alone?" he questions, closing a bit of the space we have between us.

It's hard to tell if he's the cause of the heavy beating in my chest or if it's the pot. Either way, its thumps make my senses hyperaware. His hand on my wrist, which is keeping me close to him; his cologne I'm breathing, which is a stark contrast to Tripp's; the fluttering in my stomach, which is reminiscent of the butterflies I thought died long ago.

Maybe they were, and it's Luca who just brought them back to life.

With one hand still on my wrist, his other touches my cheek and slides back into my hair. If I weren't so high, I'd push him away, stand,

and tell him he should go. But I am high, so when he pulls me toward him and kisses me, I don't resist. My eyes fall shut as he moves his lips with mine. My head dip dives as if I'm on a roller coaster. I'm spinning within my inebriation, floating freely all the way up to cloud nine where there are no doubts or regrets, only euphoria.

I'm so far from reality, doped up and beyond aroused that a single touch feels like a million, overwhelming me. So many sensations engross me that I don't even realize my frenzy until I open my eyes to find I've already tossed his shirt across the room.

His mouth is all over me, dissolving the already blurred lines. We move at a rapid pace, frantic for any kind of comfort we can get in our shared heartbreak. My hands fumble with his belt, and as one second slips into another, I shove his pants down and let him finish tugging them off his legs.

It's hard to tell if Luca is my painkiller or the dope I smoked, either way, I don't care.

It's a maniacal time warp, and before I know it, we're naked and he's nestled between my open legs, slipping a condom on. My soul screams when I grab his hips, urging him to move faster, and he does, thrusting himself inside me. The pleasure is heightened to the nth degree. I'm a myriad of sensations as we move eagerly with each other, and I swear I've never felt more alive as I do now.

Through the fog of lust and gratification, I hear the door slamming against the wall. Flashes blind me, and I pinch my eyes shut, but Luca keeps moving. Hysteria combusts inside me, and I don't know what's happening.

"Kiss me," he demands, and within the chaos, I do, all the while losing my grip on reality.

What the hell is happening?

Suddenly, there's no more weight on top of me—no more heat, no more pleasure.

Opening my eyes, my vision distorts, and it takes a few seconds to form any semblance of clarity. When I somehow manage to clear the haze, I'm met with a nightmare.

Another flash blinds me momentarily, and as soon as I realize what's going on, I go stone-cold sober.

Emma stands before me, dropping her cell phone to her side while Luca is busy tugging on his T-shirt. Frantically, I grab for my clothes and cover my body as best I can. It's madness all around me, but within me, everything paralyzes as I look on in horror.

Luca grabs his coat and then tugs on Emma's elbow. "Come on. Let's get out of here," he says, practically out of breath, but my eyes never leave Emma's.

Her face is stone, not a single readable expression can be found. It isn't until Luca takes her hand that she looks away and follows behind him.

Panic-stricken, I sit here, naked and freaking the hell out. My whole body trembles in terror and confusion, but it doesn't take a genius to figure out that I was just set up.

When my fight or flight instincts finally kick in, I jump off the couch, grab my coat, and wrap it around me. I run to the front of the office and look to the parking lot, finding Luca's car gone already. I'm too late to stop them, and nausea rolls through my stomach as I yank the blinds closed. All the heat that was just coursing through my veins a minute ago has now been replaced with ice cold fear.

My legs manage to hold me as I move back to my office and then collect my clothes, which are strewn about, and I curse myself.

What the fuck is wrong with you, Carly?

How could you have let that happen?

As I frantically put my pants back on, I pray that this is some sort of messed-up stoner hallucination and I didn't just sleep with one of my clients and that Emma didn't just sneak in here and take photos of me having sex with someone other than my husband.

Holy crap, it's only a matter of time before those photos are leaked.

Shit! Shit! Shit!

Tears spring from my eyes as my panic detonates into pure hysteria.

What do I do? How do I stop this from happening, and why did I have to be so stern with her?

My fingers tremble out of my control, and when I'm finally able to clasp my bra, I scour the small office, looking for my silk cami.

"Where the hell is it?" I mumble as I rip the cushions off the couch, but it's not there.

Dropping to my knees, I fish my hands under the couch, under the chair, under *everything* as I begin crying harder.

Another blaze of panic fires off inside me, and I begin ransacking my office, searching for my cami but finding nothing. Quickly, I shrug on my sweater before grabbing for my phone. In the process, I knock over the flowers, sending the vase crashing to the floor. Thorned roses lie in a puddle of water and broken glass, but all I can do is turn back to my desk, get my cell, and fumble to dial the number of the only person who can help me.

As the phone rings, I chew like crazy on my nails and let the tears fall freely. I'm about to have a full-blown panic attack.

"Hello?"

"Margot, I need your help!"

TWENTY-EIGHT

Carly

"What the hell happened here?" Margot questions when she walks into my office.

I've spent the past half hour sobbing and freaking out while waiting for her to get here. She's a true friend, dropping everything and coming here the moment I called her.

A new slew of tears flood my eyes, and when she turns around, I blink, allowing them to fall.

"I'm in really big trouble," I tell her, my voice trembling in fear. "That girl I told you about, you know, the one I got to sleep with Tripp?"

"Yes . . ."

"She set me up."

Slowly, I walk across the room and take a seat in one of the chairs, dropping my head into my palms.

"What do you mean *she set you up?*"

"I don't even know how to explain this because it's such a mess."

Since the couch cushions are still tossed onto the floor, she pulls out my desk chair and rolls it next to me before taking a seat.

Looking up at my friend through bleary eyes, I cut straight to the point. "I slept with one of my clients, and she must've been behind it all because she busted in and took pictures."

"She what?"

"She walked right in," I say, motioning toward the door, "and started taking a bunch of pictures."

197

"Of you having sex with your client?"

"Yes."

"Here?" she questions in disbelief. "You mean this just happened?"

"Yes! And now I'm freaking out and don't know what to do."

"Why the hell would she do that?"

"Because she's pissed off at me. I told her to stay away from Tripp, but then she kept seeing him and was demanding that I continue to pay her. I told her no, and now she has photos and I have no clue what to do."

Margot lays her hand over my knee. "Carly, you have to calm down. You panicking isn't going to help. Take a deep breath so you can think clearly."

"I'm ruined. If she takes those photos to the press, I'm ruined; Tripp too."

"Did she say anything?"

"No! She just stood there, staring at me. Then she just walked out and left."

"Why didn't you go after her? Get her phone?"

Sulking back in the chair, I admit with a defeated sigh, "Everything happened so fast and I wasn't thinking right because I got high during the appointment."

Her eyes grow wide. "What the hell are you thinking? Are you trying to fuck your life up?"

"No."

"Why are you getting high with clients?"

"I don't know," I practically wail. "Because my life is in shambles."

"Well, you're only making it worse," she scolds. "You have *got* to pull yourself together or you're going to be the front-page headline."

"I need your help. I don't know what to do."

"First off, who is this client?"

"Just a guy I started seeing a couple of weeks ago, but now I'm wondering if it was all a ploy."

Margot eyes me like I'm an idiot. "What do you mean *you're wondering*? Wake up! Of course, it was a ploy. They set you up, and you fell right into their trap. How could you have been so foolish?"

"This is going to destroy everything," I mutter. "It'll all be over."

"Not if you move fast. Clearly, this girl is out to get you, so you're going to have to reason with her, negotiate some sort of deal to get the photos and to shut her up."

"I've already given her so much money. If I pull out more, Tripp is going to notice."

"That's what you're worried about? My god, Carly, you're seriously going to run the risk of having photos of you sleeping with another man, while high, might I add, to avoid Tripp questioning you about a bank withdrawal?"

I stare at her, dumbfounded.

"Lie, for heaven's sake! Christ, tell him you used the money to make a charitable donation," she exclaims in annoyance. "But the first thing you need to do is get yourself under control and smarten up because I can't be tangled up in this. There's too much on the line for me. You can't continue involving me in all the mishaps you keep making for yourself."

I run my hands under my eyes and dry my tears, surprised that she would say such a thing when she's always been there for me—when she was the one nudging me into this ordeal. The anger is real, but it's misplaced, and even though I'm still stoned, I'm sober enough to realize it. She's right, I shouldn't be dragging her into this when she and her husband are in the public eye as well.

Turning in my chair, I see Margot leaning over my desk. "What are you doing?"

"Is this the client?" she questions as she flips through the file. "Luca Sadler?"

I nod. "Yes, why?"

"Just wondering if there's anything you could use against him," she murmurs as she keeps her eyes on the file. "He's obviously close to the girl . . . what's her name again?"

Trying to keep myself composed, I wipe away another tear, responding, "Emma Ashford."

"It says he attends Georgetown. She does as well?"

"She did, but she lost her scholarship. Why?"

She shrugs off my question, closes the file, and leans her hip against the desk. "Maybe you should just go home and get some sleep. You're a disaster. Tomorrow morning when your head is clear, you need to call her. I don't think anything should happen tonight."

"How can you be sure?"

"Because I'm good at reading people, which is something you should take more of an interest in instead of always acting so hastily." She rounds the desk and picks up one of the cushions from the floor and tosses it back on the couch. "You said you've been seeing him for a couple weeks, correct?"

"Yes."

"So, clearly, the two of them aren't as rash as you. They thought this out. If I had to bet money on it, I would say that they will move cautiously and strike when it will hurt the most."

Her words only feed my worry.

"I mean, think about it. This girl, Emma, is caught up in this too. Whatever it is they're planning to do with the photos, they will likely do everything in their power to keep her name out of it. Surely, she isn't stupid enough to risk exposing herself as Tripp's mistress."

"No, you're right. She told me that she's terrified of this getting out to the media."

"Well, there you go," she says, tossing another cushion onto the couch. "They're going to be meticulous, which works in your favor because that buys you time to figure out how to shut her down."

She continues to move about the room, straightening things here and there before picking up the card that was with the flowers. She reads it, and after a long pause, looks up at me. "What's this all about?"

"Nothing. Just my cheating husband doing his best to pull the wool over my eyes, as if he isn't sleeping around."

Her brows lift, and with a shrug, she flicks the card, sending it back to the floor.

"Your life is a monstrosity." She crushes a rose under her stiletto before resuming her spot in the chair next to mine. With a gentler tone, she adds, "Look, you're a dear friend, you know that, right?"

I nod.

"And I've always been here for you in any way you've needed me, but, like I said, I can no longer be involved in this. I'm so sorry, but it's just too risky. I hope you understand."

"Of course, I understand. I never should have asked you to put yourself on the line for me."

"I also think it would best if we stayed in our own corners for a while, at least until this passes."

She's right in wanting to distance herself from this catastrophe because, if I go down in flames for this, I certainly don't want to bring her or her husband down with me

"I'm sorry," she adds when I don't immediately respond.

"Everything has gotten so out of hand."

"Are you going to tell Tripp?"

"God, no," I blurt. "I'd actually decided to try to make it work between us, but then this happened . . ." My words fall short because I have no clue where to go from here.

Here I was, set out to prove his infidelities so I could leave him with a little self-worth and money in my pocket. But that blew up in my face and left me with nothing. If he ever finds out about anything I've been up to recently, he'll leave, no questions asked, and I'll be left with nothing.

There is only one way for me to come out of this nightmare with a shred of my dignity intact, and that is to go home and be a perfect wife and pray he never finds out.

That will only happen if I can find a way to keep Emma quiet.

TWENTY-NINE

Carly

Those pictures were taken for a reason. It's been three days of hell. I'm terrified to turn on the television, open a newspaper, or even listen to the radio. There isn't a single hour, minute, second that passes without tremendous fear that my world will come crashing down. It's the constant state of paranoia that has my stomach in knots.

I can barely eat.

I can barely breathe.

But I can't give up.

I just can't.

"Are you almost ready?"

I look in the mirror to see Tripp standing in the doorway of the bathroom as I fasten the back to my pearl earring. With a loving smile, I respond, "I'm ready," before turning around to show him my new ivory-colored shift dress. "How do I look?"

"Perfect."

Stepping in front of him, I adjust his tie and brush my hands along the shoulders of his navy suit coat. "How are you feeling?"

"Good."

"Nervous?"

"Come on now," he says with a smirk. "I'm an old pro at this. I don't get nervous."

Tripp looks into my eyes, and as much as it should calm me, there's nothing in this world that can pacify my anxiety at this point.

"I'm glad we're back on the same page. I missed having you by my side at these events."

These past few weeks, I haven't been actively involved in his campaign, and after a few big fights about it, he gave up on acknowledging my distance. But after the incident with Luca, I talked to Tripp and smoothed things over as best as I could. I admitted my insecurities, lied and told him that I trusted him. I apologized repeatedly and vowed to be better, do better, and love him better. I cried horrified tears, which he interpreted as tears of guilt for putting so much strain on our marriage. I tucked my tail between my legs and became the doormat I swore to Margot I would never be. I recognize the predicament I'm in, and I understand the woman I have to become to keep my world intact.

We made love that night, but it didn't feel right. I'm a total fraud, just as dirty as he is. Acknowledging that I've become the very thing I despise—both in life and in my marriage—was a hard pill to swallow, but swallow it I did.

Tripp once told me there wasn't anything I could do that would make him walk away from me. Of course, we were young and newly married, so I doubt he ever would have considered the web of deceit I would eventually weave around us. Still, I cling to those words like a drowning woman.

The doorbell rings, interrupting our moment.

"My parents are here," he notes, and I'm forced to bite my cheek.

They thought it would be best for us to arrive at the same time to reinforce our so-called family-first ideals. I trail behind Tripp, not unaware of the irony. My having to stand behind him and view the world from over his shoulder was something I used to find demeaning. Now, I take the spot like an obedient dog.

When he opens the front door, Eloise stands there all polished and poised, and starts right in on doting over her son and fussing over his tie that I just straightened.

"Don't you look lovely, dear," his father says before pecking my cheek.

"Thank you. It's good to see you."

"Yes, lovely." Eloise echoes her husband's sentiments as she eyes my whole look, silently picking me apart.

"Eloise, it's so nice to see you." I smile and lean forward to air kiss her cheek.

"It's good to see you supporting the campaign for a change."

My smile remains plastic as I say, "It is, isn't it. I'm thrilled that my schedule has opened up to allow me the time to be here for Tripp."

"I'm sure," she snides and then turns her attention to her son. "Well, are we ready?"

We head out to the large SUV and the driver opens the door for us. As we make our way to the event, I stay on the outside looking in as the three of them discuss the itinerary. Tripp is speaking to the students of Georgetown, giving them an inside look at what they can expect after graduation and they enter the political world. The message he will be delivering will be phony, and, later on down the road, if any of the students look back on it, they will know they had been lied to.

Every now and then, Eloise will call my attention with a condescending, "Are you listening? This is important information for you as well, dear."

To this, I smile and nod. *Yes, of course, Eloise. I hear every ounce of BS, and I assure you that I won't be an embarrassment in front of the cameras.*

When we pull up to Gaston Hall, I scan the crowd of students who are already filing in, looking for any sign of Emma or Luca. Even though she is no longer a student, this event is open to the public.

When we step out of the SUV, we are welcomed by a number of people, one being the university's president. We shake hands and exchange pleasantries before we're led inside and to the full auditorium.

"Mr. Montgomery," Olivia says formally, as if she hasn't been sleeping with my husband. "Here are the updated talking points. There were only a few minor changes that I need to point out."

Tripp turns to me. "I have to go over these notes with Olivia. Are you okay with my parents?"

"Of course," I tell him even though I don't want him anywhere near that girl. "You go. I'll be fine."

I watch as the two of them walk away, cringing when he places his hand on her lower back.

With a pleasant smile, I stand next to Eloise and make small talk with the people who come to say hello. Far too often, I catch Eloise watching me from the corner of her eye, always keeping watch to make sure I don't flounder. As if I'm a toddler she must constantly remind to be on their best behavior.

When Tripp returns, he stands at a respectable distance from me, and I smile over at him. "Is everything okay?"

He takes my hand and gives me a nod. "You ready?"

His parents are led in first and seated in the audience before Tripp is formally announced. Hand in hand, we walk onto the stage. Tripp waves to the crowd of excited students, and I stand at his side, smiling gracefully, offering a few waves of appreciation. After dropping a kiss to my cheek, Tripp takes his position at the podium and I take a seat with the university president and a few board members.

"Thank you," Tripp says into the microphone. "Thank you for having me here today. There's nothing I enjoy more than meeting young men and women, the next generation of global citizens to lead and make a difference in this world."

He delves into his speech as my eyes dart nervously around the audience, but with all the bright lights, I'm only able to see the first few rows. Everything else is a blinding blur. Olivia stands just off stage and out of sight, intently watching my husband. I wish I could talk to Margot and ask her how she does it. Turning a blind eye to the women who've found themselves in bed with my husband is killing me. I want to ask her if it becomes easier over time, but she made it clear that we shouldn't have any contact, and I have to respect her wishes.

But Olivia is the least of my problems.

Sweat trickles down my back, and I don't know if it's because of these hot spotlights or my anxiety, but I'm ready to get out of here, and Tripp has only just begun speaking.

When the informational talk wraps up, Tripp takes the microphone and steps out from the podium to take questions from the audience. Student after student asks questions, but the moment I hear, "Hi, my name is Luca, and I'm a junior culture and politics major." I lock up, petrified. "My question for you is a little personal, but I'm interested to hear how you are able to balance work and family. With a hectic campaign schedule, it must be difficult."

Oh, my god.

Squinting, I try my best to find Luca without it being obvious, but the lights are too bright.

"That's a great question, and one that isn't asked often enough," Tripp responds. "Maintaining the balance between work and family is a top priority. I'm eager to serve my country, and luckily, God has blessed me with a wife who shares that same desire. I think the best piece of advice I can give you is for you to find a partner who shares your beliefs and ambitions. My wife," he says, turning and motioning in my direction, "is a great example of what a partner should be. Supportive, patient, encouraging, and loyal are only a few of her many wonderful attributes. This isn't an easy job, but with her by my side, it doesn't seem so insurmountable."

The crowd applauds his complete fabrication of the truth, and stupid me, I clap right along with them. If only his words actually meant something.

He takes a few more questions before thanking the crowd and reminding them of the reception being held afterward.

Tripp walks over to me, takes my hand, and when I stand, we kiss. As always, it's tight-lipped and meant for the audience rather than me. I congratulate him, and we both wave to the crowd as we step down from the stage and to where Olivia is waiting for us.

As she leads us over to the reception, she briefs Tripp on something I couldn't care less about because I'm too distracted as I scan the room for Luca.

When we arrive at the reception, Tripp and I take our places to greet the students, some of whom I already know. I'm a nervous wreck, hoping to God that Luca went home and isn't here, but all hope is lost when I spot him in the far corner of the room with Emma by his side.

Ice drips down the nerves of my spinal cord and a freeze. Voices around me dull into a muted echo, and I become lightheaded. Emma and Luca talk, but the moment she looks in my direction, I sway, shuffling back a few steps.

"What is wrong with you?" Eloise scolds harshly behind her tight lips. "Pull yourself together."

I can't. Emma locks eyes with me, and I panic.

Is this the moment? Is she going to say something *here*?

Suddenly, the urgency to run consumes me, but there's no escaping.

My heart thumps so low and so heavy that it can be felt in the pit of my stomach, and I can't stop fidgeting.

"Is everything okay?" Tripp whispers, his voice chilling me even more.

No. Everything is not okay. I'm about to go down in flames, and so is this whole campaign.

With a forced smile, I lie, "I skipped breakfast. I think my blood sugar may be a little low."

"Olivia," Tripp calls. "Would you mind getting Carly a small plate of food?"

"Of course," she replies, not even looking up from whatever she's typing on her phone before she turns on her heel and disappears into the crowd.

When I look back to Emma, Luca is whispering something in her ear. She glances my way, says something back to him, and then leaves the reception as he starts making his way over to where I'm standing.

A multitude of thoughts collide in my head. I should've called Emma to get those pictures, but I've been in such a panic these past few days I haven't been able to think clearly. Plus, I've been in complete damage-control mode with Tripp, trying to get back into his good graces.

Eloise takes ahold of my cold, clammy hand. "For Christ's sake, what is the matter with you?"

I don't pay her any attention, though. I'm too busy having a silent fit of terror.

"Mr. Montgomery, it's nice to meet you," Luca says, his tone light and unburdened as he extends a hand to my husband.

My lungs constrict, and like a noose around my neck, I'm finding it hard to take in a decent breath.

I can't move.

I can't speak.

As I look on in horror, my gut twists so tightly, I have to bite back the piercing pain. Luca's eyes meet mine, and I have to grab on to Tripp's hand to keep my knees from giving way. Before he can say anything, Olivia approaches with a plate of food and does a double take at Luca.

"I didn't know you were going to be here," she says. The two of them clearly know each other.

She hands me the plate, and I whisper a jittery, "Thank you," because I can't find my voice.

Luca gives her a curt nod before excusing himself, and I have to rush off to the restroom before I collapse in front of everyone. Eloise huffs as I push by her and make a beeline to the bathroom. I lock myself in a stall and sit on the edge of the toilet, lowering my head down to my knees.

Luca knows Olivia.

Olivia knows Luca.

Holy shit!

The realization that this is even worse than I expected barrels down on me. If Olivia knows Luca, then she must know Emma too.

What the hell is going on?

A sheen of cold sweat coats my forehead and neck, and my hands shake beyond my control. I have no clue what I'm going to do, but this is bigger than anything I'm able to combat.

I'm screwed.

Plain and simple—I'm completely screwed!

THIRTY

Emma

It's strange, the shift that's taken place these past few days. I'm not even sure how I feel about everything, but it's clear that my gaining the upper hand was right move.

Establishing Luca as a client seeking help for the very issues that plague her was easy enough to come up with. I told Luca all the things Carly had revealed to me about her upbringing, her marriage, and how her marriage unraveled so that he could be someone she could relate to. We felt that was the best route to take to bring her insecurities and emotions to the surface so that he could more easily take advantage of her. Throwing in the offer of smoking pot with him was his idea. I didn't think it would work, but eventually she took the bait.

When he left to use the restroom, he was really unlocking the door for me. I waited outside her office until I could hear them. Honestly, as I waited, I had no feelings flowing through me, not even nerves. To have so many emotions and not be able to sense a single one was a little disturbing. It was as if I was so shocked that I could be *that* callus that my brain refused to acknowledge it.

It wasn't until the following morning, that I felt it—the jealousy of Luca having sex with her, the fear of taking this game to a very dangerous level, and the unease that came with my not entirely recognizing myself.

What's done is done, so there is only one way left to go: forward.

I've been sitting on the photos because Luca thought it would be best for us to lie low for a bit, allow her panic to breed with paranoia and hammer in the fact that I now have the upper hand.

Luca insisted that I go with him to the university today to hear Tripp speak. I didn't want to, but after what we had done, we both thought it would be the perfect opportunity to twist the knife in a little deeper. Again, I felt numb listening to Tripp speak, hearing his voice, and seeing Carly so pulled together at his side. Anyone on the outside wouldn't suspect that her marriage was dangling by a withered thread. She's a good actress, but that's all it is—an act.

After, he wanted me to stay and go up to Tripp and Carly so we could freak the both of them out. I couldn't do it and ended up feigning a headache before leaving. The walk home gave me an opportunity to think, and by the time I climbed into bed, I'd come to the decision that it was time to press Carly for the money she said she would get me.

Hours later, the front door opens, and I sit up in bed, watching as Luca comes straight into my room.

"What happened?" I ask when he sits next to me, propping one of my pillows behind his back.

"She freaked out when I spoke to her husband; her face went pale. But it gets better."

"What do you mean?"

"Olivia was there. Carly flipped when she saw that the two of us knew each other. She literally ran off, so I think it's safe to say that she's losing her shit."

I nod, feeling a swell of despondency come over me, and he picks up on it.

"Are you okay? I thought that would make you happy."

"I thought it would too."

"This is what you wanted, right?"

"Yeah."

His eyes scan my face as I sit here, expressionless. "Hey," he says gently, giving my arm a light tug so that I scoot to face him. "What's going on?"

My first instinct is to push him away, but then I feel the tug, the same tug that's been pulling me closer to him these past few weeks.

"Will you talk to me?"

"It just feels weird."

"What does?"

"Me," I confess. "*I feel weird . . . as if I've lost myself*." My eyes fall from him and when they return, I step out of my comfort zone and open up a little more. "I feel really lost right now. I know that I'm not, that I have you, but it's still how I feel."

"I hate that you're feeling this way. But you do have me. I'm in this with you now, okay?"

"No, it isn't okay. I should never have involved you, but I didn't know what else to do."

"Are you second-guessing this?"

"It's a little late for that, don't you think?"

"All we have to do is delete the pictures and forget it ever happened. Walk away. The money situation we can figure out later."

"I can't just walk away, Luca. I have to see this through—for my brother and myself. I'm just having a hard time becoming this person I barely recognize."

Reaching out, he slips his hand along the side of my neck. The touch soothes.

"This doesn't change who you are, Emma. You're still the same girl I met three years ago."

"I'm not," I murmur.

"You are." He pulls me closer to him. "This world ripped the rug out from under your feet, and you're doing what you have to do to adjust. Look, I'm not saying I agree with this." With a subtle flinch, he adds, "I'll be honest with you, I don't like the thought of you sleeping with that man, but I'll never judge you for it and I'll never use it against you." His other hand comes to my face, and he holds me in his palms. "I'm here, and I'll walk this path with you so you don't have to do it alone."

Leaning forward, I rest my head against his chest as he folds his arms around me, lowering us down on the bed. I want to tell him everything, tell him every detail, but as tempting as it is to be completely transparent with him, I can't—I don't know how. So, I bury it and let it be in order to protect myself. Let's face it, I have my issues, and trust is a big one.

"I won't let you lose yourself," he says. "And if you feel like you are, then you come to me."

"How can you be okay with all this?"

"Because it's *you*."

Drawing back, I look up into his eyes as he stares intently into mine.

"There's nothing I wouldn't do for you," he says.

His words loop around my heart and pull it right next to his, and it's in this very moment that I find the peace I've been lacking. His touch calms my anxiety like balm to a wound, and I can finally feel something—the fall of my heart into his. It's a powerful emotion that washes over me, taking me by surprise as it floods my system, and out of nowhere, my eyes water. I'm not one to break easily in front of others, but having him hold me instead of running away is beyond what a girl like me deserves.

Tears fill my eyes, mottling Luca into kaleidoscopic waves of color. I want to say something, anything, but the weight of what he makes me feel leaves me speechless.

Watching this shift in me, his brows furrow in concern. "What is it?" he questions, ghosting his thumb along the crest of my cheek.

"Are you sure about your feelings for me?"

Beyond my fear that we'll screw this all up is an even bigger fear of not having him love me. I didn't think I needed his love before, but I do, because it's him. He's the only one who's been able to slip between the cracks of my heart.

"I never would've told you if I weren't. I know we're both scared, but I want this—with you." He shifts down in the bed to meet me at eye level. "Tell me you feel the same because this limbo we've been in is killing me."

It's been killing me too, so I run my hand along his jaw, and with all my honesty, I admit, "I want this too."

With that, he kisses me, slow and still, pressing his lips against mine. His arms tighten around my body, and as my heart untangles, I relax, softening into his hold. I move my lips, needing more, and he freely gives it. His kisses scorch my lips, and when he glides his tongue along mine, tingles race up my spine.

We've only kissed a couple of times before, but never like this. He moves over me, and my hands get lost in his hair when he drags his lips down my neck and along my collarbone. Goose bumps lick my skin when he slides his hand beneath the hem of my top, up my stomach, and cups my breast. I arch to feel more of his touch.

I've never desired a man's hands like I do his, and being with him is unlike all the others before. Never were emotions attached, but now they are, and I don't want to imagine sharing this with anyone else but Luca.

He unhooks my bra from under my top, and when he sits back on his heels, he pulls me up with him. My eyes tether to his as I lift my arms, a silent invitation for him to undress me, and he does. Slipping my top off, he pulls my bra with it, tossing them both to the floor. His eyes cascade down my body, taking in every inch of my exposed skin for the first time. No one has ever looked at me the way he is right now—as if I'm something special to be valued. I'm not, but it feels good regardless.

He pulls his shirt over his head and tosses it aside, adding it to the pile. I meet his stance, adjusting to sit on my heels, and guide his hand back to my body. My breath kicks hard as we sit in silence, staring into each other's eyes. Seconds that feel infinite pass, melting pieces of me that this past year has hardened into ice.

I blink, and when a tear falls, his lips land along its dewy trail. He lowers me back down onto the mattress and kisses me slowly and thoroughly as the rest of our clothes are slipped from our bodies. With each item removed, I grow restless to have more of him—his heat, his touch, his power to calm and make the world right again, if only for tonight.

He touches my softest parts as if they were sacred, loving me in a way I didn't think he was capable of. The room fills with my shallow gasps of pleasure, and when the heat of his tongue tastes me for the first time, I lose all focus. Gripping the sheets in my fists, I writhe beneath him.

I reach down to grab on to his head, but he catches my hand, lacing his fingers with mine. As he loses himself between my thighs, he holds my hand tightly in his. My head lifts, and I open my eyes. He's entirely consumed, and as much as I want to watch him, the sensations become too much, and my head falls back onto the pillow.

His mouth is still on me when I hear the rip of the condom wrapper, and when he finally draws back, he spreads my legs wider. My eyes flutter open to see him staring down at me. He takes himself in his hand, and I watch as he pushes inside me.

I moan as he fills me, and when his head falls into the crook of my neck, he breathes a heady, "I love you."

It's as if everything beyond the two of us ceases to exist. He touches me in ways a woman could only dream of—with passion and purpose. He gives it freely when I am so undeserving. Yet, somewhere beneath all my vile behavior is a fragment of purity I thought was long gone until he unearthed it. So, I give it to him, handing it over with my heart as well, because he's the only one I want to give them to.

I'd give him so much more if I could.

Right now, I can't, but one day, I will.

For now, I give him all I can as our bodies move together in a way I never could've predicted.

"I love you so much," I breathe through the unbounding pleasure he's giving, and then he kisses me, stealing the words off my lips and swallowing them so they can find their home within him where they're safe. Because that's what Luca is—he's my one true place of safety, accepting me for all I am, loving me when I feel so unlovable.

With each pump of his hips, he breathes life into my soul, reminding me that I'm still alive and that I'm loved and that, maybe, just maybe, everything will be okay.

For the first time since my parents' death, I believe him.

THIRTY-ONE

Emma

Naked and warm, Luca holds me in his arms. The two of us just woke up to a snow-filled morning. I thought it would be weird, but it's the furthest thing from it. There's no awkwardness between us; it just feels right.

His hand runs along the length of my spine, and I tangle my legs with his as large flakes fall outside my window. Lazily, we kiss, his lips soft against mine. Being with Luca last night wasn't what I had expected. Never did I imagine him being as loving as he was—fervent but in the gentlest way.

Afterward, he confessed how different that was for him. It was different for me too, but the two of us have only ever had casual hookups. I can't even begin to explain how right it felt being with him.

When I sense him hardening against me, we shift to our sides and he drapes my leg over his hip. I say nothing as I reach down, not wanting to interrupt this moment to grab a condom, and guide him inside me. We're silent aside from our heavy sighs as he sinks deeper. We're skin on skin, entirely vulnerable to each other, yet I've never felt more secure than what I do right now.

In no rush for this to end, we move slowly as we quietly make love and explore each other's bodies. His breath is all over my skin, and I crave more. With my hands pressing into his strong muscular back, he flexes his arms around me tighter, pulling me closer against him. I shut my eyes and get lost in the rhythm of his body. Time vanishes into blank space as the world around me swims out of focus. The longer we make love, the more eager we become, picking up the pace, grabbing on to each other, and growing louder. The room spins, and when I open my eyes, he's right there, his damp forehead pressed against mine.

My hips meet his, harder and faster, and when he swells inside me, I rupture into a thousand fractals of ecstasy. Neither of us stops, hungry to ride out this pleasure for as long as we can before fatigue takes over and we collapse into each other's arms. Sweaty and short of breath, I rest my head over his heart, which beats wildly in his chest. Closing my eyes, I listen to its cadence as it begins to slow. He tucks me in close, and I swear I could live in this moment forever.

Showered and dressed, we finally have our first cup of coffee around one in the afternoon.

"We're all out of creamer," I say as I grin and pour the last drops.

"That's because you dump half the bottle into your coffee."

"It's good that way," I defend as he takes a loud slurp of his un-sweetened tar.

"Hey, I talked to your brother a couple of days ago, and it got me thinking. What if we flew him here to spend time with us? We could take him over to Gravelly Point to watch the planes and show him around the city."

"He can't fly by himself. We'd have to drive to Tennessee and fly back with him, but I don't have money for plane tickets."

"I didn't ask you for money."

"It doesn't feel right having you pay for all that since you just paid for our hotel."

"You're looking at it all wrong," he says. "I'm flying my friend out here to spend time with him. It just so happens that my friend is also your brother."

We head into the living room and settle onto the couch. "You know what I mean." I sip my coffee, taken aback that he would even offer to do such a thing, but even more so that he's selflessly put time into getting to know my brother on his own.

"I'm serious. Spring break is coming up in a couple of months."

"You'd really do that?"

As I cradle my warm mug, he reaches over and runs the back of his hand along my cheek, saying, "I kind of already mentioned it to him."

"Oh, God. Then we have to. You can't say something to him and not follow through with it."

"I know," he quips, and a smirk grows on his lips. The same smirk that I used to find annoying, but now find insanely sexy. Funny how things between us have changed in such a short amount of time. "Have you started looking into moving him here yet?"

"I don't feel comfortable doing that until I know there's money in the bank."

He takes a sip from his mug before setting it down. "Come here."

I scoot closer to him, nestling myself under his arm. "Speaking of, I need to talk to Carly. She was supposed to get me money a few weeks ago, but with everything going on, I haven't pushed or even spoken to her."

"Are you worried about talking to her after what happened?"

"No. She's harmless."

Before he can say anything, my phone rings from my bedroom. Handing him my coffee, I hop off the couch and run to grab my cell before it goes to voice mail. The call is from an unknown caller, and I almost don't pick up, but then I think better of it. It could be one of Matthew's doctors.

"Hello?"

"Hi, is this Emma Ashford?" a woman asks.

"Yes. Who's this?"

"My name is Liz. I work in the student financial aid department at Georgetown. Last semester, your academic advisor, Mrs. Montgomery reached out to me. We briefly discussed your financial situation, and she inquired about possible grants or loans you might qualify for."

"I already talked to someone, but I was told I wasn't eligible for anything that would be enough to cover my tuition."

"That was correct at the time, but since we've entered a new calendar year, we have more options, some that might be of interest to you."

"Really? That's great," I respond. Finally, some good news.

"As you know, these things go quickly, and the sooner you can get your applications in, the better chance you have. With that being said, I know it's short notice, but I was hoping I could treat you to a cup of coffee so that we can go over the different applications since some of them can be quite particular."

Eager to do anything to help get myself back into school, I say, "Yes, absolutely. I'm free whenever."

"Great. I actually have some availability later this afternoon. Would four o'clock work?"

"Yes. Where should I meet you?"

"I'll actually be off campus right before that, so would it be okay if we met at La Colombe on I Street?"

Shoving my hand into my purse, I retrieve a pen and scribble down the info on the back of a crumpled receipt. "Yes, that works. Four o'clock, right?"

"Yes, I look forward to meeting with you."

"Me too. Thank you so much!"

When I hang up, I return to the living room.

"Who was that?"

Sitting back down next to Luca with a smile on my face, I tell him, "The financial aid office. Apparently, some new grants became available after the new year, and they think I might quality for something that would be enough so that I could go back. I have a meeting later today to go over the applications."

"You're kidding. Shit, if this works out then that gets us out of this whole situation with Carly."

"I know. God, I need this to work in my favor."

"What time is your meeting?"

I take a quick sip of my coffee before saying, "At four."

"Man, I'd go with you, but I'll be in class. I don't get out until after five." Luca takes the mug out of my hand and sets it down. "Come on. Let's go grab a bite to eat before I have to go to the campus."

There's a lightness in my step as we leave the house. Finally, there's hope on the horizon, and I can barely wipe the smile off my face as Luca and I eat our burgers at Dyllan's. After lunch, he drops me off back at the house and then heads to class. It's hard to sit still, and there's nothing to do to help pass the time, so I go ahead and hop in my car and drive to the coffee shop.

I'm about a half hour early by the time I arrive, so I order a scone, even though I'm not hungry. Let's face it, I'm a nervous eater, and right now, I'm on pins and needles, needing to be saved from this insanely toxic situation I've found myself in.

I find a table to sit at by the windows and pick at my cinnamon scone while watching the snow fall down on the busy city street filled with people. When there's nothing left but a few crumbs on my plate, a woman with a sleek raven-black bob approaches me.

"Are you Emma?"

"Yes."

She slides into the seat across the table from me, and suddenly, I get an uneasy feeling. There are no papers, no work bag, nothing but a much-too-expensive Hermès

handbag that no one working in a financial aid office would be able to afford.

"Thanks for meeting me," she says, no longer the chipper woman I spoke with on the phone. Her expression is serious, making me very suspicious.

"Did you bring the applications?" I ask with a breath of apprehension.

"There are no applications," she states. "I don't work for the university. That was a lie."

"I'm sorry, what?"

She folds her hands and rests them on top of the table. "I'll cut right to the chase. You have something I want, and in exchange, I'm prepared to pay you whatever amount you feel is suitable."

"I don't think I have anything you could possibly want."

Leaning forward a fraction of an inch, she lowers her voice. "You have photos."

Chills needle along the back of my neck. "I don't know what you're talking about." In my head, I'm screaming all sorts of profanities, but I force myself to stay seated and not fidget.

"I think you do." She gives me a tiny, knowing smile. "The thing is, I'm aware of your agenda with Carly . . . I have my own as well. I'm not out to expose you or cause you any sort of trouble. What I am interested in are those photos that have her in such a twist. I also understand that you are in a dire financial situation, one I can get you out of."

"I'm sorry, but I don't know what you're talking about," I tell her as sheer horror bleeds through my being. Not only do I have to worry about Carly exposing me but now I have to worry about this woman, who seems far more cutthroat than Carly.

"Like I said, I have no interest in what you have going on with the Montgomeries. None at all. But I need those photos."

"I'm sorry, but I think you have the wrong person. I don't know the Montgomeries."

"No?" she questions with condescension. "Well, do you know Luca Sadler?"

My heart catapults when she says his name, and I immediately grab my purse and coat that are hanging off the back of my chair, fumbling nervously as I do. "Like I said, I think you've mistaken me for someone else. I don't know what you're talking about."

Before she can say anything else, I'm out the door and rushing to the parking garage, half-blinded by panic. My pulse races, and I quicken my step. The second I see my car, I break into a run and, once I'm locked inside, start it, and throw it in reverse. White-knuckling the steering wheel, I make my way out of the garage and head straight home, all the while looking in my rearview mirror, paranoid.

When I'm home and safe in my room, I take a moment to catch my breath and replay that whole situation in my head. That's when fear morphs into fury, and I want to punch Carly right in her face for opening her stupid mouth.

Pulling out my cell, I dial her number, but after only a couple of rings, she sends me to her voice mail. I hang up and call her right back. Again, I'm sent straight to voice mail. When my third attempt is also rejected, I slam the phone down on my bed and brace my head on the edge of my palms as I freak the fuck out!

Too terrified to think about who else she's told, I try to take in a steady breath. Knowing that there are people who know about the affair and the pictures increases the chances of me being exposed, the very thing I was trying to avoid.

I'm not sure what to do, but I do know that I have to shut Carly up.

Picking up my phone, I call Carly's office at the university.

"Academic advisory office. How can I help you?"

"Hi, is Mrs. Montgomery available?"

"No, I'm sorry. She's already left for the day. Can I take a message?"

I hang up on the girl, open the photos on my phone, and scroll through to the pictures of Tripp's calendar. When I see that he's here in the city for the next two nights, there are no second thoughts.

I bolt off the bed, grab my keys, and get back into my car. Anger has me about to fly off the handle as I make my way to Maryland. I shouldn't be driving as fast as I am in this snow, but all I can think about is getting to Carly.

An hour ago, I was excited and hopeful. I should've known better than to think for one second this world would cut me a break and grant me a reprieve. Instead, that phone call turned out to be my worst nightmare.

Since Carly is clearly inept, it's up to me to fix this total clusterfuck of a situation.

The sun no longer illuminates the dank, cloud-covered sky as I make my way closer to Carly's house. I've been here once before, but everything looks different at night. I make the turn that leads me to her home, which sits on a large piece of land that's surrounded by woods and backs up to the bay. I slow to a stop when I see the glow of house lights.

I take the keys out of the ignition and toss them next to my purse in the passenger seat before picking up my phone. She has one more chance to talk to me before I resort to pounding on her door and yelling until she opens up.

The call goes to voice mail, and I grit my teeth as I step out from my car and make my way up the stairs that lead to the front door. The lights are on inside, so I know she's home. I ring the doorbell and wait impatiently, but no one ever comes.

I ring again and wait.

Ring again.

Ring again.

Her avoidance only serves to piss me off even more. Walking back down the stairs and onto the drive, I look up at the house, but before I can shout her name, my phone rings from my coat pocket.

Pulling it out, I see it's Luca.

"Hi, Luca."

"Hey, I just got out of class and wanted to know how your meeting went."

Already feeling a monumental amount of guilt for involving Luca in this mess, I make the choice not to tell him about Liz. "Um, good. I'll talk to you about it when I get home."

"Where are you?"

Anxiety infects me, and in my struggle to figure out if I should lie to Luca or just tell him the truth, I walk aimlessly. I hate that he and I have taken this huge step to be together, and here I am, a constant deceiver.

"I'm actually at Carly's."

"At her office?"

I continue to pace nervously, walking across the snow-covered lawn. "No, I'm at her house in Maryland."

"What are you doing there? Is that even a good idea?"

"Yeah. Like I said before, she's harmless," I tell him before spouting off yet another lie. "She has the money she owes me, but by the time my meeting was over, she had already left work. So, I decided to just come out here and pick it up."

"When will you be home?"

"I don't know, she lives kind of far out here. Maybe a couple of hours."

"What about her husband?"

"He's staying in DC. He isn't here," I respond before placating, "Don't worry about me. Everything's fine."

"Are you sure?" I hate the uncertainty in his tone.

"Yes," I assure as I mindlessly stroll out onto the dock, unable to keep my feet still. "Like I said, I'm going to talk to her really quickly and then I'll be on my way."

"Okay. I'm going out to The Tombs with some buddies, so I'll probably be out late."

"I'll just see you tomorrow then?"

"Yeah. Call me when you're heading back to the house."

"I will."

We hang up, and when I slip the phone back into my pocket, I look out over the water, which is frozen in a solid sheet of ice. A few random flakes of snow float down, and I shiver against the frigid night, wrapping my heavy wool coat more tightly around my body. Turning around, I stare up at the house. There's a light shining through the large window on the second floor.

A shadow crosses.

The light goes off.

THIRTY-TWO

Carly

I t's good to finally be home after a stressful afternoon. I was assisting a student with his schedule and Emma kept calling. Even though I should've taken the call, knowing what she has hanging over my head, I didn't. To be honest, if it had only been one call, it wouldn't have spooked me, but it was several.

Standing in front of my dresser, I'm slipping my earrings off when the doorbell chimes. It catches me off guard. It isn't like we live close to any neighbors. We're pretty secluded out here. I look over to Tripp's nightstand where the small monitor to the security cameras is. When I see it's a woman, I step closer to the screen and gasp.

It's Emma.

The doorbell rings again, and I step back, irrationally paranoid that she can tell I'm watching her through the camera.

I don't move, hoping that maybe she'll just go away, but she rings the doorbell again and again and again.

When she finally turns and walks down the stairs, I release a hard breath.

Thank, God. She's leaving.

She then stops short of her car and pulls out her phone. I continue to spy on her as she wanders across the yard, talking to someone. When she curves around to the back of the house, I go to my window to get a better look.

What the hell is she doing?

My fear shifts into agitation as I watch her walk toward the dock, and I just want her gone. She has to leave, but with her being as persistent as she has been today, trying to get ahold of me, I don't see how I can continue to avoid her. I'm going to have to face her.

I tell myself to get it together and harden up before hitting the lights and making my way down the stairs. Silently giving myself a pep talk, I head out the back door and find she's still standing on the dock, but she's no longer on the phone. It takes her a moment to hear me walking through the snow to get to the dock, and when she does, she's pissed.

"What the hell, Carly? Why are you ignoring me?"

"I'm not, it's just been a hectic day. I was going to call you tomorrow," I lie as I approach her. "What are you doing here? How do you know where I live?"

She cocks her head. "Your husband. This isn't the first time I've been here." Her eyes turn to daggers. "Care to tell me why you opened that stupid mouth of yours?"

"What are you talking about?"

"I met your friend Liz today."

"Who's Liz?"

"Stop bullshitting me! You told her about Tripp and me! About Luca and the photos! Are you fucking crazy or just dumb as shit?"

She spits her words so fast that it takes me a moment to grasp on to them. The only person I ever told those things to was Margot.

"Clearly, you suck at choosing your friends. Did you know that she called me and offered to pay me for the photos? It seems I'm not the only one you've ticked off."

Holy shit.

My mind races in every direction possible, I can't even think straight as she continues.

"You do know that you aren't only putting me in danger—you're implicating yourself too. It's like you just want everyone to know what we've done!"

"And what about Luca?" I lash back.

"Unlike your friend, he'll keep his mouth shut." She turns away from me and paces farther down the dock. She rakes her hand through her long hair before turning back with more anger in her eyes. "This is all your fault!" she screams. "You dragged me into your fucked-up life, and because you can't keep your mouth shut, my reputation—*my life*— is in your hands and your untrustworthy little friend."

"You expect me to feel sorry for you?" I snap, furious at this girl's audacity, furious that Margot would go after those photos. "You set me up!"

"You paid me to be your husband's whore! And then you decide to renege on your word."

Her yelling echoes through the night, and I'm terrified some-one—anyone—might hear her. "Lower your voice, for Christ's sake," I seethe, following her as she nears the end of the dock. "And you're wrong. I never reneged on anything. I paid you exactly what we agreed on and you threw a tantrum when you couldn't get any more out of me."

When she turns to me, her face is drenched in a savage wrath I've never seen in anyone before, and it strikes a fear unlike I've ever known.

"I want my money," she demands in an eerie low tone.

"I-I don't have it." My words stammer out of me as fear wilts my brave façade.

Glaring at me from under her furious brows, she grits out, "I'm going to ruin you."

"Fine!" I shout. "I'll go inside and grab my checkbook, and then you have to leave."

She rights her spine and takes a step toward me, but her foot lands on a patch of ice. All too quickly, she loses her balance and falls off the edge of the dock. There's a loud *crack* followed by a splash, and when I run to the edge, she's trapped under the ice. Shock cleaves its way right through to my core, and everything inside me paralyzes as I watch in horror.

Her hands push against the ice as she fights, finally finding the edge of the hole. She gasps, and it's so loud that I shift back an inch.

"Help me!" she shrieks, flailing her arms and clawing along the edge of the ice, but she can't get any grip. Her hands slip all over the ice while she continues to cry, wailing for my help through her chattering teeth, but I can't move.

"Please!" she screeches before she chokes on a mouthful of saltwater, gargling and coughing as she slips beneath the surface for a second before popping back up. "Help me, please!"

But I can't. All I can do is stare at the woman who holds my future in her hands. She has the power to destroy me entirely—destroy my whole world, and there isn't anything I can do to stop her. I never would've guessed her to be the virulent girl she turned out to be.

Attempt after attempt, she flails wildly, trying to pull herself up, but the ice only snaps beneath the pressure. The water must feel like a million razors slicing into her flesh, stabbing her over and over and over. I step back as her blood-curdling cries of terror cut through the night, and I just need her to stop. I can't take it anymore as she begs for her life.

Stammering back a step or two, I can't think around the noise she's making and wish that she would simply give up on her fight because her fate is sealed.

As if in a trance, I bend and grab the thick fibrous rope that's connected to the massive crab trap that's on the dock.

This is it; this is the ending to my nightmare.

I pull it toward me, allowing the wiry cage to scrape along the dock. Slipping my fingers through the metal wires, I pick it up and step back to the edge. Her screams quiet as she gargles and chokes, barely able to keep herself above the surface, her lungs taking in more water than air. When her head bobs back up, I take back control and save my life by slamming the crab cage down on top of her with every ounce of force in me, grunting loudly as I do.

The night goes still.

I've put her out of her misery.

Aside from an owl hooting in the distance, there's no sound, no movement, nothing.

After a moment, I step forward and find that I can barely see her floating under the shell of ice. The force of the blow must have shoved her back under, and in the corner of my mind, I wonder how long it will take her to sink.

I'm not me, stuck in an alternate world that isn't real, I'm not sure how to even find myself.

I simply stand, with no feeling, no thought, no conscience, and I watch. For what? I don't know, but I can't tear my eyes away from her frozen body, the splintered ice, and the crab trap.

A gust of wind howls through the bare trees, stirring my hair, and something inside me snaps. My eyes blink, and suddenly, I'm able to move, taking a step back as the scene sinks into me, waking me up.

Oh my God.

Terror breeds inside me; its unrelenting fangs biting into my very soul and flooding it with its poison.

I killed her.

Holy shit! I killed her!

My hands cup around my mouth as I stumble back. I can't even process what I'm looking at or what just happened. The only thing I can grasp on to is the fear rumbling inside me. Every part of my body shakes beyond my control, and I flee.

Sprinting as fast as I can, the tears streaming down my face turn to icicles carving into my flesh. Revolting adrenaline races through me as I take the porch steps two at a time. As soon as I'm inside the house, I collapse to my knees and wail so loudly it deafens me.

What have I done?

I'm too scared to look outside, too scared of the gruesome scene out there. I could've helped her, could've reached out my hand and pulled her out, but I didn't. No, what I did was abominable. If I had just left it as her drowning, I might have been okay. I might have been able to spin it as her having slipped and fallen in without my knowledge and been done with it.

I might have been able to live with that guilt.

But I'm not sure I can live with this guilt. What I did was far, far worse than not offering help, and there's nothing I can do to rewind time.

It's done.

My throat fills with curdled bile, and I cry even harder, scared to death and unsure of what to do. All I do know is I have to run. I have to get as far away from here as possible.

I stand too quickly and find dots dancing in my vision. Lightheaded, I sway and press against the wall until it passes. When I'm sure I won't fall, I make my way up the stairs and to my bedroom, where I grab my purse and then rush back down the stairs, turning off all the lights as I do. When I flee out the front door, I come to a grinding halt when I see her car.

"Fuck!"

With no time to waste on thinking, I pull on the passenger-side handle to find it's unlocked. And to my surprise, her keys are lying in the seat. I grab them and go around to slip into the driver's seat. Her scent is all around me, and I don't think my heart could possibly hammer itself against my ribs any harder than it already is. My hands are tremoring so hard that it takes me a few attempts to get the key into the ignition, but I eventually get the car started.

Speeding down the drive and turning onto the main road, I talk to myself, repeating over and again, "You're going to be okay. You're going to be okay."

But what if I'm not?

Shaking my head, I tell myself to focus because I have to figure out what to do with this car. I scramble through my head, which does me no good since I can't think straight. When a car passes going in the opposite direction, I freak.

Leakin Park is a place notorious for having bodies dumped in the woods, but if I abandon the car there, it would look suspicious. I have to get rid of it entirely. Then I remember a beautification project in Oliver that Tripp was involved in with The 6th Branch. They may have planted some trees, but it's still sketchy and filled with criminals. It's always the focus for outreach programs because it's *that* impoverished. It's nowhere I would ever want to find myself, but I don't have any better ideas. The moment I dump it, it'll either be stripped for parts or stolen to be used in someone else's crime. If it isn't and the police find it, they'll just chalk it up as another crime and peg it on an unfortunate minority.

As I drive through Baltimore, I pay close attention to all the blue lights that mark the police surveillance cameras. Good thing about Oliver is that the cameras are all basically dead. I know that because I was on the committee that was denied the grant to have them all replaced. I just need to make sure I find a good spot to ditch the car, which doesn't take me long.

I pull into a dilapidated shopping strip with no blue lights in sight and park the car, but I don't get out. This isn't a place where a woman like myself should be walking around, especially alone and at night.

I pick up my purse and dig out my cell. Opening my internet, I find a taxi company and call in for a car to meet me at the gas station I passed a block away.

"Your taxi will be there in ten minutes," the operator tells me, and when I hang up, I wonder what I should do with Emma's purse, which is still in the passenger's seat.

I decide to leave it and the keys as an incentive for someone to steal the car. In the meantime, I pull out my winter gloves from my purse, slip them on, and begin wiping my prints off the gearshift, steering wheel, and everything else I've touched, making sure to rub down the outside passenger's handle as well.

Once I'm somewhat satisfied, I tuck my purse under my coat and walk as fast as I can down to the gas station, avoiding eye contact with the few random people I pass. I stick out like a sore thumb, a woman begging to be robbed, so I walk even faster. Before I even make it to the parking lot, I can already see the taxi getting close.

Thank God!

When the taxi pulls up, I've settled down enough not to look too suspicious, I think.

"Where to, hun?"

"The Jefferson Hotel in DC."

"So, what's a lady like you doing walking the streets this late at night? It's dangerous around here."

"Long story. I just need to get to DC," I say, brushing him off, and he takes the hint.

He punches the info into his GPS, and a minute later, we're on our way.

There's no way I can go back home and no way I'd be able to make the drive in my current condition, so I settle in for a really long taxi ride.

DC is where Tripp is, and right now, I need him, so that's all that matters. He really is all I have in this world, and I'll take comfort wherever I can find it. I used to have Margot, but how could I possibly trust her after what she did. I would be stupid to think she was trying to get the pictures from Emma to help me. She was clear that she needed distance from me, so why would she purposely put herself right in the middle? No, she's clearly up to something, and if I had to take a wild guess, that something is probably her husband. Conrad is so incredibly ambitious about getting into the White House that I don't doubt he would take down anyone who posed a threat if the opportunity presented itself, which in this case, it has.

I can't be certain, but my gut is telling me that whatever Margot was trying to do was to further her husband's campaign.

Dirt on me would be like a golden ticket in her hand.

I sulk deeper back into the seat and stare out the window, letting the passing lights lull me into a trance. My mind no longer torments me as we drive into the night. It's as if it's completely shut down on me. I've taken a total one-eighty—sheer panic to detached. My only hope is that Emma sinks quickly and that her car is completely dismantled by sunrise.

Despite my despondency, my stomach is still a knotted wreck. None of this seems real, but I know what I saw, and I know what I did. Nonetheless, I'm numb to it all right now. Maybe I'm in shock; I don't know.

About an hour later, the cab is pulling up to the hotel. When we come to a stop, I pull out my wallet to pay the exorbitant fair, and cringe when I realize I don't have enough cash.

"You okay?" the driver questions, watching me in the reflection of his rearview mirror.

"No, I'm fine," I respond.

A tidal wave of panic crashes down on me when I swipe my credit card through the reader, all the while praying this doesn't come back to bite me in the ass.

Once inside the hotel, my first stop is the restroom, where I check myself in the mirror. My face is splotchy, and my eyes are bloodshot, but I can't fix either of those things. What I can do is cover them with a lie. Quickly, I wash my hands and splash some cold water on my face before going to the front desk.

"Welcome to The Jefferson," the young woman greets. "Are you checking in?"

"No, my husband, William Montgomery, and I are staying in one of your suites," I say as I slide my driver's license to her. "I've misplaced my room key and can't remember our room number. I've tried calling, but his cellphone must be turned off."

"No problem, Mrs. Montgomery. Give me just one second," she says, buying my lie as she punches away at the keys of her computer. She then activates a new keycard and hands it to me inside an envelope with the room number written down.

"Thank you so much."

"Enjoy your night."

I take the elevator up to his floor, and as I'm making my way down the long corridor to his suite, I see Olivia walking toward me. When she lifts her attention from her phone, I catch her eye but neither of us say anything as we pass each other. Looking over my shoulder, my bleak heart reminds me that I'm not the only one, but that's a burden I can no longer stray away from. I'm on the brink of destruction, and he's the only one I have to hang on to. I may be second best or even third, but it's better than nothing at all.

When I knock, he answers, and I begin to cry.

"What are you doing here?"

I fall into his arms, the mere sight of him awakes everything inside me, and I just need him to hold me.

"I'm sorry for not calling first," I quietly weep. "But I just needed to see you."

We walk into the living room and take a seat on the couch together before he does exactly what I need him to do; he wraps his arms around me and holds me against him.

"What's going on? Why are you upset?"

"I've just . . . I've been sitting at home thinking about how we've gotten so off track," I tell him, saying what I think he will easily believe. "And I realize that it was me. That I've been the cause of us falling apart, and I'm so sorry."

"Carly, no. You can't blame this on yourself. You aren't the sole cause at all."

"I am. I know how hard you work and how much you do for me, and I let my insecurities get the better of me. I feel so horrible for all the accusations I've made against you."

"Look at me," he says, holding my face between his hands. "One thing you need to know is that I love you—*you*—and no one else. But I'm to blame as well. I never knew how busy this campaign would keep me, and I hate that my crazy schedule and long hours have been so difficult on you."

"I just want us to go back to when we were happy and not fighting all the time."

He releases a heavy sigh with a hint of a smile. "I do too. I miss you, and I miss us."

And with that, he kisses me. I take it greedily because, if what happened tonight ever gets traced back to me, I'm going to need him by my side. Without him, I don't have a fighting chance to save myself and avoid spending the rest of my life behind bars. So, I vow to be the best wife I can no matter how much I have to sacrifice.

THIRTY-THREE

Luca

I expect to see Emma's car when I pull into the drive, but it isn't here. After a second, I remember telling her to call me, but when I check my cell, there's nothing. Last night got a little crazy with my friends, and I wound up getting too drunk to drive home, so I crashed at my buddy's house.

I'm already calling her cell when I walk through the front door, but it goes straight to voice mail.

"Em," I call out, but there's no response, and when I go into her room, her bed doesn't look as if she slept in it.

It's only seven thirty, so it isn't inconceivable that she's out grabbing breakfast. While I wait for her to return, I jump in the shower and clean up, even though I feel like complete ass.

As I'm brewing coffee, I try calling her again, but still, it goes right to her voice mail. It's now after eight o'clock. If she ran out to grab food, she'd be home by now. Worry creeps in, and when I take a sip of my coffee, I think back to last night. She was at Carly's house, but where is she now?

Thinking for a moment, I resolve to call her only other friend, even though she's the last person I want to talk to. I just can't shake the uneasy feeling I have.

"Hello."

"Olivia, it's Luca."

"Hey, what's up?"

"Have you heard from Emma? She isn't home, and I can't get ahold of her."

"No, I haven't talked to her in a few days. Is everything okay?"

I avoid her question, asking, "Is William with you?" because if Emma's with him, that would explain her whereabouts. Although, since we got the photos of Carly, she no longer has a reason to be carrying on her affair with him.

"Yeah, he's in the conference room. Why?"

Setting my coffee down on an end table, I take a seat on the couch as I grow more worried. The only place I know to look for her would be the last place she said she was at. "You think you could do me a favor?"

"I guess it depends. What do you need?"

"I need William's home address," I tell her.

"Why?"

I can't tell her why, though. It's already suspicious enough that I'm even asking. "I can't say. I just need you to trust me."

I'm met with silence on her end.

"You there?"

"Yeah, I just—I shouldn't be giving out his information. Does this have to do with Emma?"

"Can you just give me his address?" I push.

Sighing into the phone, she resolves, "I'll text it to you."

"Thanks." I hang up, and sure enough, a few seconds later, my phone chimes with his contact information. I plug his address into my navigation app, and get the directions. Shit, she wasn't kidding when she said they lived far.

I'm normally not one who reacts quickly, but something is telling me to go to Carly's home. It's an unsettling feeling I can't shake, so I take one last gulp of my coffee and grab my keys.

The drive feels much longer than it should, and as each mile passes, I grow more concerned. I start questioning my decisions from last night. I should've checked my phone and called her when I decided not to come home. If I hadn't drunk so much, I would've gone home sooner and started looking for her last night instead of this morning.

The roads got bad last night with the snow that came through, and I find myself distracted as I scan the ditches and shoulders for her car.

Shit, what if she got into a wreck?

I press my foot down on the pedal to speed up, and when I turn off the highway and draw closer to Carly's house, I've almost convinced myself that she must've gotten into an accident.

When I pull into the circular drive, I look at the impressive home before getting out and heading up to the front door.

I ring the bell and then wait, but when no one answers, I ring again. I pull out my phone and try Emma one more time, but her battery must be dead because it doesn't even ring, just goes straight to voice mail.

I walk back down the front porch steps and scan the property. Her car is nowhere to be found, and it doesn't appear as if anyone is home either. I consider calling Carly's office to see if she knows where Emma is, but I choose to walk the property instead. I'm not sure why, but something isn't right.

There's a dense fog in the air with no footprints in the fresh snow, aside from my own, as I make my way around to the back of the house. Nothing is disturbed, and everything is quiet and peaceful. Clearly, she isn't here.

Looking out at the bay, which has frozen over, I can just make out the form of a large boat that's along the side of the dock. There's a dense fog that practically sits on the icy water's surface. Curiosity pulls me down the property and onto the dock, confused as to why they don't have it lifted out of the water at a marina during this time of year.

My foot slides, and as I regain my balance, a large rope that's tied to a piling catches my eye. I follow the line down the dock and find a large crab cage sticking out of the ice. Grabbing the rope, I tug, but the cage is hung up on something. I yank a couple times, and when it comes loose, I pull it out of the water and notice something caught within the wiring of the trap. I squat down and almost topple over when I see a wad of hair tangled in the hex mesh.

My gut hallows, and I quickly crawl to the edge of the dock on my knees and look down at the hole where the trap has broken through the ice. The surface is at least three to four feet below the dock, and with the recent snowfall, it's hard to see anything. I lie down on my stomach and stretch my arm down. It's too far for me to reach, but it's close enough for me to see that something is trapped beneath the ice. It's hard to make out what it is, but when a gust of wind cuts through, it takes enough snow with it that I can make out the form of a hand.

"Fucking, shit!"

I pop up to my knees and shuffle back on my hands, my heart pounding like a beast.

For a split second, I question my sanity, wondering if I just spooked myself out or if there's really something in the water. Creeping back over to the edge, I peer over, and freak the fuck out when I see it again. Panic fires off inside me when I make out the thin gold ring on the first finger, the same ring that Emma wears on the same goddamn finger.

Adrenaline detonates deep inside me, and I panic. Pushing myself out farther, I dangle my chest off the dock and reach down as far as I can, but I can't even get close to her.

"Fuck!" I grunt helplessly as sheer hysteria takes me hostage. I scream her name, but there's no way I can get to her, but I know it's her. If I lower myself onto the ice, it'll crack and I'll slip under too. With how low the surface is, there's no way I'll be able to pull myself back up. I'd drown.

"Emma!"

She's trapped under the ice, and I'm powerless to get to her. Tears build in my eyes as I look on in horror, unable to digest what I'm seeing.

But I see it.

Right here in front of me.

There's no way I'm imagining this because she's *right fucking there!*

Crazed delirium stifles my head, and I go into shock. I can't even think straight as my pulse races in pure insanity. My chest heaves against my shallow breaths, and for a moment, my vision blurs.

Pushing myself up from the dock, I look to the crab trap and grab on to the wad of hair—her hair. The very hair I used to drop kisses into because I was too much of a coward to cop to my feelings and kiss her on the lips.

Tears fall, and there's no doubt, not a single one, that this wasn't an accident. There's no reason for that cage to have been in the water. Visions terrorize me when I think about all the possibilities, but they all funnel down to one thing—one person—Carly.

Panic bleeds out of me and rage starts to consume. I stand, my hands in fists, and I charge up the dock and toward the house. I bang on the back door, and when no one appears, I punch the glass so hard it shatters, slicing through my knuckles, but I don't feel a thing. There's nothing left of me but fury as I break into the house, broken glass crunching beneath my heavy boots.

Knowing that either she or her husband could come home at any moment, I race through the house as blood drips off my fingers, finding myself tearing through the large desk in the den. In one of the drawers, I discover a revolver, stopping me dead in my tracks. I release the cylinder to find each chamber is loaded. With the gun in my hand and no sign of anyone here, I run back outside, but something stops me from going out to the dock.

I slow my steps and drop to my knees in the bitter snow as I stare into the fog that veils the monstrosity in the water. My lungs strain against my erratic breaths, and with the gun gripped tightly in my hand that's still bleeding, it all becomes too much, and I release a godawful barbaric scream. My strained voice rips through my vocal cords like barbed wire, echoing into the sky, and when I deplete all the air in my lungs, I drop my head and lean forward. I can't even think straight. Tears fall from my face as a vicious storm erupts within me, taking all my rationale hostage.

I want to go to her, pull her out of the icy water, and hold her until she's warm, but what good would it do?

She's dead.

There's so much roiling inside me that I can't even find the sadness

I know is in there. I'm unable to grasp on to a single emotion. It's a maniacal assault to my system, and I swear to god I'm going to fucking kill
Carly.

With tears dried on my face, I stand and stare down into the
dense cloud that blankets my fucking heart that's submerged in the water. That girl is my everything, and there's no question that I will make
that woman pay for what she's done.

I debate calling the police. I'm not blind to the Montgomery
wealth that can afford the country's best legal team, plus his political
status. People get away with murder every day.

I won't let that happen, not after what that bitch just took away
from me. No amount of justice will ever be enough, but if justice is going to be served, I'm going to be the one serving it. I'm going to fucking
annihilate Carly.

Turning around, I look up at the house. I contemplate going
back inside, waiting for them to get home and killing them—both of
them, because William is a piece of shit just like his wretched wife. I
cringe when I think about him putting his hands all over Emma, him
undressing her, him kissing her, him fucking her. The thought alone
makes me to want to put a bullet in his head.

In an instant, my eyes catch something that silences those
thoughts and makes me pause.

There is a security camera under the eave on the back of the
house. My legs, which are numb from the snow, lead me closer to find
the camera is aimed right out toward the dock. I scan the property and
find a few more cameras as I force myself to slow down and think.

Frozen in place, I continue to stare into one of the cameras.

And then it hits me.

When I get to my car, I toss the gun onto the passenger seat and
grab my phone. Running on sheer panic, I easily find her number because it was the last one I dialed. Throwing the car in drive, I pull away
from the house to head back to DC.

It only takes a couple rings for Olivia to answer.

"Hey, Luca. Any word from Emma?"

"I need another favor," I say, still short of breath.

"Are you okay?"

"Listen, are there people around?"

"Um, yeah, why?"

The phone starts to slip in my bloody hand, so I quickly place her on speakerphone, and tell her fervently, "I need you to go out to your car."

"Why?"

"Just do it."

There's shuffling around on her end, and it takes a few moments before I hear the chirping of her alarm followed by a door closing.

"Okay, I'm in my car," she says, and I can tell she's nervous. "What's going on, you're scaring me."

"I need you to do something for me, but I need your word that you'll keep quiet, and no matter what, you have to promise me that you won't involve the police."

"What are you talking about?"

I turn onto the highway. "Promise me, Olivia."

"I-I . . . yeah, okay, I promise."

"William has security cameras at his house," I say, and she's nothing but silent on her end. "He most likely has an app on his phone that's connected to them. I need you to get his phone and see if there's a way for you to send the videos. If there is, I need you to email them to me. I only need the footage from last night."

"Luca, what's going on?"

"I can't explain anything right now, but I need your help. I wouldn't be asking you if it wasn't important. Can you trust me?"

She hesitates and doesn't respond right away, but then she gives in reluctantly. "Yeah . . . I trust you."

"When you email them to me, make sure you email them from William's campaign headquarters' email account, not yours. And not a word to anyone, okay?"

"Okay."

Ending the call, I drive the rest of the way home completely disconnected. It's as if I'm stuck in an alternate universe or something. Maybe it's shock, but it has me completely severed from reality. I'm withdrawn from all emotions, completely numb to the core as I head back to the city.

An hour and a half later when I pull into my driveway, I can't recall the drive home. With Emma's car gone from here and at the Montgomery's as well, I can only conclude that it's been disposed of. It's probably sitting at the bottom of the inner harbor.

I blink, and when I open my eyes, I'm inside the house.

I blink again, and I'm sitting on Emma's bed.

Another blink slams me back into existence.

She's all around me, her smell, her voice, her touch. My eyes close, and I slip off the edge of the bed and onto the floor.

My cell rings, and when I answer it, it's Olivia.

"Did you get it?"

"I think so. I was able to share a secured link to the videos. I sent it to your email."

"Thanks. I owe you."

"What's on the videos that's so important?"

With a heavy exhale, I tell her what I can, "Look, you need to know something. Emma's missing," I lie, not wanting anyone to know where she is or that she's dead. "I'm telling you this because I'm about to call the police, and they'll most likely want to talk to you. Whatever you do, do not mention anything about the security videos you just sent me, understand?"

She's quiet, but it spans for longer than what I'm comfortable with. "Olivia?"

Her voice cracks, and I can tell that she's crying when she asks, "Luca, what's going on? Are the Montgomery's involved?"

"Whatever you do, don't ever mention this video," I repeat and then quickly hang up. I open my email, and sure enough, I have the secured link waiting in my inbox.

When I click on it, it takes me to a home screen that gives me six different camera options. There are two options that would've caught what happened: Backyard and Dock. I click on Dock and it brings up the last twenty-four hours of footage, so I drag the toggle on the video player to fast forward. It takes a few minutes until I catch something. Hitting play, I watch, and there she is, Emma, standing on the dock alone. The video is pixilated, but it's clear enough for me to tell that it's definitely Emma.

Leaning in closer to the screen, I watch, and soon Carly walks into the frame. There's no sound in the video, but it's clear they're arguing. I then see Emma fall into the water. I rewind a few seconds to watch again, but it isn't until the third time that I realize she slipped on something, most likely ice.

I stare in horror as Carly stands over her and does nothing. Not a fucking thing. And then she reaches down and grabs the rope to the crab trap and picks it up. She brings it over her head and then slams it down.

My stomach caves in on itself, and I drop the phone. Tears fill my eyes, blurring the world around me, and I couldn't possibly feel any emptier than I do right now. Words can't even begin to describe my feelings for that girl. Fuck if I didn't love her from the moment I met her, but I was always too damn scared to say anything because I knew I wasn't good enough.

She was so perfect, and I was nothing but careless, screwing random girls who never meant shit to me. I was worthless next to her, but that didn't stop me from loving her the best I knew how—as a friend. Although she was always so quiet and closed off, she was vibrant and full of life in her own reserved way. Others could never see it, but I could. All I could ever see was her.

But then her parents died and she lost herself. She completely shut down, and I felt helpless. That was when she started pushing me away. It wasn't until she moved in here with me that I heard her cry for the first time. She would wait until late at night when she thought I was asleep, but I wasn't asleep. Shit, sometimes I'd force myself to stay awake just to listen to her because I hated the thought of her suffering all alone. It was my pathetic way of being there for her.

Hell, even my parents loved her. My mother would talk about her often. She always hoped that I would pull my head out of my ass and ask her out. I just can't believe it took me so long.

Two nights ago, she finally opened her heart and let me in.

Two nights ago . . . and now she's dead.

Finally, being able to have her changed everything about me. If I could go back, I would tell her exactly how, but I was nervous. I feigned it well, but shit, making love to her was scary because I had never in my life allowed myself to be that vulnerable with anyone. But I should've said more because she deserved to know how special she was, how much I truly did love her and that I had loved her for years. I'll always love her.

All I ever wanted was her—every piece—including her fragments, her bad days, her broken hopes and soul aches. The pieces so small that they lost their place when she would put herself back together after every heartbreak she ever suffered.. I wanted it all, and two days ago I was on my way to having it all and now . . .

Dropping my head in my palms, I cry for the girl who never deserved any of this. All I ever wanted to give her was everything that had been taken from her.

God damn, I love her.

My phone rings next to me, and when I wipe my eyes, I see it's Matthew calling. I stare at his name, but I can't move. I can't answer because, what the hell am I going to say? The ringing eventually stops, and it's in the hollow silence of this moment where I vow to take care of him.

He was Emma's world, and even though she was too prideful to ask for help, I'm not. I'll talk to my parents, and we'll figure it all out, but I just can't deal with that right now. I can't deal with anything when I feel like dying myself.

I swear to God that I will make Carly pay for what she's done. I will fuck her life up in the most unimaginable ways, and I'll make sure I do it slowly so that she suffers.

There's no way I'm going to let that piece of shit get away with this. Fuck no!

I call Olivia back.

"Luca, I'm freaking out over here," is the first thing she says when she answers my call.

"I need one more thing."

"Tell me what's going on," she demands.

"I need you to listen to me."

"Have you been crying?" she asks, but I avoid her question.

"I hate to involve you in this, but I am going to email a file to William's campaign headquarters' account, and I need to make sure that you are logged in so you are the one who retrieves it, okay?"

"I don't know if I can do that because there are lots of people here who have access to that email."

"Can you temporarily change the password? If you do that, by default it'll kick everyone off until they log back in, which they won't be able to do."

"Yeah, I can do that," she says.

"Stay on the phone with me and let me know when the password has been changed."

"Okay." Her whispered voice rattles. "I'm doing it now. Just give me a minute."

"When I send this file, I need you to email it to William's wife, Carly, and then delete it from the email and make sure it's off the computer as well, okay?"

I give her these instructions, not bothering to tell her not to watch it. I know she will, and when she does, she'll have a million questions.

I need this to happen *now*. I'll deal with Olivia later.

Her voice is addled with nerves when she responds, "Okay, it's done."

Putting Olivia on speakerphone, I open the video and fast forward to when both Carly and Emma are on the dock. With my screen recorder on, I record my own copy of the video, only the small clip that matters.

"All right, I'm emailing this over right now. When you get it, move fast."

It's silent on her end aside from the sound of her clicking the keys on her computer. My heart races as seconds pass, and when I hear her gasp, I know she just watched it.

"Luca?" My name is a frightful whimper.

"Just send it."

Her breathing becomes erratic, and a moment later, she mutters through the tears I'm sure are spilling down her face, "It's sent—"

I cut her off before she can say anything else. "Don't lose your shit, Olivia, and whatever you do, don't tell a soul about what you just saw."

"But—"

I hang up. It's all I can do because how can I attempt to makes sense out of what she just saw when I can't make sense of it for myself?

I have to keep moving though.

I have to make the call I've been dreading. The call that will make all of this real. I'm sick to my stomach as I look up the number, but when I find it, I hesitate before making the call.

More tears come, and then the line connects.

"Metropolitan Police Department."

"I need to report a missing person."

THIRTY-FOUR

Carly

It's been two weeks of hell.

I can't sleep because, when I close my eyes, I see her in the water.

I can't eat because, when I do, my stomach coils in sharp pains.

I can't look at myself in the mirror because I'm terrified of the murderer staring back at me.

After going to Tripp at The Jefferson, I returned home the following afternoon to find that the house had been broken into. The glass to the backdoor had been shattered and drops of blood trailed through the first floor. There was also a lot of blood outside in the snow. My first instinct was to call Tripp and then the police.

I didn't do either.

I can't do anything to draw attention to myself after what I did. For God's sake, there's a dead girl out back.

Shortly after I had cleaned up all the glass and blood, I mustered up the courage to go out onto the dock to find that her body had sunken and was no longer on the surface. Morbidly, I breathed a sigh of relief, which was short-lived when I got back inside to see I had an email notification. Someone had accessed our security cameras and emailed the video of me killing Emma. What was worse was that it came from Tripp's campaign email address.

Seeing that video threw me into a maniacal anxiety attack that took me a while to claw myself out of. Once I calmed down, I realized that whoever had sent that footage was also likely the same person who'd broken in. So, I pulled up the footage from the cameras and that was when I discovered that it was Luca. He was on the dock, he was inside the house, and then he was staring straight into the camera. He knows, but who else has he told? He doesn't have access to Tripp's campaign email . . . but Olivia does.

I've been on edge ever since. There isn't a single person in my life who I can trust anymore.

Olivia knows Luca, who knows Emma, who knows Margot—or, should I say *Liz*?

It's a tangled web there's no escape from.

My hands are tied. I can't do anything about the break-in. Luckily, I was able to get someone out the following day to replace the glass, and when Tripp came home a few days after, he was none the wiser.

But things only got more complicated when Detective Arroyo showed up at my university office last week. Being Emma's advisor and therapist, it made sense that he would want to talk to me. I was taken down to the police station and questioned. I answered the best I could, lying when I needed to, and when it was over, he let me go home. I haven't heard from him since. I figure they are calling in everyone who was linked to her in for questioning.

Much like my neglect in telling Tripp about the break-in, I didn't tell him about my trip to the police station. If he's been called in for questioning, he isn't saying anything either.

As far as the police are concerned, at this point, it's a missing person case.

I don't know how things got so out of hand so fast. Honestly, I try not to think about it because what's done is done, and overanalyzing it won't bring Emma back.

I killed her. In a strange way, it doesn't even feel real. I know it happened, I know what I did, but it still doesn't feel as if I'm the one who did it.

To distract myself, I've been focusing my energy on being a better wife. Tripp and I have made love more in these past two weeks than what we have this past year. Our fighting has lessened, and we're finding our way back to each other. But with that being said, there's still the ever-present cloud of calamity that hangs overhead. I wonder if it'll always be this way, if I'll ever escape the horror of that night.

"I just got off the phone with my mother," Tripp says as he strolls into the living room where I've been sitting and watching a cooking show.

It's Sunday, and I was able to convince my husband to take a day off from the campaign. So today, we are simply hanging around the house, being lazy.

"What did she have to say?"

"When I told her that we didn't have any plans for the day, she invited us over for dinner. What do you say? Do you want to go to DC tonight and have dinner with them?"

I paste a smile on my face and lie, "Yes. That sounds wonderful."

"Okay, I'll go give her a call back and let her know."

After he leaves the room, I pick up the remote, shut the television off, and head outside. The sun is shining brightly for a change, and when I get to the bottom of the porch steps, I tilt my head back to soak in the faint heat through the bitter cold. Needing more of the fresh air, I decide to walk down the long driveway and check the mail. After I collect a few letters and the university newspaper that I have delivered to me, I make my way back toward the house.

When I hit the steps, I startle when I see the crab trap that should be on the dock sitting next to the porch swing. Turning around, my eyes dart around the property, but there isn't anyone there. I take the last two steps up to the porch and slowly walk over to the trap, trying to figure out what has been haphazardly shoved inside it. Slowly, I approach it, and then my heart catapults.

My silk cami.

The one I couldn't find after having sex with Luca is shoved inside, tangled in the wires. I panic, the pit of my stomach hollows, and I quickly maneuver the cage, find the opening, and shove my hand inside, dropping the mail from my other hand. The fabric gets caught on a wire as I try to fish it out, and I panic a bit more, well aware that Tripp is on the other side of the door. When my fingers get close enough to fist the material, I rip it out. Rankled in white-hot anxiety, I grab the trap and toss it over the railing onto the side of the house. Wadding up the tattered cami, I lift the lid to the large trunk where I keep a few gardening supplies and bury it toward the bottom.

After I pick up the scattered mail, I wipe a bead of sweat from my forehead, take a deep breath, and glance down my driveway before going back inside. Tripp is in the kitchen, riffling around in the fridge. I do my best to get my heart rate under control as I reclaim my spot on the couch and slip the rubber band off from around the newspaper.

This is my new life, I guess, Luca taunting me and me having to deal with it and play normal. I'm not sure how much longer I can go on constantly looking over my shoulder, knowing that he knows. Not only does he know but he also has proof. The fear of being exposed as a cheater doesn't even compare to the fear running rampant in me of being exposed as a killer.

When I open the paper, I'm reminded, once again, that there's no escape for me. I stare down at the headline that reads: "Georgetown Student Still Missing."

Her photo takes up most of the page, and I swallow hard against the terror that's silently erupting inside me. Her fibrous eyes stare up at me, haunting me, and I jump when Tripp enters the room.

"Didn't mean to scare you," he says with a light chuckle and then takes a seat next to me. He leans over to see what I'm looking at, reads the headline, and then asks, "Do you know that girl? Was she one of your students?"

My eyes fly to him as he stares at the photo of Emma, but it's when he looks up at me that something inside me shifts—my intuition.

I scan his face for some sort of tell, a hint of something—anything, but there's nothing, and I go cold.

"So, do you?" he asks again, exposing every single truth within his expression.

He doesn't know her.

EPILOGUE

Three months earlier . . .

I t was a cold and rainy night, and Tripp found himself in his usual spot when he would stay the night in the city. The Jefferson was his hotel of choice, rich in history and opulence. He was a hard worker, but he was born with expectations already on his shoulders and didn't know any other way around it. Tripp Montgomery was a legacy from the start, groomed for a life in politics, he took the path that had already been laid for him seriously.

There was always a sense of inadequacy that resided in him, the fear that he would never become all that his parents desired, that he would never measure up in their eyes. But he never questioned his wife. Carly loved Tripp beyond measure. When he met her, he knew she would be the one. Carly was a woman with no expectations, she was content living her simple life and working her simple job. He knew that, with her, he could be himself without the pressure so many others put on him.

"Another one," Tripp told the bartender at Quill, the lounge on the ground floor of the hotel.

It was his favorite place to work late at night. He preferred it over being locked away in his suite. When a fresh glass of scotch was set in front of him, he took a sip before returning to the speech he would have to present in a couple of days. He read it again and made some notes, just a few changes here and there before removing his glasses and pinching the bridge of his nose as if to ward off the first twinges of a headache.

"May I?" a young woman questioned before she sat next to him.

"Um, of course . . . yes."

She smiled in a way he had become all too familiar with. He came across girls like her all the time. The ones with ambition in their hearts and ill intentions in their souls. Tripp was a man of power—a well-known political legacy—who girls would flock to as if he were some sort of a conquest. He wasn't interested in any of that.

Never had been.

"Working off the clock?" the young blonde asked.

He glanced over to the girl who looked young enough to be his daughter. "In my line of work, there are no clocks."

He listened to her as she ordered a drink, "Grey Goose martini, up, stirred, with a twist," and laughed to himself. Such a sophisticated drink for someone her age. He smirked, amused at the act he clearly saw through.

"So, no clocks," she said, "how do you know when to stop?"

He turned to look at her, and as she reached for her martini glass that the bartender just set down, his eyes caught sight of her cleavage. Momentarily, he became distracted. He was human, after all, and although she was young, she was a beautiful woman with soft bone structure and deep-green eyes.

"I'm not a man who likes to stop." He then went back to his speech.

"I'm Emma, by the way."

"Tripp," he responded without a glance her way. Truthfully, he just wanted to concentrate on his work so that he could go to bed at a decent hour.

Emma then reached over and plucked a small piece of lint off the shoulder of his dress shirt. He watched as her hand lingered on him for longer than what he was comfortable with, striking a nerve within the already exhausted man.

"I don't mean to be rude, but I'm tired and have a lot of work that I need to get done," he told her, hoping she would get the hint, and she did. Emma dropped her hand and took another sip of her drink.

Sure, it boosted his ego to have an attractive girl flirting with him, but Tripp was married and adored his wife. Their marriage may have been strained for months on end, but he loved her nonetheless. Carly had been trying the limits of his patience lately, hinting at her suspicions that Tripp was giving into temptations, but that couldn't have been further from the truth. And although their once peaceful relationship had turned tumultuous, the idea of cheating on her was . . . unthinkable.

He could only hope that after the campaign came to an end, they would be able to get back on track. Tripp knew that he needed to be more understanding of his wife's insecurities, but with a schedule that never stopped, by the time he would walk through the door, he had no more energy left. It was making him wonder if he had it within himself to even be running for governor.

Not needing any more distractions, he began packing up. "It was nice meeting you," he told Emma politely before grabbing his briefcase and his scotch and heading up to his room—alone.

Emma sat there, defeated in her attempt to seduce the man running for governor of Maryland. *The poor guy has no idea that his wife put me up to this*, she thought to herself. Tripp wasn't anything like Carly had told Emma he would be. He was nothing like the snake she had described at all, but that wouldn't stop Emma from making Carly believe he was the lying, cheating bastard of a husband she suspected. She knew she needed to be smart about it, and she was. Emma was graced with a rock-solid surface most couldn't see through, making her the perfect match for the unassured Carly.

Instead of making a second attempt with Tripp, Emma would lie. And lie she did.

EXPLORE OTHER TITLES FROM

e.k. blair

www.ekblair.com/books

FOLLOW
e . k . b l a i r

Instagram:
www.instagram.com/ek.blair

Facebook:
www.facebook.com/EKBlairAuthor

Twitter:
twitter.com/EK_Blair_Author

Goodreads
www.goodreads.com/author/show/6905829.E_K_Blair

Bookbub:
www.bookbub.com/authors/e-k-blair

ACKNOWLEDGEMENTS

To my fans, I cannot thank you enough for continuing to love my characters and support my stories. Your loyalty means the world to me. The greatest joy is being able to open my heart and share what's inside with you.

To my husband, none of this would be possible without you. I know I say that a lot, but it is so very true. You are my support, my best friend, my partner in crime for life. Thank you for all you sacrifice in order for me to follow this passion of mine.

Sally Gillespie, you are one of my biggest blessings! The time you give me is simply incredible. Thank you for helping me in the creation of this story. It wasn't easy, but together we made it happen!

Ashley Williams, wow! How do I even thank you properly? You make my words strong, even though you bust my balls to do so. From the early mornings to the late nights, and everything in between, you are always there for me. You are an amazing editor and friend!

Josh, thank you for taking an interest in this book and fueling my creativity through our phone calls. You helped make this story even better!

Liz, thanks for taking the time to walk me through a few of my scenes for accuracy. I really appreciate your ideas and the insight you gave me!

Bloggers, there are too many of you to name, but each and every one of you are equally important. Thank you for your undying support.

A big thanks to my PR team, Give Me Books Promotions, my cover designer, Emily Wittig, and my formatter, Stacey Blake.

Thanks to each one of you!